You Won't Miss Me 'til I'm Gone

The Long Journey Beyond the Shroud

JAAK TALLINN

Copyright © 2023 by Earl Horntvedt.

ISBN: 979-8-89090-1-613 (sc)
ISBN: 979-8-89090-162-0 (eb)

All rights reserved. No part of this book may be reproduced or transmitted in any form or by any means, electronic or mechanical, including photocopying, recording, or by any information storage and retrieval system, without permission in writing from the copyright owner.

The views expressed in this work are solely those of the author and do not necessarily reflect the views of the publisher, and the publisher hereby disclaims any responsibility for them.

EXPRESSO
Executive Center 777, Dunsmuir Street Vancouver, BC V71K4
1-888-721-0662 ext 101
info@expressopublishing.com

TABLE OF CONTENTS

El Nichupté Laguna 3
Shanty Side Of Town 14
Barracuda Bay, Belize, & The Beach 21
Oil And Water 33
The Second Coming 41
Checkup In Chetumal 53
Agents, Amigos, Angels, & Saints 61
Damage Control 71
Island Hopping To 'Habana' 88
Gino's Lounge 104
Row, Row, Row Your Boat 118
Prado Esplanade 129
The Citadel 144
Small Blue Planet 159
Tromsø Triskelion Tryst 170
Beyond The Shroud 183

President Ronald Reagan once famously said, *"The nine most terrifying words in the English language are, 'I'm from the government and I'm here to help."* Ronald Reagan, 40th president of US (1911 - 2004).

This book is dedicated to the many fine men and women in governments worldwide, who are working hard to make 'governments' better and smaller, … so that eventually, they barely exist at all.

PROLOGUE

In the preceding novel, we traveled with Jack Redhouse on his mystical motor yacht (*Victory Liner 504, by Jaak Tallinn*), after he met up with his old sailor buddies Sanjo Casagrande and Frank Valero at the '*Jack of Clubs*' sports bar in Topeka, Kansas many years after they were all discharged from the US Navy. In the current sequel, '*You Won't Miss Me 'Til I'm Gone*', we find Jack Redhouse where we left him in the last story, back on his boat down in Cancun, Mexico ready to tackle the next adventure with his pals.

Sanjo's wife Marissa Marikit (aka *Cassandra*), a dancer/hostess friend of all three sailors from the *California Club* in Olongapo, Philippines, and two of Jack's other lady friends from the '*Jack of Clubs*', Carol Mulhaney (*Pernicious*), and Sarah Reid (*Enchanté*), who had all joined the crew on earlier cruises in the Caribbean, were now content to remain in the states for the interim, while Jack took a break from the action to begin exploring new business opportunities in the Gulf of Mexico and Central America.

A string of lifelong struggles had led Jack to theorize that 'life was like a business'. There was 'profit and loss, risk and reward', and it required investment in time, resources, and assets to realize benefits. To live well, … good cash flow was required, especially if lady friends were included in the mix. More money in, less money out, was needed to satisfy expenses, and payroll. Jack felt that it was important to invest in his own welfare as well as others, for sustained growth and prosperity. That philosophy prompted Jack to develop the *Redhouse Ranch* as a producing asset near a small airport outside of Topeka, Kansas where he kept his 50-year-old blue and white Cessna 170 'tail dragger' airplane in a Quonset hut hanger there. While contemplating his next moves, Jack and his friends believed that 'the Saints would provide', and everything would work out okay in the end, in their individual quests for independence.

With conspiracies circling his crown like a confluence of crows in a cornfield, Jack found that a little 'Irish diplomacy' (the ability to tell a man to go to hell, so that he looked forward to the trip), went a long way toward diffusing tensions. In reality, Jack's friend Sanjo Casagrande tailored the skill to better effect, ... which he learned from his Irish mother Anita Kelly, who hailed from the high desert plains of Roswell near Albuquerque, New Mexico.

In this sequel, Jack continues his search for truth, happiness, and a promise for a better tomorrow. Why was it that the world around him was so sodden with sadness, fear, disharmony, acrimony, and dishonesty, he wondered? Where could he run to, where could he hide? Should he 'just adjust' to the interminable intractable conditions, or did a better world exist elsewhere, in a lesser known, yet long forgotten realm?

Time would tell.

EL NICHUPTÉ LAGUNA

"A man is happy so long as he chooses to be happy." — Aleksandr Solzhenitsyn

It was early October, and Jack Redhouse could feel the whisper of the offshore breeze whistling through his whiskers as the autumn air warily arrived. The wind was a welcome relief from the harsh heat that had harassed him during the summer months of his surreptitious, if somewhat secluded sojourn, as Jack adjusted to the local weather and waited for the forecasted space weather events, prior to the normal hurricane season.

On that particular morning, he awakened refreshed from a nightlong nap aboard his motor yacht *Victory Liner 504,* berthed at the *Barracuda Marina* in Cancún. Jack had enjoyed his quiet evening hours slumbering peacefully in his well-worn rack listening to the water lap up against the hull of his boat near the dock. The more he rested and relaxed, the more he was able to think with a clear head. So, after stretching his limbs and wiping the sleep from his eyes, he pulled up his favorite easy chair next to the metal desk in his stateroom, poured a hot cup of coffee, opened his laptop to browse his morning e-mail, and scanned the local weather. He connected his VPN through Bucharest, Romania and took a few sips of rich Colombian java (with a slice of lime), to activate the villi in his GI tract. The hot coffee helped him clear his head while also easing some of the joint pain that he was feeling, giving Jack the added bump that he needed to begin his day.

After checking the morning mail, he moved into the head to rinse off in the shower and reconcile his other morning business. He showered and shaved, leaving a stubble of a beard, flossed between his teeth, dried between his toes, dressed, then sauntered aft to the galley to enjoy a snappy breakfast of oatmeal, grapefruit juice, English muffin, and melon. He poured a second cup of coffee from the galley, added a pinch of ground turmeric with some cream, and returned to his berthing space to check the current weather while scrolling through the local news. He made a mental note to call Frank Valero, … but he didn't need the note. He found Frank's number on his smart phone and dialed it. Frank's voicemail instructed him to leave a short message; so he did. He then reclined in his treasured leather chair to ponder the day ahead. They would talk later.

Jack had been flying solo aboard his boat for about a month since Frank Valero, Sarah Reid (aka *Enchanté*), and Carol Mulhaney (aka *Pernicious*) had all returned to Kansas after their last trip south along the Gulf coast. Sarah would return to Cancun in a couple of weeks to be with Jack and darken her Irish freckles, while Carol Mulhaney decided that she preferred to stay up in Topeka with Frank to help him run the '*Jack of Clubs*' sports bar near the local Topeka airport. Carol was dancing less, and running the club more, while Sarah conversely decided to spend more time later with Jack down in Cancun, … as Carol and Frank got to know each other better back in Kansas. Their lives had taken a U-turn during their many extended days, nights, and close encounters at sea; so they adjusted accordingly. Their little ventures were getting longer as well as more expensive, and began to seem more like work, so they all traveled less frequently.

Travel had become a royal hassle anyway, with the many TSA security checkpoints and DHS flash inspections in a fast changing world, so they all went about their business independently to get the job done. In the minds of Jack and his pals, no laws were being broken, so minor adjustments became routine, and by controlling their own thoughts and actions they could maintain their independence, as well as their individual freedoms. To be free, was to be happy, but it was also a personal choice. The checkpoints were just another bullshit government predictive programming mechanism put in place to keep citizens corralled like cattle, and probably wouldn't work in the long run anyway; but until people realized that they were being duped, and truly didn't need 'big government' in the first place, control actions would most likely continue.

If governments were able to control thoughts, they could also control actions. That was how people, corporations, and governments derived their power, in any case. As a result, there was a constant clash to control the minds of others to acquire more power and conquer more territory. The 'powers-that-be' wouldn't be content until the world was constrained like a favorite glossy golf ball clamped tightly within a confused and corrupted tight fisted grip.

Jack's old Navy pal Sanjo Casagrande and his wife Marissa (aka *Cassandra*), had joined Jack and the group on other Caribbean cruises in the past, but were eventually content to return to Duluth to enjoy the north country up near Lake Superior. They liked the slower paced life and the meat-and-potato pasties in the pleasant north, and would often just opt for an occasional 17-day holiday down to Albuquerque in the winter months to visit Sanjo's mother, Anita Kelly, and escape the more serious snow. Nevertheless, they mainly liked their slower paced life up north, especially after purchasing a comfortable little red and cream-colored Dutch roofed bungalow with blue swing-out arched windows overlooking the big lake on a peninsula near downtown Duluth, close to restaurants, shopping, and entertainment, to enjoy their golden years.

Jack Redhouse, for his part, enjoyed his 'alone time' on the boat since it allowed for a slower paced routine, a chance to devote more time to tackle some needed maintenance on the boat, and was a welcome respite. He had installed a small reverse osmosis water purification system onboard that converted seawater to fresh water, for use underway and in port, which greatly improved the quality of life aboard the boat. Using a small check valve and a spray wash wand, with a 3-way ball valve at the water inlet, he had rigged up a freshwater wash-down system to power wash everything on board 'YP-504' to keep her in tip-top shape. Jack enjoyed that. He also appreciated the extra time he had available to sketch drawings and paint pictures, as well as practice his knot tying skills; activities held over from his earlier days in the Navy.

Nevertheless, Jack's lifelong search for contentment continued to elude him. He had found external happiness; but it was the internal happiness that left him wanting. He had surrounded himself with many fine possessions, traveled to countless curious and alluring lands, and achieved a multitude of life long goals, yet felt arbitrarily assigned to a vacuous vessel and a saddened soul. Jack's earlier years had been blissful. People had seemed to be more positive in his younger years, and often went out of their way to help one another; the world was a different place back then. More recently, there were just too many people in constant conflict, possibly influenced by external forces, with too much personal friction between them, to realize much peace and harmony. So, it was partially a spiritual assimilation that Redhouse sought.

His trip to Finland a few weeks earlier to meet with his Russian pals had energized him as he vowed to get back into shape mentally, physically, and spiritually. The spectacular sauna on the sixth floor of his 'old world' hotel in Helsinki, with it's massive wood beamed ceilings, stunning tiled shower area, muted surroundings, and plenty of steam, helped Jack to dial down some of the stress and remove the toxins accumulated during the prior six months. The 'Finnic' cuisine amid the Baltic ambience of the abundant boulevards and proud people of Helsinki made his holiday travel all the more satisfying, as Jack explored his ancestral surroundings. Likewise, his subsequent trip to Estonia to retrieve his new e-Residency ID card at the 'Politsei' Border Guard station in Tallinn, and explore that enchanting old city with a university setting, helped Jack to revive and restore his mostly melodious and metaphysical demeanor. Furthermore, his shipboard encounters with complete strangers aboard the *Tallink* car ferry during the crossing through the Gulf of Finland took him back to his old Navy days. The fact that he could also enjoy a tall glass of *'Lapin Kulta'* draft beer at the bar in the main lounge, while listening to the shipboard band, added to the adventure. The trip also put him in touch with his Russian pals who were located just around the corner in St. Petersburg, Russia, and who had expressed an interest in Jack's work to help with 'Business Development' projects there. The proximity to the Gulf of Finland was an added plus, as the closeness allowed travel to St. Petersburg by boat, rail, or automobile through the border town of Narva, if needed.

The fact that Estonia might soon be offering their own 'cryptocurrency' called the 'estcoin', might allow entrepreneurs with e-residency status to set up new global 'virtual businesses' with other blockchain technologies as well. 'Estcoins' might be a good alternative to relying on corrupt central banking systems in any case. The 'estcoin' would compete with other digital based currencies like 'Bitcoin', 'Ethereum', and others that were making their debut, but the world was changing, and Jack needed to change with it. So, 'estcoins' might provide a future option for Jack if central banks didn't block them.

Still, what was it going to take to make Jack happy? Toys weren't cutting it anymore; although he did truly enjoy his boat, his old 'straight tail' airplane, and the many other amenities at the 'Redhouse Ranch' in Kansas. He also had plenty of money for his basic needs and wants, plus extras. He found that the women in his life were often confused, conflicted, and complicated, with more of his money going to pay for their many needs and wants, regardless. Perhaps that was a trait that attracted Jack to those women in the first place; a desire to set things straight, and do some good in the world. So, what was it that would actually made Jack happy? That was his curious conundrum.

For his part, Jack didn't need much money for his day-to-day expenses in any case. He didn't eat or drink as much as he used to, was debt-free, and lived on his motor yacht much of the time. He did most of his grocery shopping in the local markets where he pulled into port, and kept a small freezer and a walk-in cooler on board to store food. The boat did actually use a considerable amount of diesel fuel when underway, but the cost was a business expense and was included within his calculations for the 'cost of sales' under his company account. His ranch in Kansas was also a producing asset, which paid for itself while contributing to his revenue stream and income. Yet, he felt blessed (but not necessarily happy) to be alone in Cancun for a few weeks of reflection and renewal. To be honest, the whole team needed a bit more space after spending some time at sea; so a foot planted on familiar turf while strolling to the market in the fresh morning air for some fresh fish or fruit, or plopping into a pub for a pint, felt like fun. Like a corked bottle of champagne stranded on a hot summer deck, where an increase in temperature causes an increase in pressure at constant volume; As the cork is popped, the gas explodes through the narrow neck of the bottle in a spontaneous spray of instant gratification. Pulling into a new port was a lot like that.

Thus, sometime after noon, when Jack had sufficiently spruced up and finished his chores, he threw on a fresh pair of blue jeans with a cotton shirt, donned his ball cap, then grabbed his new cell phone as he stepped off the quarterdeck and sauntered down the peninsula to find the nearest watering hole. In this case, it was *'Guillermo's Grill'* which was located just a couple of hundred meters south of where his boat was berthed, overlooking the Cancun Nichupté lagoon.

Guillermo's Grill was a 'top drawer' steak and seafood place with a relaxing ambience, great stonework all around, lots of glass, and wood beamed ceilings in the interior, with a fantastic bar that featured a stunning view of the lagoon from the outside deck. Jack had met several of his old Russian and Panamanian pals at *Guillermo's* a couple of times in the past to talk business, make plans, and just relax. In that place, and on that day, Jack chose to be happy.

Jack stepped inside *Guillermo's Grill* and sauntered up to the bar while elucidating on how much he admired the milder weather. He then ordered a *Modelo cerveza* from the bartender who wore a white nametag with black scripted letters that just read 'Seumas'. As Jack sat there, taking in the warm surroundings and practicing his 'Spanish' at the bar, Frank Valero returned Jack's earlier call.

As he recognized the caller's name and number, Jack answered the call. "Frank, … *'Hola amigo'*, it's good to hear from you. Thanks for returning my call. How's everything going up at *el rancho Redhouse*?", asked Jack.

"Great Jack! Everything's fine up here. It's good to hear your voice. How's your little slice of paradise down in the lagoon?" replied Frank.

"It's pretty nice down here too, Frank! The weather has cooled down a bit, and there's a slight offshore breeze. I'm sitting here at the bar at *Guillermo's Grill* with Seumas enjoying a *frio Modelo Especial* overlooking the bay. What could be better? How are the girls making out?

"They're doing well, Jack. Sarah plans to fly down to the Yucatán sometime next week to join you in the good life, while Carol and I bust our asses up here at the farm" Frank said with a laugh.

"I feel your pain, Frank. How's the club doing? All copacetic?, asked Jack. "You bet. Running like fine-tuned clock, or a well-oiled *Glock*. Regular customers are coming in often, ... and new faces showing up all the time from out of town. The economy may be going to hell, but this place is hopping. Go figure", Frank said with confidence, again with a laugh.

"That's good to hear, Frank. I'm looking forward to Sarah's visit. It will be good to share some time down here with someone who appreciates my sensibilities. Although, I do very much enjoy my loneliness and quiet time as well. I need the balance", he said.

"That's a good way to put it, Jack. I mean, what's it gonna be, ... sensitivity, or success?"

"Ha-haa, right Frank. A young gal that I dated in our twenties, who eventually passed her bar exam to become a lawyer, once told me that every successful guy that she ever met was a real prick. So, what do women really want? Do they want that 'sensitive' guy, or would they prefer to spend some time with a real prick? Can they have it both ways? I'm sure that many of them try. In any case, we all have to live with ourselves", said Jack.

"By the way, you can reach me at this number while I'm down in Mexico. You can buy these cell phones pretty cheap down here at the local OXXO convenience stores in Cancun and load them with a couple hundred minutes on a 'pay-as-you-go' basis for about $20 bucks; so it's quite convenient, ... and I can always switch phones if necessary. On top of that, you can track my location if I give you an access code. It's a pretty slick option for guys like us. Very clean." said Jack.

"Yeah, that could come in handy", conceded Frank.

"Yes, in fact, let's check it out. Send me a request from your smart phone with your GPS tracking app, and I'll send you an access code. Then you can track my location on your phone to see if it works." suggested Jack.

"Good idea, Jack. I'll send the request out shortly", agreed Frank.

Soft music played in the background on the restaurant's sound system. Erik Clapton singing *'Autumn Leaves'* drifted through the sunlit stillness of the segmented rooms while a few people chatted in scattered groups around the grill,

... and the water off the lagoon sparkled through the clear glass plate windows causing the slate-colored stacked-stone archways to dance.

The Autumn leaves, Drift by my window, ♪♪♪ *The Autumn leaves, of Red and Gold.*

I see your lips, the summer kisses, ♪♪♪ *The sun burned hands, I used to hold.*

"Anyway, I think that Sarah would enjoy taking a break from her dancing routine at the club, and getting back together with you for a while", Frank confided. "She also said that she needs a little more sun, so I think she's ready for a holiday", suggested Frank.

Yes, it will be good to have Sarah back down in Cancun in a week or so, thought Jack, where he could appreciate her dance moves more attentively. Frank could hear the muffled music in the background through the phone, and thought Jack was probably getting the rest that he wanted. They talked a bit more and agreed to keep in touch via their cell phones through text messages until they could talk again. Things were going well from their adjacent perspectives. 'Autumn Leaves' was followed by Rod Stewart singing, *'Let it Snow, 'Let it Snow, 'Let it Snow'.*

https://www.youtube.com/watch?v=LAdmdunWvsA

"OK, thanks for the update Frank, and for getting back to me", said Jack. "We'll talk again soon".

"Great Jack! Take care, and call me any time", answered Frank. "In the mean time, I'll text you if anything urgent comes up", he said.

"Hasta luego, *Señor*". "Si, Hasta luego, Mister", they responded to each other.

The geopolitical situation back in the States, as well as the rest of the world was a mess, and Jack and Frank felt like big changes were on the horizon. Nothing was safe. People were voting to break away from 'big government', with its 'one world order' mentality controlled by the corrupt criminal reptilian actors within big institutions and NGO's, and were opting instead for nationalistic structures. There was also some talk about the United States breaking apart in the future and becoming a series of individual sovereign republics, with parts of the country joining with Mexico, some states like Michigan and Wisconsin with Canada, California with Canada or Asia, and the East coast becoming part of Europe. Also, Europe was breaking apart into separate states once again with countries voting to 'stick with their roots' to control the runaway immigration into the EU from Africa and the Middle East. The US Dollar was on the verge of collapse due to mountains of debt, as were other counterfeit fiat currencies, and there was also talk of the Federal Reserve, the IMF, and the World Bank going 'belly up' in bankruptcy with a return to sound money coming from the US Treasury. A new 'Continental Dollar' had already been designed and printed, and was awaiting distribution. How was that going to work? Nobody seemed to know. So, they were all on edge, ... and clueless in a dimensionless matrix. But, from a funny and lop-sided point-of- view, that's the way they liked it. Foot loose, and fancy free, with plenty of possibility; kind of like the Wild West, ... with its numerous native attractions.

The question was, 'Where was the world headed'? Or, as Winston Churchill said about Russia during World War II in a radio broadcast in October 1939, "*I cannot forecast to you the action of Russia. It is a riddle, wrapped in a mystery, inside an enigma; but perhaps there is a key. That key is Russian national interest.*" The United States was beginning to look a lot like that, as autumn arrived, and the climate slowly changed.

With those thoughts in mind, Jack ordered a New York strip steak dinner and another *frio Modelo cerveza* from '*Seumas*' the bartender, while he pondered the past, and peered out over the shimmering lagoon.

"Thanks for taking care of me, Seumas", said Jack. "Don't mention it Jack, it's my job. The customer always comes first, and my shift ends shortly anyway", responded Seumas.

Upon finishing his dinner and drinks, Jack paid his bill, took another look past the expansive bar window to the lagoon beyond, and for a moment, thought he saw a flash of the future; or perhaps it was a pane of the past; or maybe it was just a crack in the wall of reality leading to the truth. As Jack left the restaurant, he found Frank's text requesting a GPS access code on his cell phone, then sent a code back to Frank before stepping into the afternoon sun and out of Guillermo's Grill heading back up the peninsula toward his boat. Feeling satisfied and well adjusted, perhaps even a little bit happy and mystified, as well as a bit groggy, he decided that it was probably time for his afternoon siesta.

His situational awareness was usually pretty keen, but his street smarts were somewhat soft on this occasion, as he didn't hear the quickened steps of the two hombres coming up fast behind him as he passed a delivery truck. The next thing he felt was a blunt tap on the back of his head before he went down like a sack of fresh fish. Thus, he didn't quite make it back to the boat.

Just Adjust

Some might say
We chose this place
Before the earth was dust.

And, some would say
That's just not so;
The old ones rose through crust.

My brother says that we must do,
just what we think we must,
And therefore, should consider most,
the things that don't go bust.

He also said that life's a trust,
And, that his mind is toast;
And of all the things he ever lost,
His mind, he misses most.

Our thoughts get tossed
From to, through fro,
we ponder, and we fuss.
But after all is said and done,
They're adjusted, as discussed.

Transcending all dimensions
Through all things frivolous
In existential furor;
It's just ridiculous.

Dost thou live forever?
Or did we just get thrust
From somewhere long forgotten,
And tossed beneath the bus?

It really shouldn't matter
Since most roads lead to thus;
The seven mountained city
with its frankincense and lust.

In constant contravention,
with manifest mistrust,
Consensus in all circles says
We just must just adjust.

Jaak Tallinn Adjusted; May, 2015

SHANTY SIDE OF TOWN

'Victorious warriors win first and then go to war, while defeated warriors go to war first, and then seek to win' - Sun Tzu, <u>The Art of War</u>

Back at the ranch near Topeka, Frank Valero felt energized after his short phone conversation with Jack, and was glad that Jack sounded content. He would pass the good news on to Carol and Sarah. They had all been working hard at the ranch and the *'Jack of Clubs'* sports bar to keep both operations running smoothly for Jack, since he was the one that kept them all in sync, living well, and on the straight and narrow. Frank also sent out the request for an access code to Jack's local cell phone in Mexico to allow him to track Jack's location on GPS, as Jack had requested. Sarah would be glad to hear that Jack was doing well because she had planned to head down to Cancun the following week to take a well earned break from the 'Sport's Bar' scene.

Frank hadn't been all that familiar with the day-to-day operations of either the club or the ranch, having come from the Louisiana shipyards following his 'Navy days' with Jack, but he was a good manager. That is, he knew instinctively how to plan, organize, staff, lead, and control operations to get results. Carol knew the internal workings of the 'Jack of Clubs' quite well having worked in all areas wearing different hats (or pants, shorts, or skirts), so she pretty much managed the club with Frank overseeing the entire business and making some of the critical decisions when his input was requested. Since Carol Mulhaney and Frank Valero were also part owners in the 'Jack of Clubs' they had a vested interest in making sure that the business was profitable. Sarah, not so much, since she just worked there as a waitress and dancer. Ray Forbes, the foreman at the *'Redhouse Ranch'* outside of Topeka, had been husbanding Jack's whole farm operation in Kansas for many years under Jack's supervision, working independently to get the daily chores accomplished. As Ray liked to say, "Chores Come Hell or High Water", and they had to be completed regardless of weather, personal problems, or other concerns. Ray Forbes always 'Got 'er done'.

So they were busy, and hadn't quite noticed, or weren't very surprised that Jack hadn't gotten back to them for a couple of days after his call. After all, Frank had just spoken to Jack earlier that week. So, Frank was a bit bewildered when he received a voicemail message from Jack's cell phone a couple of days later, from *someone* other than Jack. Frank remembered their conversation about switching to the pay-as-you-go cell phones, so thought maybe Jack had exchanged his earlier phone for a new phone. Frank had also received an earlier text message from Jack listing an access code. So, Frank was confused. Be that as it may, the message from the new caller was quite clear and somewhat puzzling. The voice message simply said, with a distinct Mexican accent, "Hi, we're friends of Seumas, and we've got Jack! Call if you want him back.", then hung up.

Meanwhile, in another part of Cancún, north of the posh hotels, and away from the '*Zona Hotelera*', Jack sat in a hot, remote, stale, and somewhat stinky cinderblock storage building on a dirt and gravel side street, bound to a bench where his new 'breaking bad' amigos had spirited him away for safe keeping. Miguel and Ignacio had been watching Jack for several days, had followed his regular routine, and after bundling him away in their delivery van were determined to extort some sort of ransom from the old gringo that had landed on their sacred turf. After all, anyone that could afford their own boat, as well as dine regularly in a place like *Guillermo's Grill* must have some extra loot lying around, they reasoned. What they didn't quite understand was that Jack was the wrong guy to mess with, even in Mexico. That was true of Jack, but was also true of Jack's close friends in the states.

In any case, Frank Valero was understandably concerned with the voicemail message left from Jack's cell phone a couple of days following their conversation. He sent a text message back saying, "*Let's talk! You are making a big mistake. Coming down to Cancún for a friendly chat*". And with that, he booked a flight to Cancún ahead of Sarah's visit, and contacted his Russian and Panamanian buddies in the area as well as dropping a line to his old Navy buddy 'Crazy Joe' Melnik, who was always happy to help. 'Crazy Joe' was one of Frank's old steaming buddies that could wrestle his way through some tricky situations, could handle the stress, was looking for a 'project' anyway, and was quite handy with various types of ordnance and firearms. 'Crazy Joe' would meet Frank at the airport in Cancun for a friendly 'meet and greet' and would find a way to work around the Mexican thugs to get Jack back. Their foreign pals from Panama would also meet Frank and Joe in Cancún when they landed, with some state-of-the-art electronics for tracking cell phones via GPS monitoring equipment, as well as a few other special tools specific to their immediate task.

Frank, Crazy Joe, and the rest of their team all met up at a hotel in Cancún close to the International airport on the morning after they all arrived, for a short strategic '*logisitics*' discussion. They also rented a couple of cars, one mid-size and one SUV, at the airport in case they had to split up during their surveillance. They knew that they needed to act quickly since Jack had been missing for a few days by then. All the same, their job was made easier thanks to the 'acceptance code' that Jack had sent to Frank a couple of days earlier to allow Frank to monitor the location of Jack's cell phone. They didn't know whether the phone was still with Jack's abductors, but were hoping that it was. So, their first action item was to enter the acceptance code into Frank's GPS phone 'app' to locate Jack's cell phone. It showed that his phone was changing locations, allowing them some quick 'real time' reconnaissance to determine who was in possession of the phone, as well as assess the threat level before walking into harm's way. Or, as *Sun Tzu* wrote in *The Art of War*, '*Victorious warriors win first and then go to war, while defeated warriors go to war first, and then seek to win*'. If the threat was small, they decided that they wouldn't finish off the two guys that had taken Jack, … just rough them up a little to send a clear message. After all, they were in another country and wanted to avoid the cops if possible. They had heard some of the stories about corrupt Mexican cops and crusty jails before. Frank and Joe had also both stood plenty of shore patrol duty in their Navy days, so they knew how to handle a nightstick effectively to take someone down.

Thanks to the phone app, within a few hours after they arrived, Frank, Crazy Joe, and their two friends found an older white delivery truck with two guys in their late forties near a liquor store on the north side of Cancun, while tracing the signal from one of their rental cars. They watched from a distance as the two thugs exited the store with what appeared to be some sandwiches and beer, and hopped back into the truck heading down some back streets to a remote residential neighborhood in the northern section of the city. They stayed back at a safe distance while tracking their path via the cell phone app. The area was full of concrete-block houses, shabby half-painted apartment buildings, and other small ramshackle cinderblock buildings scattered among a few retail stores in a haphazard, comingled kind of way. The area looked poor, and like many places south of the *Rio Grande*, many of the buildings appeared crude and 'unfinished'. They kept a close watch on the two guys to see whether they might lead them back to Jack's location to possibly allow the team to extract Jack before confronting his assailants. Their planning and patience would pay off.

The four of them watched from a distance as the two scruffy thugs entered through the back door of a remote dishwater-white cinder block building that appeared to be abandoned. A few minutes later they parked their rental cars about a half block away hidden from view, and watched the building in two teams from different angles, checking for access or a clue to Jack's whereabouts. As dusk approached, they decided to wait until it was a bit darker outside to move in close. From a distance, they tried to track their movements to watch for an opening. They also decided to call Jack's phone to see if his captors would pick up and discuss terms, ... if there were going to be any. They reasoned that, if they could negotiate their way through the process, it might be less chaotic when they actually moved in for Jack. That might be a bit tricky in any case, since it could arbitrarily remove the element of surprise. On the other hand, if they worked it right, they hoped it would force the abductors to make some stupid mistakes.

With that decision made, they watched the building covertly, and as darkness fell over the northern reaches of Cancún, Frank then pressed the call button for Jack's cell phone and heard three rings before someone picked up. *"Hola, Who's this?"*, the caller asked plainly. "Hello, I'm a friend of Jack," answered Frank. "I got your text message! Is there something we should discuss?" asked Frank. "Yeah, we got your buddy here!" came the reply. "You can have him back for

$50,000 dollars cash", he demanded. "That's a lot of money", said Frank. "But it can be arranged. Let me talk to Jack". With that, they put Jack on the phone for a few seconds. "Frank, is that you?" and Frank said "Yes, Jack. Hang in there! We'll work something out very soon!", as they quickly pulled the phone away from Jack again. Frank said to the guy on the other end, "How do you want to work this?" To which the thug replied, "We'll call you with instructions tomorrow", and then hung up again.

So from that short exchange, Frank and his team determined that the callers were with Jack, and were probably in the building that they were watching remotely, and would call sometime the following day to make the exchange. However, Frank and his team weren't going to wait until morning, but were going to get very 'up close and personal' at the first opportunity. The building was tightly wrapped with little access other than a back door and two boarded up and steel-barred windows, with some junk leaning up against the outside cinderblock walls, near a few tall weeds. There was however, a vent on the roof that they found through their initial surveillance. They also brought with them a small fiber-optic camera device with a wire probe that could be inserted into a crack to check the interior layout. Using a small connector that fit into the bottom of a smart phone, the operator could view the interior of the space on his phone's display screen. Pretty slick! The camera would help them with their game plan. As night approached, one of the Panamanians was able to sneak quietly up to the side of the building unnoticed, and furtively insert the camera optic through a small crack in one of the boarded up windows to get a better view of the inside, as well as Jack's location in the far corner, and snap a couple of pictures with the phone set on 'silent'. They drew a quick layout of the interior, agreed to a plan, and then moved into position for a possible assault. They carried a couple of solid oak, 22" long night sticks, and one of the Panamanians, as well as Frank, carried a small Bersa Thunder .380 with a noise suppressor, that was also supplied by their pals. They gave Crazy Joe a 'concealed carry' Taurus model '180 Curve' with laser, in .380 ACP, just in case the situation turned 'froggy'. Actually, Joe would have preferred his own Smith & Wesson .357 magnum revolver that he kept at home, but it would have been difficult to get that into the country on short notice; So Joe was glad to have the little Taurus instead.

They would create a diversion and hope that one of the guys would get curious enough to investigate. Then, they would make their move at the right moment. If they were lucky, they could quickly toss a stun grenade into the building, either from the topside vent or the door, breach the back door, and rush the two guys while covering Jack within about 30 seconds. It was a bit risky, but if their luck was better, one of the two guys might investigate a disturbance outside the building and come out the back door to make the extraction easier yet. Either way, they were going in within the next two minutes.

Their luck quickly paid off again as they put their plan into action. One of the Panamanians took one of the rental cars, revved the engine hard outside the building, then slammed the gears into reverse and smashed into the side of the building near where Jack was tied up in the back corner. Frank, Crazy Joe, and the other Panamanian friend were all in position as one of the thugs, Ignacio, panicked and immediately rushed out the back door of the building with a pistol in hand to check the commotion. He went down hard as Crazy Joe, ready at the back door used the night stick to smash his shins and slam the back of his head in the darkened alley as the thug shot past him. Ignacio went down hard and fast without a peep. At that point, with the back door still ajar, they kicked his pistol away and stashed it, then simultaneously tossed a stun grenade into the center of the building before rushing to both interior sides with their weapons drawn after the blast went off. The other guy, Miguel, didn't even see it coming. As he stood up and grabbed a hammer off the wooden bench, Frank shot him in the right leg just above his kneecap with his Bersa Thunder .380, then knocked him out cold to the floor with a quick barrel to the head near where Jack was seated. Jack was sitting quietly tied to a heavy wooden bench in the corner with a big grin on his face as they cut the tape and plastic tie-wraps from around his legs and ankles. He said, "Frank, I owe you one". Frank just smiled. Amazingly, the whole plan went off without a hitch, nobody else was shot, and no other person outside the building ever saw or heard a thing.

The men then quickly extracted the two coldcocked banditos after binding their hands and feet, stuffed a sock in their mouths secured with duct tape, then tossed them into the back seat of a rental car at the rear of the building after searching for more weapons. While binding their hands, Joe also noticed that Miguel had a tattoo on his right hand that looked like a snake and a cross, intertwined together. A similar tattoo was also scribed on the right side of Ignacio's neck. Beneath the symbol were the words *"Esse non videri"*. Joe would try to identify the marks at some later date to determine their meaning and origin. They also tied a 'CAT' tourniquet around Miguel's right leg to stop the bleeding in the rental car. The whole extraction exercise took less than five minutes to complete as they all slipped away in the darkness back to Jack's boat at the *Barracuda Marina* in Cancún, located just 20 minutes away to the south.

BARRACUDA BAY, BELIZE, & THE BEACH

Esse non videri - "To be, rather than to seem"

Frank would need to call Sarah Reid to postpone her trip down to Cancún for a week or so. She would be disappointed, but as Ray Forbes liked to say, "Chores Come Hell or High Water". Frank, Jack, and Joe would need to get some answers first. Business, … before pleasure.

When the five pals and their 'breaking bad banditos' arrived back at the Marina with the two rental cars, they parked as close to Jack's motor yacht as possible. Using a small cart and a tarp that they had on board, they wheeled the two thugs out to the boat and swung them on to the main deck, then took them below to the engine room. They heaved the cart on board and stowed it below as well. The two Panamanians drove the rental cars further away to an adjacent parking lot, cleaning up any blood in the car as best they could, then returned to the boat. They would call the rental car company in the morning to give them the location since they had no intention of returning to Cancun anytime soon. The cars were charged to a Panama company credit card in any case. Then, with their two new passengers taken below, they decided that it was time for some night time 'big game' fishing somewhere out in the Caribbean for a few days to sort out the details and get some answers. They wanted to keel haul the two hombres that had kidnapped Jack, but decided that it would be better to get some additional information first, like what did they know, when did they know it, and who put them up to their disdainful deeds; or were these two clowns just operating under their own initiative? Also, how did

Seumas Santaña fit into the picture, or did they just throw his name out there for grins?

With little time to waste, Jack started the main engines from the bridge while Frank pulled the mooring lines onto the main deck, and Joe and their two Panamanian pals boarded the vessel. Following that, they quickly cracked the throttle, along with a vintage bottle of blackberry brandy as the boat got underway heading south out of the marina toward Panama. Their plan was to meet up with their Russian friends, turn these blokes over to them for further interrogation, and take their two Panamanian pals back home. The fate of the 'stowaways' would be determined later.

Jack felt relieved to be back behind the wheel of his boat again, as they all headed south into the darkened waters of the Caribbean away from the lagoon. With Cancun and the *Barracuda Marina* dissolving into the horizon behind them, Jack began to reflect on the past few days, thankful that the situation had worked out favorably. He recited a short prayer thanking God and any of the angels and saints that he could think of, for watching over him, and also asked for safe travel. So, what was it going to take to make Jack happy, he mused? He had a lot of time to ponder his precarious position over the past few days while being bound to a wooden bench in a scant little shantytown shack in the northern slums of Cancún, and decided that the best way to resolve his present dilemma would be to identify the things that were making him *unhappy* in the first place; then eliminate them. That would be a good first step.

As Jack began to focus on the task at hand, the whole team began to unwind and felt more at ease as they ventured further out into the open waters of the Caribbean, putting some distance between themselves and the tenuous trouble. The salty sea air seemed to satisfy some deep-seated sensibilities as the group settled into a regular routine and downed a couple more shots of brandy. The two Panamanians, Eduardo and Fernando, had been sent to Cancun by Jack's Russian friends, Garry and Zak, after Frank had learned of Jack's abduction and called them. The team was now heading down to visit their Russian friends in Belize after Jack sent a text message apprising them of their current status. The Russians sent a text back saying that they were presently in Honduras but were planning to be in Belize on business, so it might be more convenient to meet with everyone there. In that case, the two Panamanians could fly back to

Panama City from whichever port they eventually pulled into. Jack agreed and welcomed the shorter trip after a hard week, and was delighted with the change in plans since they all needed to get some rest. Jack would hit his rack first for a few hours, as Frank took the con, and as Joe went below with the two Panamanians to help keep an eye on their prisoners.

Jack, Frank, and 'Crazy Joe' had all been friends for many years as all three had served aboard the same ship in the South China Seas as 'snipes' (engineering group) during their Navy days, decades earlier. All three were familiar with the internal workings of ships and how to maintain them. After his discharge, Frank returned home to Louisiana and landed a job working at a large shipyard in New Orleans building US Navy and commercial ships. The shipyards were always happy to hire ex-Navy guys like Frank Valero because they knew their way around ships, equipment, and construction. In fact, it wasn't much of a transition at all. When his sailor buddies Jack Redhouse, and 'Crazy Joe' Melnik were discharged, they had contacted Frank as they made the transition from military to civilian life, and stayed in touch throughout the many years since then. They could also rely on Frank to lend them some quick cash if they needed it while they found their footing again back in the states. So the relationship continued as Frank entered the 'Sports Bar' business with Jack after retiring from the shipyard, and Crazy Joe kept in touch with his Navy pals as well.

As they made their way south, one of the Panamanians, Fernando, the taller of the two, appeared to have some medical training, as he was able to dig the .380 slug out of Miguel's right leg above the knee while he was still groggy. Actually, being unfamiliar with the Bersa, Frank's aim had been a little bit off so the slug hadn't penetrated the bone to any great extent, and was easily removed. The other Panamanian, Eduardo (they called him 'Eddie') was more of a 'special ops' sort of guy; shorter, but stocky and fast, who also seemed to know a bit about treating gunshot wounds. They kept the two captives tied up below in the engine room where they had set up a couple of cots, as they rotated the watch around them. Joe tied a strap around Miguel's torso, and his legs below the knees, to help restrain him while Fernando operated. Eduardo assisted Fernando as they made their prisoners more comfortable. Eddie also poured some brandy on the wound to help cleanse it, but he may have just seen the technique in a movie and was curious to see how Miguel would react. in any case, after the slug was removed, they inserted a few stitches, then dressed the wound with gauze and a bandage from the boat's first aid kit to help it heal. As an added precaution, Jack provided Joe with some pain pills left over from an earlier operation in Panama, to help calm Miguel's nerves and ease the agony. When their two prisoners came around again the boat was well out to sea, so Joe gave each of them, Miguel and Ignacio, a shot of brandy to show some compassion, dampen their senses, and loosen their tongues a little. It seemed to work, because they both began to talk.

While Jack rested, and Frank took the controls, Joe kept the two Panamanian's company as they changed the watch around their two captives. Frank would take a nap after Jack returned to the bridge. Then, it would be Joe's turn to nap while Frank kept their Panamanian pals company. It wouldn't take them long to reach Belize in any case, traveling at a steady 10 to 15 knots; maybe a couple of days. They would have to navigate around some shoals but weren't too overly concerned with the boat having a draft of about 1.8 meters. As long as they stayed out in the open water, and with weather permitting, they could make good time. So as they motored south down the coast, Joe questioned the two captives as they began to explain their motives for abducting Jack. Their Panamanian pals helped Joe with the interrogation since some of the testimony was in Spanish, and their 'English' was limited, or so they said. According to their statements, it was mainly their own idea to shanghai Jack after the two thugs saw him sitting in the bar at *Guillermo's Grill* enjoying his steak dinner and beer. They had been watching him for several days as he walked between his boat and the bar and decided that it would be a good way to garner some quick cash. That was their initial story. Joe asked, "How does Seumas fit into the picture?" to which they replied that they "just made it up" to tie in their relationship with Jack's location, and to emphasize to Frank that they were serious when he called. They hadn't thought the plan through very thoroughly; it was more of a spur-of-the-moment decision. They had done this type of thing before but were never caught, so thought it would be a piece of cake. They said that they knew 'Seumas' from the bar because they made frequent food and beverage deliveries to *Guillermo's Grill* for a local vendor. He "knew nothing about it" they said, and "by now Seumas was probably wondering why Jack hadn't been back to the bar for a few days". It was a good story; but was it true? Joe then asked them what they had planned to do with Jack after they received the ransom money? They just looked at each other with a blank stare, then looked back at Joe and said nothing. "Were you going to snuff him?" asked Joe. Miguel, who was feeling a little pain from his gunshot wound looked at Joe contentiously and shrugged his shoulders. "That was the plan!" he confessed. It would not have been the first time. Joe and the others would have more questions for the two thugs later.

After Jack awoke from his nap, he began to feel more levelheaded about his current situation and his station in life. He felt as if he may have 'turned the corner', as he vowed to eliminate many of the things that were making him unhappy. He needed to simplify things, he decided; Make some changes, and perhaps get away for a while to ruminate on the rudimentary aspects of his new reality. Reflect. Get rid of some baggage. Disappear. Vanish. Become invisible. Maybe spend some time on a beach. Now that he had slept awhile, he felt more refreshed. He needed to put some things behind him, and start over.

With that thought in mind, Jack decided that he might just put the boat into port at San Pedro on the *Ambergris Caye*, slightly north of Belize City instead of the larger port near the city. They could dock at *'Amigo's del Mar'* where the coastal ferry came in, as well as fly out of the San Pedro airport if needed. They could also take on fuel and pick up some supplies in port for the next leg of the trip, or wherever else they decided to 'steam' to next. San Pedro also had a decent beach as well as several hotels if they decided to just 'kick back' for a few days. He would discuss the plan with his Russian friends to see whether they agreed with his proposal. Jack also knew that he should contact Sarah Reid (*Enchanté*) at some point to give her their current status and try to meet up with her in Cancun, or elsewhere. What to do, what to do, what to do? He should at least call her to let her know that they were OK. Touch base, so to speak. Then he wondered whether he was beginning to add more 'baggage' to his life; baggage that he was trying to jettison in his quest to simplify his life. He would need to deal with those individual requisites later.

As they made their way toward *Ambergris Caye*, Jack sent a text message to his Russian contacts to gauge their reaction to a possible rendezvous in San Pedro instead of Belize City. The Russians liked the idea. The change in plans would get them out of their current routine and help them avoid the city for the most part. They could either fly into the main hub airport, or directly to a smaller airport in San Pedro from their current location. The ferry from the city to San Pedro was an hour-and-a-half boat ride if they chose that option. Then they could meet Jack, Frank, Joe, and the Panamanians at one of the hotels in San Pedro. The Russians would set it up and get back to Jack. With that done, Jack dialed up Sarah Reid to say 'Hello', and get her input. It was the right thing to do.

"Hello Sarah, it's Jack" he said when she answered her cell phone. She could see that the call was a 'private number', and was curious. She was a bit surprised to hear Jack's voice. "Well, Hi Jack, where are you calling from", she asked.

"We're down around Quintana Roo", said Jack. "Not sure exactly", he continued. "We left out of Cancun last night and we're making our way toward San Pedro Island at the moment. I believe that we're about forty or fifty miles off the coast heading south. I'll have to check the charts", he said.

"Well, how are you?" she said. "Frank told us that you were having some trouble down there, and that he was flying down to Cancun with 'Crazy Joe' to take care of a problem." Sarah said, sounding a bit concerned. "He asked me to hold off on flying down there for a few days until we heard back", she said.

"Yeah, we had some trouble. Not sure what Frank told you. But, it's all taken care of now for the most part. As a result, we had to leave Cancun in a bit of a hurry, and we have to meet with some people down in Belize for a few days; then, I'm not exactly sure what my plans are after that. I can tell you more about it later. Are you still planning on heading down this way?" he asked.

"Well, yes!" she said. "If it's OK with you, I'd like to fly out of here in the next couple of days. I was just waiting to hear back from you".

"Ok. That's why I'm calling. I think you could fly down to Belize City or San Pedro Island in a few days to meet with us there, or I could call you after we settle this other business, and make more definite plans in that case. Whichever you prefer." Jack responded.

"Terrific!" She said. "I'll check the websites and plan to fly down to Belize in a few days" she said. "I'll text or e-mail with my flight itinerary as soon as I have it". "I'm looking forward to seeing you Jack, as well as working on my tan", said Sarah. "It's getting rather gloomy up here in Kansas, and I need a break. Can't wait to see you!" she repeated.

"OK, Sarah. That works for me. Let me know when you set things up, and I'll plan to pick you up when you arrive. We'll keep in touch through this cell phone number by text or phone call. Sound good?"

"Yes, Jack. Good news! I'll text you as soon as I can set it up, and I'll let Carol know what's happening so that she's in the loop" Sarah exclaimed, and with that they ended the call and began to make future plans.

Victory Liner 504 scouting the Caribbean coast in the early years

It was late afternoon on the second day heading south, so with the call to Sarah out of the way and in play, Jack decided to go back to the galley and brew a fresh pot of coffee, as well as a few simple cold cut sandwiches for the crew and prisoners. By now, Joe had found a spare rack and was taking a well-earned nap, while Frank was up on the bridge steering the boat and watching for trouble. Jack would take some coffee and a sandwich up to Frank, make another sandwich for Joe for after his nap, then take a few more sandwiches aft to the engine room where their Panamanian pals, Eduardo and Fernando were taking turns keeping a close eye on their prisoners. Before heading up to see Frank, Jack stopped in at the head, then went down to his rack to pick up his old Model 64 Smith & Wesson, .38

Special revolver that he kept under his mattress for insurance. He trusted his own firearm over the guns that the Panamanians had brought. Besides, they had their favorite pieces, and he had his. He checked the chamber for rounds, then stuffed the S&W in his belt in the middle of his back and pulled his shirt over the piece outside his pants to conceal it. He also checked that he had his 'Browning' folding pocketknife in his right pocket that his Dad had given him when he was a boy in Minnesota, and that he usually carried with him. Now, he felt prepared, and could take care of business if needed. 'Hope for the best, and plan for the worst', he thought to himself. After that, he stopped back in the galley to pick up the coffee and sandwiches and headed up the ladder to the bridge to speak with Frank.

In the wheelhouse, Frank Valero was in his element as he maneuvered the boat through the rolling waves, and enjoyed trying to maintain the best course toward San Pedro. He stayed far enough out from the coast to avoid obstacles on his course while following the charts and his GPS, … but close enough to the coast to conserve energy and make the most headway. Frank estimated their position to be about forty miles out from the coast, and maybe thirty miles northwest of *Banco Chinchorro*. It was a challenge that he very much enjoyed. He loved boats, loved working on them, and loved operating them. He had worked on them for decades in Louisiana and loved everything about boats, … and it was a great diversion from Kansas, the ranch, and the 'Jack of Clubs'. He was on top of his game. Up on the bridge, Jack mentioned to Frank that he had called Sarah (*Enchanté*) and that she would probably be flying down to Belize in a few days to meet up with them. Sarah would also talk with Carol Mulhaney (*Pernicious*) to let her know that Jack, Frank, and Joe were all doing well and had pretty much settled their business. Jack had earlier mentioned to Frank that they might meet the Russians in Belize City or San Pedro, so it was best to head for *Ambergris Caye* for the present; so that's the information that Frank used to set his current course. Frank was glad to hear that Jack had spoken with Sarah and he could cross it off his mental list of 'things to do'. It felt good to be singing out of the same hymnal. With that, they talked a bit more about what they should do with their 'extra passengers', and Jack told Frank that he was still 'mulling it over' but would try to address that little detail shortly.

"What are ya thinkin' Jack? asked Frank.

"I haven't decided yet", answered Jack. "I had a good nap, and that allowed me to toss this around in my head a bit", he said. "I'm having a little problem with turning these guys over to our Russian pals. I hate to lay this headache on them. It really isn't their concern. I think they're just trying to help us out of a jam. Or, perhaps they have some ideas of their own about how to resolve the situation, or use these guys for something else. I'm not sure. But, I spent several days with these Cancun clowns and I have a pretty good idea how they think. They certainly didn't intend to cut me any slack when this was over", Jack said 'matter-of-factly'. "I don't owe them anything, but I'm not sure where we're headed with them now", he said. "I'm going to head down to the engine room and take Eduardo and Fernando some sandwiches and coffee, as well as something for our 'stowaways' and try to get a few more answers. I'll let you know how things work out." Jack gave Frank a quick salute, and said, "We'll talk later, Mister", and went below.

Jack then headed back down to the galley, grabbed the sandwiches and the fresh pot of coffee that he had made moments before, and headed down to the engine room. He also grabbed a couple of glasses from the galley to pour some shots for the two tough guys. He found Eduardo and Fernando in the engine room barely able to keep their heads up after the long hours spent over the past day, and night before, as well as that day. By then it was dusk on the second day out to sea, so he suggested to Eduardo and Fernando that they go find themselves a spare rack somewhere and crash for a while. Jack said, "I'll take the watch for awhile, … you boys try to get some rest. I'm relieving the watch". Eduardo and Fernando quickly devoured their sandwiches and coffee, said *"Muchas gracias, Jack"*, then headed out of the engine room to find a good place to take a long snooze.

Miguel and Ignacio had their legs and hands bound tightly and were sitting up against the hull on the port side of the boat away from the noisy engines, with their feet straight out, trying to get comfortable. After Eduardo and Fernando left the space, Jack pulled up a short stool that was sitting nearby, looked at his two captives sitting against the hull, and just stared at them for a couple of minutes while he ate his sandwich, sipped his coffee, and pondered his next move. He threw two sandwiches on to Miguel and Ignacio's laps to give them something to focus on, since he figured that they hadn't eaten in a while. They appreciated the gesture, but knew from Jack's body language that this wasn't going to be a social visit. After finishing his sandwich, Jack took another slug of coffee, then sauntered over to a side cabinet and pulled out the bottle of Blackberry Brandy along with the two shot glasses that he had in his left pocket, and sat back down on the stool. This was the first time that Jack and the two tough guys had been alone in the same space together, 'up close and personal', since they had tied Jack to a bench for a couple of days in a Cancun warehouse after knocking Jack on the noggin and dragging him to the 'suburbs'. This time, the boot was on the other foot.

Jack reached into his right pocket and pulled out his knife, then cut the thick tie-raps that bound the hands of the two tough guys sitting against the bulkhead. This allowed them to eat their sandwiches, while leaving their legs tightly bound. He thought that they might try to pull something stupid, so he also yanked the Smith & Wesson from his back belt and held it snuggly in his right hand, while resting it on his knee so that they better understood his immediate concern. The two thugs nodded their understanding, and began chewing on their dinner.

Jack then poured each *bandito* a shot of Brandy, holding the bottle in his left hand with the shot glasses clutched between his knees, then scooted the filled glasses over to the *bastardos* to help them wash down their sandwiches. Looking the two of them square in the eyes, he broke the silence.

"Payback's a bitch, boys" he said. "You don't feel as smart as you used to, do you?" he asked sardonically. They just stared back, wondering what was coming next. After spending the better part of the past week together, the three of them all understood each other pretty well, and the two thugs began to feel a gurgling in their wrenching guts as they downed the shots of brandy along with the last bites of their lunch.

"Now that the boot is on the other foot", Jack continued, "What would you two clowns do if you were in my position?" he asked. They just stared back at Jack suspiciously.

"Actually, amigos, you don't have to answer that", he said. "I've had plenty of time to ponder that same question over the past 24 hours, and I've decided that you both have a decision to make. So, the question will be answered pretty quickly after we take a short walk", he said with some certainty. "Besides, you two hit me over the head pretty hard when you threw me into the back of your van last week, and I don't believe that was part of the original plan", said Jack.

By now it was getting darker outside as Jack cut the cord around their legs with his pocket knife and backed away from the bulkhead a few feet, while holding his revolver in his right hand, signaling for them to head aft up the ladder to the fantail where they could discuss the issue more. "Let's go!" Jack demanded, as they walked ahead of him toward the stern of the ship. Jack stayed close behind, but held back a bit in case they tried something clever. He had Miguel walk ahead of Ignacio since it was slow going for Miguel with a wounded leg. The painkillers that Jack had given Miguel helped, and allowed a smoother transition. The two amigos didn't know what to expect, but began to hope for the best, ... yet feared for the worst, as the three of them ascended topside.

Up on the after deck, motoring south at about 10 knots in the somewhat chilly evening air, they could hear and feel the water rolling up against the hull as Jack motioned them to the back of the boat. The yacht was moving slow enough for the two gangsters to take a flying leap off the fantail, and lift themselves up out of a bad situation. As the three of them stood there staring anxiously at each other on the rear deck, Miguel and Ignacio thought that Jack would just shoot the two of them on the spot and dump their bodies to the sharks; But Jack thought that might be rude, and didn't really want it to end that way. And, although Jack thought justice might be served in that 'payback' sort of manner, he also remembered his ship's motto from his Navy days, *'Judicemur Agendo',* and decided that *'Let us be judged by our actions'* should be followed whenever practical, as he kicked a couple of old unmarked orange and white flotation rings over toward their feet.

"Here's the way it works, boys" announced Jack, "If this were turned 'round the other way, and it was *you* holding the gun, and it was *me* that had kidnapped and beaten you, and planned to steal your money, then kill you, ... I'm not so sure that you would be as considerate with my life as I'm going to be with yours. But, as it happens, I'm not wired that way, ... so I'm going to give you a sporting chance", he said, as he pointed his revolver west toward the Mexican coast.

"Out there to the west is a body of land, a reef actually, off the coast of *Quintana Roo,* called *Banco Chinchorro;* if you take those flotation rings and start swimming now, maybe you can make it to the shoals by sometime tomorrow. There are no guarantees in life; however, if you stay on my boat, we're heading south to meet a couple of very nasty Russian friends who helped bail me out of this mess, and they might not be as forgiving as I am. *¿Usted entiende?* So, without further adieu, … the choice is yours. You've been fed, you've had a shot of brandy to help you stay warm in the water, and your time is running short. So, what's it going to be *mis amigos*, sink, or swim?" Jack asked incredulously.

Miguel and Ignacio looked at each other soberly, considered what they had put Jack through over the past several days in Cancun, thought about their options, and in an instant threw the flotation rings over the starboard side, and sprightly jumped into the Caribbean after them. Jack could see their heads bobbing in the tumbling surf as they swam smartly to the orange and white rings disappearing in the distance, as *Victory Liner 504* steamed steadily south. Jack then wondered how many barracudas, crocodiles, and sharks might be lurking around the reef at night, especially with Miguel's damaged leg; then, headed back up to the bridge to see how Frank was getting along. Jack felt that he had handled the matter in the best way possible under the circumstances. He had identified two of the things that were making him *unhappy*, and removed them from his 'to do' list. His load felt lighter as he returned to his rack to stow his revolver until he needed it next time.

OIL AND WATER

> *"Man will never understand woman and vice versa. We are oil and water. An equal level can never be maintained, as one will always excel where the other doesn't, and that breeds resentment."* - Dionne Warwick

It is often said that oil and water don't mix. Oil is thicker, with a higher viscosity; so oil normally floats on top of water when the two try to occupy the same space in standard atmospheric conditions. Nevertheless, we see them together a lot; like men and women, or vowels and consonants, or lights in the darkness; an irascible, immiscible, incontrovertible mixture of incidentally incompatible components.

Jack's Russian friends, Garry Odonavich and Zakhar Maxikov were in the oil refinery, brewery, and bottled water businesses (pumps, tanks, pipes, valves, and controls), as well as other 'sideline' businesses in Latin America, working primarily in Panama; but also spent some time in Ecuador, Cuba, Venezuela, and Honduras, as well as the Caribbean islands. They originally moved to Panama to explore gold and copper mining ventures with some Chinese affiliates there, but as their exploits expanded, their companies compounded to include more 'process systems' type businesses.

Garry and 'Zak' first met Jack when he was working as an Engineer in the Middle East years earlier, but they continued their contact with him as he returned to Kansas to open the 'Jack of Clubs'; ... his 'Sport's Bar and Strip Club' in Topeka. As a partner in the 'Jack of Clubs', Frank Valero knew Garry and Zak from working at the club, while their friend 'Crazy Joe' had never met either one of the them, ... but was about to make their acquaintance. Jack's Russian friends also consulted with Jack as they set up their own 'Sport's Bar' operations in the Caribbean; so the team had sundry jointly owned, comingled, 'cash rich', but bodaciously broad business ties that also benefited Jack. For example, customers at the various clubs always seemed to enjoy the sumptuous Kansas City strip steaks supplied from the *'Redhouse Ranch'* outside of Topeka, almost as much as they delighted in watching the bountiful slim-waisted, long-legged waitresses in short shorts, that danced and delivered drinks to the tables.

Meanwhile, south of the Texas border, the presence of more Chinese and Russian workers was palpable, as those two nations strived for better relationships with their Latin American partners. As 'BRICS' members (Brazil, Russia, India, China, and South Africa), both the Russians and Chinese were effectively pushing for more geopolitical control near North America in their constant quest for energy, power, and resources. Their proximity to the United States was prominent as they repositioned themselves. Some of it was 'pushback' prompted by America's continued expansion against Russian and Chinese national interests. The US Federal government had perniciously positioned NATO forces in a ring around Russia, as well as threatened China's 'One China' policy, so, in a perspicuous counter-play, Russia and China were pushing into America's playground by putting people in places like Cuba and the Caribbean, as well as Central and South America, as payback. In essence, a *'quid pro quo'*.

So, Garry and Zak were part of that putsch, but were also Russian agents in a sense. The combination was complicated, and sometimes conflicting and confusing, but still congenial. That was Crazy Joe's impression as well, as he met the two Russians for the very first time. Joe was pretty adept at sizing people up at first glance, so his initial reaction was that they looked a bit malicious, but otherwise seemed 'OK'. If they were good enough for Jack and Frank, they were good enough for him; so allowed them the 'benefit of the doubt'. Be that as it may, he hadn't formed a firm opinion about either one of the gentlemen prior to meeting them, since he had only heard a few quick stories from Jack and Frank.

Although Jack called them his 'Russian pals', Garry Odonavich was actually from Belarus, a separate state near Russia that also bordered on Latvia, Lithuania, and Poland. Garry's father was Russian, but his mother was American, so he spoke almost perfect English. In fact, if you didn't know his background, you might think that he worked selling European cars at a dealership in Milwaukee. His 'English' was just that good. Zakhar Maxikov, on the other hand, hailed from St. Petersburg where they made the famous *Lomonosov* porcelain tea sets, as well as *Raketa* watches, and other fine products. St. Petersburg is also on the Gulf of Finland, quite close to the Finnish and Estonian borders. Notably, after working in the Middle East with Jack, Zak had been very active in projects in both Finland and Estonia, working with the Finnish Consulate. Later on, the three of them, Garry, Zak, and Jack had all reconnected again as Jack opened his club in Kansas and began to develop other businesses in the Caribbean and Latin America. To complete the circle, Garry and Zak then contacted Jack to help them set up their own clubs in Central America after observing Jack's significant success in Topeka. In any case, they also worked with the Russian government to help expand influence in Latin American countries. So again, it was a bit complicated and confusing, but generally congenial, as is often the case in these matters.

 On the third day after they left Cancun, with a temperature hovering around 90°F and high humidity, *Victory Liner 504* approached the port of San Pedro on the *Ambergris Caye*, slightly north of Belize City. As the *'Amigo's del Mar'* pier came into view, Garry and Zak were already standing on the dock in their shorts, sandals, and tropical shirts awaiting the boat's arrival as the surf broke across the reef about a thousand feet offshore. And, as chance would have it, as they drew nearer to the dock, Sarah Reid (*Enchanté*), called Jack to say that she was planning to fly into Belize on Friday, the day after next, to join their party. So, everything was beginning to fall into place as the group planned their reunion. The Belize Water Taxi pier for the trip over to San Pedro was a ten-minute cab ride from the main airport, so Jack recommended that Sarah take the hour-and-half water taxi directly from Belize out to San Pedro after she landed, to expedite the meet. Sarah agreed, opting for the convenience as well. Their Russian pals had already reserved several rooms and a suite at the '*Sandy Beach Villas*' hotel for the group, as their ad proclaimed 'All Hotel Rooms & Villas with Beach & Ocean View '. As they guided their motor yacht through the shoals, Joe Melnik was perched on the forward deck taking depth soundings to avoid surprises, as Frank scanned the nautical charts to avoid any reefs, sand bars, or other obstacles, while Jack dialed down their cruising speed a bit, to nudge the boat toward the landing.

 Coming alongside the pier at *'Amigo's del Mar'*, Joe stepped off the main deck with a line to secure the bow, then positioned a couple of bumpers between the boat and the dock, as Jack cut the engines. He extended a hand to Garry and Zak as they helped to secure the stern and tie a couple of hitches around the cleats on the dock. That was the first time that Joe actually met Garry and Zak face-to-face, but his first impression was favorable. They would grab a few supplies and some beer, then motor down to the pier nearer to their hotel for future convenience, and take their bags over to their rooms. If diesel fuel was available at the dive dock, they would buy a couple hundred bucks worth; otherwise, they might try to get a fuel truck to come out to the hotel dock from the local airport, or wait until they reached the next big port to take on more fuel. Jack made a note to investigate later.

Jumping off the boat onto the pier near the hotel while grabbing their bags, they strolled down the dock toward the hotel trying to lose their sea legs. As they walked, Garry looked over at Joe and asked "Where are the two prisoners, Miguel and Ignacio?' To which Joe just replied, "They didn't make it". Nevertheless, Joe wondered to himself *'How does he know their names?'* Joe was sure that Frank or Jack never mentioned the names of their two captives over the course of the past few days, but he would first check with Frank and Jack before jumping to any premature conclusions. Still, Joe was puzzled by the brief exchange.

Upon checking into the reception area of their quaint little beach hotel, the crewmembers were assigned individual rooms from the hotel clerk with most of them doubling up, like Fernando and Eddie, Garry and Zak, as well as Frank and Joe. Jack would double up with Sarah after she flew in on the following Friday. So, after getting their rooms, they all agreed to meet in the bar area (about fifteen minutes later), after getting settled. It was during that brief interlude that Joe had an opportunity to discuss his question with Frank. How was it that Garry and Zak knew Miguel and Ignacio's names if they had never met them? Frank had no idea. They would ask Garry and Zak directly when they met them for drinks in a few minutes. They would save the beer they bought for later.

Down at the bar, Eddie and Fernando ordered local *Belikin* beers, while Frank and Joe ordered Bloody Marys, and Jack ordered a pitcher of rum punch. Garry and Zak ordered a couple of tropical Vodka Martinis. They all ordered sandwiches or fish plates as well. The group briefly discussed their travel plans since Eddie and Fernando's work was finished, and they had plans to fly back to Panama on the following Friday. Garry and Zak also found few reasons to remain in San Pedro since there were no prisoners to interrogate, and they preferred to return home to take care of their other businesses. There was a gas shortage crisis in Mexico, which affected their oil refinery business, but their bottled water business was booming. They were also in the middle of negotiations related to a stake in some copper mines since they believed that the future was in copper as the automobile industry switched to electric cars (instead of gas or diesel), and believed that fossil fuels were on their way out. Nevertheless, they would probably hang around for a couple of days to enjoy the laid-back atmosphere of San Pedro, and perhaps say 'Hello' to Sarah when she arrived. Otherwise, they would leave Jack, Joe, and Frank to get on with their normal routines. Eventually, after taking a few more sips of their drinks and having a few more laughs, Joe popped the question to Garry.

"Say, Garry, when we were walking down the dock from the boat a short while ago, you asked 'where are Miguel and Ignacio, the two prisoners', correct?" asked Joe. "Well yes, we expected to see them when you pulled in so that we could question them", said Garry, a bit sheepishly. We are a little surprised that they are not with you. What happened to them?" he asked, with Jack looking quite surprised by both the question and the answer.

"Well, the short answer is that they took a swim. They thought they could get here more quickly that way", Joe shot back, sarcastically. "Actually, Jack can give you more of the dirty little details on that, … I was napping at the time", continued Joe. "But, more to the point, how did you know their names?" Joe asked pointedly.

Garry Odonavich and Zak Maxikov looked at each other somewhat chagrined, and a bit red in the face, recognizing the significance of Joe's question; then Zak responded in a believable tone, and a slight Russian accent saying "We heard their names from Sarah", which caught them all by surprise. "Now, that is a surprise", said Jack. "I don't recall mentioning their names to Sarah when we spoke on the phone" So, they were all puzzled by that revelation. How did Sarah know their names they wondered, as they all sat there stunned staring at their drinks, trying to remember their earlier conversations with Sarah? Jack was sure that he had never uttered their names since he had only spoken with her once in his call from the boat on the way to Belize. Prior to that, he was in the process of being rescued by the others who were casually circled around him at the table in the bar.

Garry and Zak knew Sarah Reid (*Enchanté*), and Carol Mulhaney (*Pernicious*), from the 'Jack of Clubs', as they were two of the 'out-of-town suits' that his good friend Sanjo Casagrande had recognized standing with Jack and *Pernicious* at the bar in Topeka, when Sanjo visited them from Minnesota well over a year ago. Garry and Zak had traveled to Kansas during that same period to learn more about the *'Jack of Clubs'* operation, as they were setting up their own clubs in Latin America. So, all of these revelations begged more analysis. Stepping back a bit, Jack, Joe, and Frank all wondered a) How did Sarah know the names of Miguel and Ignacio, Jack's two captors in Cancun, b) Why were Garry and Zak talking to Sarah about the abduction, and what was their relationship with her, c) Who else knew the names of Miguel and Ignacio (maybe Carol Mulhaney, by now), d) Who else had Sarah been talking with, that might also know something about the abduction, and e) how were all of these facts related? Did Sarah know Seumas?

Looking back, Sarah Reid had also met Seumas a couple of times at *'Guillermo's Grill,'* from their many trips down to Panama in *Victory Liner 504* over the past few years when they were all working in their 'money exchange' business. In fact, his full name was 'Seumas Santaña' and many of the regulars on the *'Zona Hotelera'* strip knew him since he had been working at several different bars on the Cancun 'hotel peninsula' for the past fifteen years or more. So, was Seumas also involved in the plot after all? And, was Sarah also talking to Seumas? Wow! Jack decided that he needed more rum punch, and poured another glass from the pitcher sitting in front of him. It tasted a lot like the 'Mojo' that he and his sailor pals used to drink in Olongapo, during their Navy days, and went down easy. So, again, the question came back to Sarah and Seumas.

"Garry, or Zak", Joe continued, "How well did you know Sarah? I've never met her myself. I understand that she was also Frank's girl for a time before she switched over to Jack, and she also goes by the name of *Enchanté*, at Jack's club in Kansas. Is that right?" Joe inquired. "I'm just trying to get all of this straight since I'm kind of new to the bunch this time around. Jack and Frank and I haven't seen each other for quite a few years, so my curiosity sometimes gets the better of me" he explained. "Was she pretty active at the bar?" Joe queried, trying to make a point. "Well, yeah" said Zak. "She was always very friendly, if you know what I mean. She was a great dancer, and Garry and I spent quite a bit of our travel per diem on her for dinner and drinks, … and dances", he added. "We learned a lot from her, so we've kept kind of close since then", he revealed. Actually, that was no surprise to any of them, so there was no point in pressing the point any further. They all knew that Sarah Reid (*Enchanté*) was quite the party girl, who just liked having fun. In fact, they were all looking forward to her visit on Friday. "This sounds like it's going to be a fun trip", said Joe. "I can't wait to meet Sarah myself! She sounds like my kind of babe". He finished, with a laugh.

"OK, so let's get down to brass tacks", said Frank. "What did Sarah say to you about Miguel and Ignacio, and when did she say it", he asked. Garry responded, "Well, when we heard about Jack getting grabbed in Cancun from you Frank, we wanted to know whether anyone had heard any news. At one point, I called Jack's club to talk to you, but you had already left for Cancun to meet Eddie and Fernando. Sarah answered the phone so we spoke with her. She told us that two guys named Miguel and Ignacio had abducted you, and that Crazy Joe was flying down with you to meet with Eddie and Fernando. So, that's where we heard the names. We thought that *you* gave them to her", said Garry, almost apologetically.

"Well that's all very interesting", posited Jack. "Sarah should have some important facts to share with us when she flies in on Friday", he said. And with that, he poured another glass of rum punch and gazed out across the water at the surf swept shore, watching the waves break over the reef, anxiously looking forward to Friday. They would all kick back and take in the local sights until Sarah arrived, as they continued their conversations and planned their evening around visiting some of the other local pubs and clubs.

Now, Jack was the kind of guy who felt that he could accomplish anything that he attempted in life, … if he just put his mind to it. The fact that Jack grew up in northern Minnesota, the land of Paul Bunyan, and 'Babe' the Blue Ox, immersed in countless lumberjack tall tales about super-human accomplishments, may have had an impact on his philosophy and behavior. Although, he was probably just as influenced by his Dad, who gave him his first pocketknife when he was a boy; a 'Browning' folding pocketknife, that he usually carried in his right pant's pocket. At the ripe young age of six, his Dad told him that 'every young man should have a good pocketknife', and gave him the Browning. He used it to play 'Mumbley Peg' with the other boys in the neighborhood for entertainment and would often win the game flipping his knife where he wanted it to land from a variety of positions. He could also flick the knife out of his pocket quickly with the blade out after lots of practice, a skill that often came in handy if he wanted to make a point. A couple of weeks after his Dad gave him the knife however, his Dad had to confiscate it from Jack for about a week, after a neighbor complained that young Jack had been chasing some nasty little kids around their neighbor's house for hassling Jack's younger brothers. Jack was sure there was a lesson in there somewhere since the neighbor kids avoided his little brothers after the incident, and certainly went out of their way to avoid young Jack as well. So, Jack was a guy that took care of niggling little problems when necessary.

But 'problems', were part of the problem that Jack felt he should eliminate in his quest to find happiness. It seemed to Jack, that everybody else's problems ended up being Jack's problems. Perhaps it was Jack's own fault. In any case, Jack now found himself facing additional problems that he must try to resolve. In all fairness, he was hoping that some sort of cosmic wave would wash over all of humanity to crystalize their consciousness into a sort of 'universality', whereby all would possess the same understanding, or pansophical knowledge, or energy, and be immersed in a feeling of freedom, comfort, and love. Maybe that would make him happy. After all, weren't they all living in the 'Age of Aquarius' anyway? He felt as if he had been there before. It also troubled him that Sarah knew Miguel and Ignacio's names. What was up with that?

The Pier in San Pedro, Ambergris Caye

THE SECOND COMING

> *"The secret of happiness, you see, is not found in seeking more, but in developing the capacity to enjoy less."* -
> Socrates, 469 BCE

On Friday, Sarah Reid (aka, *Enchanté*) landed at the airport in Belize in the late night hours after a seven-hour flight from Kansas City, wearing a pair of tan khaki culottes, a loosely buttoned white blouse, and light purple pumps with ankle straps. Her reddish hair was a bit disheveled from the trip, but looked cute braided with a ponytail in back, bound with a light purple bow to match her pumps. She booked a room at a nearby 'villa' hotel for the evening to catch up on a quiet night's rest, as she planned to take a cab and ferryboat ride out to San Pedro on the *Ambergris Caye* the following morning. She sent a short text message to Jack after checking into the hotel, telling him that she had landed in Belize and would meet him 'sometime tomorrow'. Jack was glad to hear that she had arrived safely. She had a couple of stiff drinks at the bar, and hit the sack for the evening.

Sarah had a lot on her mind and was looking forward to meeting up with Jack again. She speculated that he might have some questions related to his recent abduction, and she needed to explain some things that had occurred in her past before she began working at the club. In the early years, when she first began dancing at the *'Jack of Clubs'* in Topeka, working with her good friend Carol Mulhaney (aka, *Pernicious*), she had her eye on Jack, but didn't want to offend her friend Carol who was dating him at the time. Because they would party out at Jack's ranch regularly, she also had a short fling with Jack's old Navy buddy Sanjo; but due to personal conflicts, as well as other activities with Jack, she eventually began seeing more of Frank Valero after he split up with his wife, Yolanda. After a time, and partially as a consequence of their many shipboard parties and trips down to Panama, Carol Mulhaney eventually developed a fondness for Frank, so Jack and Sarah developed a countervailing close relationship as well. It was somewhat confusing, and complicated, but not uncommon. During their many seafaring sojourns, they occasionally made port calls in Cancun where they also ran into Seumas Santaña from time to time, the bartender at *Guillermo's Grill*.

So, Seumas Santaña, who actually grew up in Loredo, Texas after he and his illegal immigrant parents breached the Texas border from Mexico to find work, had in his earlier years been a member of a disreputable biker gang called '*Los Santos*'. The gang was notorious for running drugs, booze, guns, hookers, illegal immigrants, and/or anything else that paid well across the border, and was also well connected with other biker gangs, as well as some Russians, Chinese, and corrupt politicians in the southwest United States along the US-Mexican border. Their symbol, which was often tattooed on a hand, arm, or neck, featured a snake, or 'S' overlapping a large cross '✝' to indicate their affiliation with the pack.

As many people know, *Tijuana* (near San Diego, CA), *Juarez* (near El Paso, TX), and *Nuevo Loredo* (near Loredo, Texas), are all well-worn crossing points between Mexico and the USA. Be that as it may, *Loredo* in particular, is a main artery for transit between the two countries, as it is situated on Interstate I-35 between San Antonio, Texas and Monterrey, Mexico *("La Ciudad de las Montañas")*, the central corridor between Mexico and the USA spanning hundreds of miles north through mid-America including Austin, Waco, and Dallas, Texas, Oklahoma City, Kansas City, and Minneapolis, and continuing north to Duluth, Minnesota (almost to Canada), a substantial and sometimes snowy city situated on a major international shipping port on Lake Superior. Duluth was also 'home' to Sanjo Casagrande, a good friend of Jack, Frank, and Joe from their Navy days. Also situated near I-35 extending south, half the distance between Duluth and Monterrey sat the 'Jack of Clubs' in Topeka, Kansas making it a good 'stage coach stop' on the way to and from Mexico, as well as a place to relax and let off a little steam. The route was well used by the *Los Santos* network for their many 'trade deals' within a vast, well linked, and well funded operation, and was a convenient tool for those desiring to conduct nefarious 'over-the-border trade' between the two culturally diverse countries. And, that was just on the surface.

Indeed, there are those who posit that beneath the earth's crust exists a vast and sophisticated other world 'underground network' of tunnels, colonies, DUMBS (Defense Underground Military Bases), and high-speed transit systems between the North and South American continents, as well as beyond, betwixt, underneath, and between the several continents of the world that may have existed for tens of thousands of years, and are still used to this day. Nevertheless, this may be news to those unfamiliar with personalities like Helena Blavatsky (aka, *Yelena Petrovna von Hahn*) from the Ukraine and the leading theoretician of Theosophy in her day, or Alexandr Aksakov, Edward Bulwar-Lytton, Countess Hella von Westarp, Nikola Tesla, René Guénon, Nicholas Roerich, the artist and mystic, Maria Orsic (aka, *Maria Orschitsch*), and others associated with the Thule Society, Vril technology, and/or various other old world postulates, as well as Agharta, a legendary lost culture situated somewhere in the earth's core, central to many of these underlying beliefs. A very well written book authored by Alec Maclellan in 1982 (reprinted in 2001), entitled *'The Lost World Of Agharti: The Mystery of Vril Power',* offers a thought provoking composition of the many stories and adventures associated with travel to/from the inner earth. If one combines these events with that of a story about a Norwegian father and his son who sailed into a northern opening of the 'inner earth' and lived there for a couple of years, and is documented in a book that was written by Willis George Emerson in 1908 entitled *'The Smoky God: Or The Voyage To The Inner World',* the reader can follow the exploits of these two Nordic explorers upon sailing through a large entrance to the Earth's interior at the North Pole. Following is an introduction to the book on the 'Amazon' website;

'Olaf Jansen, a [Norwegian] fisherman from Sweden, and his son, sailed by accident through the North Polar opening into the Hollow Interior of the Earth, and lived 2 years among its people. Olaf Jansen claims this is his true story as revealed to Willis George Emerson in confidence. He tells of a race of Super Giants, 15 feet tall, far advanced scientifically, who treated them with the utmost kindness. He lived in peace and harmony and traveled all over their country. He claims they returned through the South Polar opening. The book tells a fascinating story, with pictures, charts, and maps. It's up to you

to believe or disbelieve their story. They swear it is true. We heard about this book and their journey, and searched all over the United States and Europe to find a copy. Now at last, we have found a rare old copy and are reproducing it exactly as written, with no changes. It must be read, to be appreciated. We [Amazon] recommend it highly.'

As indicated in an excerpt from the novel; *'The Smoky God: Or The Voyage To The Inner World'* by Willis George Emerson, originally published in 1908;

Olaf Jansen's Story

My name is Olaf Jansen. I am a Norwegian, although I was born in the little seafaring Russian town of Uleaborg, on the eastern coast of the Gulf of Bothnia, the northern arm of the Baltic Sea.

My parents were on a fishing cruise in the Gulf of Bothnia, and put into this Russian town of Uleaborg at the time of my birth, being the twenty-seventh day of October, 1811.

My father, Jens Jansen, was born at Rodwig on the Scandinavian coast, near the Lofoden Islands, but after marrying made his home at Stockholm, because my mother's people resided in that city. When seven years old, I began going with my father on his fishing trips along the Scandinavian coast.

Early in life I displayed an aptitude for books, and at the age of nine years was placed in a private school in Stockholm, remaining there until I was fourteen. After this I made regular trips with my father on all his fishing voyages.

My father was a man fully six feet three in height, and weighed over fifteen stone, a typical Norseman of the most rugged sort, and capable of more endurance than any other man I have ever known. He possessed the gentleness of a woman in tender little ways, yet his determination and will-power were beyond description. His will admitted of no defeat.

I was in my nineteenth year when we started on what proved to be our last trip as fishermen, and which resulted in the strange story that shall be given to the world, -- but not until I have finished my earthly pilgrimage.

Although many books have been written about the inner earth over the past hundred years or so, and a quick computer search could turn up evermore lore, it's also true that some of this information began to appear more recently as a Russian Patriarch from Moscow, a US Secretary of State, and a famous US Astronaut, among others, began visiting the South Pole; and as more discoveries about a 'lost world' began to surface from beneath the frozen, but slowly thawing continent of Antarctica, where an ancient civilization may have begun to rear it's fascinating (if not Fascist) head.

Needless to say, there are numerous 'unknown unknowns' relative to the way that the 'unreal' world works in the penetralia of underground realms. Conspiracy theories abound between, betwixt, beneath, and beyond the bellicose redoubts of these truculent and tremendous tunneled tracts. What secrets are satisfied by the saddened souls that sagaciously serve these sardonic sectors? If a sun does indeed shine at the core of Gaia, is a sun also central to the soul, or are secrets held that are not so easily dissected? Both Jack and Sarah began to assimilate these axioms in their individual quests for cheeriness, but were satisfied that they had, not yet, their souls to sell (and were not for sale), which served to intoxicate their reticent contentment.

So, on Saturday, Sarah Reid awoke to a sunny day and grumpy stomach eager to visit Jack. She showered and shaved (her underarms, legs, and other areas), flossed between her teeth, dried between her toes, got dressed, then took the stairs down to the lobby to enjoy a quick breakfast of oatmeal, juice, English muffin, and fruit. She poured a cup of black coffee from the 'free' pot in the lobby, and returned to her room to check her e-mail prior to catching a cab to the ferry for the crossing to San Pedro on *Ambergris Caye.*

She summoned her sixth sense as she sought to slow things down a bit with Jack. Perhaps it was the suddenness of the sunny and sultry Caribbean air as she exited the small villa hotel, or the slower paced beat of Belize Bongos that allowed her to languish in a few new rules of engagement. She was young, and had been moving fast, while at the same time, '*Time*' seemed to be standing still. Nonetheless, she really did feel that it would be better to slow things down with Jack. To take their time to understand, know, and enjoy one another more, while exploring each other's personalities and perplexities in a more purposeful way; in essence, … to lavish in the luxurious lap dance of life.

The ocean ferry ride from Belize was refreshing for Sarah. Toting her roller bag, wearing a pair of tan khaki shorts over her cute little booty, and a pair of high tie leather sandals with a long lime-green tank top to match the calypso-like community around her, she took a fast cab ride over to the coast, bought a one- way ticket to San Pedro, and boarded the boat about 45 minutes later. She enjoyed being on the water again skimming across the crystal clear blue Caribbean seas, as she began to realize that 'she wasn't in Kansas anymore', and could actually begin to relax.

The ride was swift, as the island ferry soon pulled into the pier at *'Amigo's del Mar'*. Jack was waiting at the end of the dock as the passengers marched along the wooden planks in the salted and sunny haze, and exited the ferry on their way to hotels and bars along the beach. The two anxious lovers embraced each other in a long awaited hug as Jack grabbed her bag, pecked her on the cheek, and put his other arm around her waist while they meandered back down the beach to the Villa hotel. The 'boys' were all sitting in the hotel bar as they walked up the beach to greet them. Garry and Zak, as well as Fernando and Eddie were all planning to fly out later that same day from the small San Pedro airport, but wanted to say 'Hello' to Sarah first before they left. Sarah would remain with Jack, Frank, and Joe as they made other plans in the following days. Jack ordered a round of drinks for the entire group as they positioned themselves around a table near the bar overlooking the beach, and began to get chummy with Sarah once more. It was good to see her freckled little face again.

As Jack brought a pitcher of 'Mojo' over to the table, and the others ordered beers or wine, Jack, Frank, and Joe wanted to know how Sarah just happened to know the names of Miguel and Ignacio before they themselves knew. What was up with that? Sarah, anticipating the question, quickly answered that she had heard the names from Seumas Santaña, who had been rather close to the two *hombres,* as they had all been members of the same gang in their early days, and had been delivering supplies to *Guillermo's Grill* in Cancun on a regular basis. Sarah had also known several of the other gang members personally in her younger years, and that was part of what she wanted to explain to Jack.

Joe Melnik had not yet met Sarah Reid (aka, *Enchanté*), but had heard several stories. Needless to say, Joe was favorably impressed by her first appearance, and he very much liked the attractive young woman that was then joining them for drinks in that very tropical environment. She was certainly a welcome surprise after spending the past week with the other partners in crime. The Panamanians had the same first impression as Joe, since they too had not met Sarah previously. Of course, Sarah and the others were all old friends from The *'Jack of Clubs'* in Topeka and from the various visits to Central America, so they needed no introductions. Nevertheless, Joe had questions for Sarah that he thought needed some clarification. So he jumped ahead with his questions first.

Joe; "Sarah, I'm very pleased to finally make your acquaintance", Joe began with a blush; taking a sip of his frosty *Belikin* beer. "I've heard so many good things about you", he said. "Jack and Frank have told me so many stories that I feel like I've known you for years; but of course, we've never met. So, I'm curious, … this bunch has been through a lot over the past week or so, between here and Cancun, - and you already know a lot of that story, - but frankly speaking, there are a lot of unanswered questions that I believe may need some further clarification", he said. "So, maybe you could do a little 'backfilling' for us, and tell us how you happened to hear the names of the two guys before we did, that assaulted Jack, and perhaps help us better understand the events over the past week, as well as help us to get ahead of whatever might be coming our way next." he said.

Sarah; "Hahaaa, I'm very pleased to meet you as well, Joe!" Sarah said with a chuckle, unsurprised by the question, and with a wide welcoming grin. "And, I'm looking forward to knowing you better too!" she said. "I thought that you all might have a few questions about that, so I would be happy to try and fill in the blanks of that little riddle", she said, sounding a lot like Holly Hunter, the movie star. "The fact is Joe, I was worried about Jack!" she said emphatically. "When I heard from Frank that Jack had been kidnapped, I called Seumas Santaña down at *Guillermo's Grill* because I knew that Jack had dinner there on occasion, and his boat was parked a short way up the pier. Frank also said that Jack had called him from *Guillermo's Grill*, and that Jack was sitting at the bar with Seumas when Frank called him back. I wanted to know whether Seumas had any information about Jack, and Seumas told me that he hadn't seen Jack, or

Miguel, or Ignacio, after Jack left that day, but that he suspected there might have been some 'funny business' since none of them had been back to the bar since. Seumas also knew their background from their younger years, as they had all been members of the same gang long ago. So, I may have read more into his response than necessary, but it sounded to me like Miguel and Ignacio were somehow involved." Then she said, "I also knew some of the gang members myself from my early years, since we were all brought into these various 'exotic dancer clubs' together through the *Los Santos* gang members that recruit young ladies all the way up and down I-35. After all", she continued, "it's not by accident that Carol and I landed at the *'Jack of Clubs'* in the first place. Where do you think all of these pretty little girls come from?" she asked. "By the way, Jack knows all of this very well." she said; as Jack stared back from across the table looking a bit bewildered. "And, who do you think is funding all of these gangs to find these girls?" asked Sarah as she stared across the table at her two Russian pals, Garry and Zak. "On top of that, who do you think turns their heads the other way in the local government when they try to do something about the strip clubs that lace the interstate all the way up and down I-35? Can you say mucho 'kickbacks', tax free cash, and political campaign money?" she continued. "So, I don't really have the whole story Joe. But I think that I can connect some of the dots, and put two and two together if I try hard enough!" she finished with a grin. "How about you?"

Jack: "So, Sarah, are you saying that all of this trouble started at the club?"

Sarah "Well, I'm *suggesting* that it's a good place to begin looking. These two guys may have been acting on their own initiatives, or they may have had more help, or there may be an ulterior motive", she counseled. "Who had a motive, and what was it? Can we follow the money? Maybe someone wants to shut down the *'Jack of Clubs'* to fund their own enterprise, … and taking you out Jack, might lessen the competition, speaking from a marketing perspective", she postulated.

Frank: "So, why did they want $50,000 then?" asked Frank. "Were they in it for the money, or was that just part of the con; Perhaps, as a cover, or maybe a contribution for the real purpose behind the abduction?"

Sarah: "I'm not sure Frank. You might want to ask Miguel and Ignacio that question", she said. "By the way, if that's who jumped Jack, what ever happened to them? Are they somewhere back in Cancun, or did you take them somewhere else?" She asked. "The last time we spoke, Jack just told me that you guys had some trouble. I'm just guessing at all the rest. We agreed to meet here in San Pedro, ... and so, here I am. I'm thrilled to be here, but you were going to tell *me* what happened up there. I just wanted to get some sun, have some fun, and get together Jack", she said.

Joe: 'Well, to answer your first question Sarah, the last I remember, Miguel and Ignacio hadn't quite made it back to *Quintana Roo* after their evening swim when they bailed over the side of the boat on the way down here" he said. "But, I don't know the whole story since I was napping at the time. Perhaps Jack can humor us on that particular point" he finished, knowing the facts quite well.

And with that, Jack retold the whole sordid story about how he had let down his guard coming out of *Guillermo's Grill* over a week ago, and how he was held captive for a couple of days in a stark stone house in northern Cancun tied to a bench, and how his pals around the table had all done such a terrific job of pulling Jack out of a bad situation to bring them to the point where they were all then sitting around the table at the beach. Still, there were several unanswered questions that needed to be resolved relating to how the whole situation began. And, to get to the bottom of it, they believed that they might need to have further discussions with Seumas, Miguel, and Ignacio, which could prove to be difficult under the circumstances. So, Jack began to wonder whether the two bad apples had ever actually made it to shore in *Quintana Roo*, and whether he might run into them again somewhere down the road. He now wished that he had asked more questions when he had their undivided attention aboard the boat, while also thinking that he might have to 'backtrack' a bit to see if they had made it to shore. He also thought that perhaps he should have turned the two thugs over to Garry and Zak after all, or better yet, taken them out when he had the chance. Hindsight was 20/20. There was more to this story than any of them really understood.

Following their conversation, and as they finished their drinks, Garry and Zak, along with the two Panamanians Fernando and Eddie, all said their farewells to the bunch, then caught a cab from the hotel out to the small local airport in San Pedro for their trip back to Panama. They left their weapons on the boat with Jack since they didn't want to try to board an aircraft with their small arsenal. Jack would keep them safe aboard the boat until he could return them at a more convenient place and time. Jack had a short conversation with all of his pals before they departed, thanking them profusely for their assistance in saving his hide, as well as letting them all know that he would be sending them some separate 'compensation' for their help in the matter. They would also be in touch shortly to consummate some additional 'deals' as they tried to plan their next moves. There were still plenty of unanswered questions, but they all felt that they could move forward from that point in time.

Meanwhile, back at the hotel bar, Joe was busy being entertained by Sarah as they began to learn more about each other's background. Joe felt comfortable around Sarah, and she was warming up to Joe. Nevertheless, Sarah was still with Jack, and was looking forward to being with all three of them, ... Jack, Joe, and Frank as they planned their next moves and enjoyed their current surroundings. Be that as it may, to Jack, it was business as usual since he believed that 'life was like a business'. There was profit and loss, risk and reward. He needed cash flow. More in, ... less out, to meet expenses and payroll. 'We invest in ourselves, and in others as we grow; Yet, constantly struggle to know ourselves better as we hope and pray that 'the Saints will provide', and that everything will work out OK in our quest for independence'. So ultimately, what was it going to take, to make Jack happy?

Some of Jack's favorite songs were playing in the background as Jack pondered his next moves. The songs on the sound system included 'Nice and Easy' by Frank Sinatra, followed by 'Beyond the Sea' by Bobby Darin. 'Perhaps it should all begin with a quick call to Seumas', thought Jack, ... to see whether he had heard from either Miguel or Ignacio. That information alone might tell him a lot.

Or, Jack could invite Seumas to visit them down in San Pedro, which might work even better. After all, the Mexican cops might be looking for Jack back in Cancun, and may have even been 'in on the caper', he thought. Best not to take any chances on the local authorities for now. Yes, he would call Seumas and invite him to visit them in San Pedro, he decided.

It was just after noon when Jack dialed the number at *Guillermo's Grill*, and as luck would have it, Seumas was still at the bar working his normal shift. He was surprised to hear Jack's voice. "Hi, Jack", said Seumas, as he took the call. "We haven't seen you around here in awhile. Is everything OK?" he asked. "Sarah called down here about a week ago looking for you, and I told her that I hadn't seen you, and a couple of our delivery guys for awhile. You all disappeared around the same time, are you alright?" he asked.

"Yes, I'm fine Seumas. I had a little bit of trouble after I left the Grill a couple of weeks back, but we took care of it. Actually, it did involve your 'delivery guys' Miguel and Ignacio", Jack revealed. "Have you heard from them lately?" Jack continued.

"No, Jack. You're the first one I've heard from. But it's good to hear that you're OK. What can I do for you?" he asked.

"Well, as I said, the trouble involved your delivery boys, and I'd rather not discuss the matter over the phone at the moment." Jack responded. "I'm currently down in San Pedro with Sarah and Frank for a few days, taking in some fun and sun. What's your situation up there Seumas? Can you take some time off and meet with us down here in San Pedro? There are a few details that I would like to discuss with you, and I'd rather do it here, than up in Cancun. I'm not sure that we'll be back up that way anytime soon, under the circumstances. We have a few other stops to make now that we're down this way", Jack explained, cautiously.

"Sure, Jack. I can do that!" responded Seumas. "I could use a break anyway right about now. Someone else can take my shift for a couple of days. I can take the '307' highway down to Chetumal in a few hours when I get off work, and take the water taxi over to San Pedro tomorrow if you like. Would that work?" asked Seumas.

"Terrific" responded Jack. "Dinner, drinks, and a room are on me, Seumas. We look forward to seeing you. Maybe you can help us fill in some of the blanks", he said.

"No problem Jack. What are friends for? Like I said, I need a break anyway; and it will be good to see you all again. I'll catch up with you in San Pedro sometime tomorrow!" Seumas finished, and said goodbye. Then, after he ended the call, Seumas made a couple other phone calls to some old friends.

Glory be, and Hallelujah!" thought Jack. "*Maybe now, we'll get some solid answers and this whole problem will go away!*

Jack wondered whether a good answer would actually make him happy, as he hummed the tune to 'Nice and Easy Does It'.

https://www.youtube.com/watch?v=YnvXSSv2vqU   https://www.youtube.com/watch?v=5bRAtV-jgoQ

In the recesses of Jack's cerebellum, Leonard Cohen sang 'Hallelujah', as Jack made his way back to the hotel bar on the beach to locate Sarah and Joe.

View of 'Villa Hotel Dock' in San Pedro

CHECKUP IN CHETUMAL

"Never miss a good chance to shut up." ~ *Judge Roy Bean*

Ignacio Escondido and Miguel Parás were not strong swimmers, but they weren't quitters either. Their salvation had been the orange and white flotation rings tossed from *Victory Liner 504* before they jumped overboard. As the motor yacht faded below the horizon while steaming south toward San Pedro, the banditos continued to bob up and down in the water for several hours as they swam toward the coast. A research vessel exploring the coastal shoals near *Banco Chinchorro* eventually spotted the two ex-*Los Santos* gang members still clinging to their flotation rings, and pulled them on board. When the skipper of the vessel asked them how they landed in the water, 'way out in the middle of the Caribbean', the two banditos responded that they 'fell off a boat', but were going to meet a guy named '*Seumas*' in Chetumal, so he decided that they were just delusional from spending the night in the bleary brine, and took them into port to be examined by a medical professional.

Whether Sarah knew it or not, she had hit the nail on the head, ... and someone was searching for a bigger hammer. Jack's business was attractive for the cash flow that it generated, so Jack was a target; But, why? Well, because global credit was drying up. And, if credit ever quit, world economies would grind to a halt; and those left looking for a chair when the music stopped would be those without hard cash or precious metals. Who would take credit cards at that point? The 'Powers-That-Be', the world banks, the IMF, the FED, and perhaps large corporations were banning cash and tracking payments for tax purposes. Who would take

'*American Express©*, *MasterCard©*, or *Visa©*' cards if there was no cash in the bank to back them up? Credit was either backed by fiat currencies, or nothing. It wasn't rocket science; it was finance. It didn't matter whether companies sold food, cars, diesel fuel, refined oil, bottled water, dried beans, or popcorn, ... if customers couldn't get the goods with credit or cash, the consumer side of the equation would collapse. The dirty little secret was that very little real money existed in banks anyway, just 'numerical digits' linked to numbered accounts in cyberspace.

Venezuela, Cuba, Brazil, most of Latin America, and Mexico, not to mention Russia (and some of the BRICS), were already on their backs economically. They had banned $100 dollar bills in India, and were proposing 'cashless societies' in Europe and elsewhere. How was that going to work? World economies had either tanked, or were in the process of caving. Only China, and some 'Western' countries like the US, Europe, and Japan struggled to keep up, but made up the rules as they ricocheted along. The truth was, there really was no real 'money'; only credit, backed by worthless paper (fiat currency), with trillions in world debt backed by empty promises and derivatives (gambling based on futures, options, and warrants), as countries kept printing counterfeit currencies like there was no tomorrow. Everyone owed everybody else. It was the greatest Ponzi scheme in the history of planet earth, ... but few knew it! Well, ... some did.

Economically, the world was at war. What would sell after world markets crashed? Beans, bullion, booze, bullets, bunkers, and blow. What wouldn't be selling? Everything else. Food, shelter, and clothing (also transportation and fuel), were all required for life support; but without credit, how would trucks, ships, and trains deliver goods to where they were needed; and how would those products be purchased? Were blockchain currencies, precious metals, and barter an answer? Indeed, unbeknownst to others, Russia had already implemented their 'Masterchain' strategy to circumvent (or ultimately replace) the US dollar as the 'Reserve Currency' to conduct business and eliminate central banks using 'blockchain' technologies like 'Ethereum'. People, prognosticators, and pundits alike would be pummeled with problems as 'powerful intermediaries' along with policies and procedures perished. Big bankers, big government, and PhD economists had provoked the plunder by inflating counterfeit fiat to pay for pork-barrel projects and protracted promises. The more that governments grew, the more work was pulled away from the private sector with printed money stolen from taxpayers to satisfy corporate avarice. The problems multiplied, and concerns grew. Concerns, that easily eclipsed the issues that Jack was facing.

In any case, there was a scramble for cash. As a restaurant, bar, and strip club that also supported Jack's ranch as a resource, the '*Jack of Clubs*' and the '*Redhouse Ranch*' were as close as it gets to being a producible asset, with plenty of free cash flow and arable land. Jack, Frank, Joe, Carol, Sarah, and their buddies knew it, … and so did Seumas!

So after their little swim, as Ignacio and Miguel checked into a local health clinic in Chetumal, the examining nurse practitioner found them to be in relatively good health, other than the bullet hole above Miguel's right knee. Miguel told the nurse that a 'barracuda bit it', but she didn't believe him. Nevertheless, she understood the significance of the prominent tattoo on his right hand that looked like a snake tangled up in a cross, and decided to drop the subject altogether. The wound was healing pretty well, so she applied a new sterile pad with salve, gave him some more pain pills, and sent the two packing with few questions asked. They found a cheap motel near the waterfront in Chetumal, close to a local liquor store, and settled in for further instructions.

Nevertheless, as they relaxed and reflected, Miguel and Ignacio began to question their own 'cheeriness' related to events over the past few weeks. Floating for too many hours in the caliginous waters of the Caribbean, deflecting their fate as fish bait, they began to ponder their own perverse paths to propitiation. Indeed, they began to wax repentant for the copious wrongdoings conducted throughout their sorry lives. At night, as they rested, they were visited by obscure otherworldly entities introducing long forgotten scenes from a distant past that arrived uninvited. Added to that, was an invasion of fifth dimensional and higher vibrational light rearranging a world of darkness that demanded deductions for their dastardly deeds. Their ubiquity was a mere metaphor of past lives transcending through a transmuting continence of impending restitution and resurrection. Meanwhile, Seumas was now on a glide path to Chetumal to check on the two conflicted comrades to communicate his own acute discomfort with their callous crimes. As he careened south along the Caribbean coast from Cancun to Chetumal in his 'tricked out' Toyota RAV4 with large chrome exhaust pipe extensions trumpeting his discontent, Seumas felt both contempt and compassion for his forlorn and felonious friends. He did not want to appear overly judgmental, yet he recognized the resultant ramifications if his two close compatriots were to identify the hierarchy involved in their nefarious plot.

All the while this drama was dragging out, Frank Valero began to long for Carol Mulhaney and the *'Jack of Clubs'* in Topeka. The whole group had for weeks been on a mission to save Jack, so their mutual affability began to abscess. Feeling the fray, Frank made his exit plans during their few days in San Pedro after his Russian and Panamanian friends had rotated back to Panama since he wasn't needed in Central America any longer. Carol Mulhaney would be glad to have Frank back at the bar to help with chores and chats at the 'Jack of Clubs'. Thus, Frank decided to fly back to Kansas out of the local San Pedro airport a couple of days earlier than originally planned, following their friend's departures. That would leave Jack, Joe, and Sarah to continue their shared adventures exploring each other as well as some obscure islands to the south.

Within a day's boat ride from their current coordinates, just off the northern coast of Honduras, sat several reclusive hotels, resorts, and beaches on the islands of Roatán, Guanaja, Útila, and other ports around Turtle Bay, that were often Jack's 'go to' getaways during his island hopping junkets. Jack, Joe, and Sarah had discussed visiting a few of the outlying islands for more relaxation and renewal after they finished their business in Belize, but Jack would need to make his rendezvous with Seumas first to try to learn the reason for his abduction in Cancun. Little did he know that Seumas was on his way to meet with the bad boys first, prior to his scheduled rendezvous with Jack.

Now, it has often been said that each of us is surrounded by a unique and individual 'aura' that can be sensed by others, that helps to define our 'selves' as we traipse through the titillating tarmac of life. Is there some sort of electromagnet force, chemical reaction, 'polar' attraction, or otherwise peripheral potential energy that attracts or repels one person to (or from) another? Do light and dark forces exist asymmetric to a less visible aura in another dimension that can conversely be observed by those possessing a higher vibration? Who can tell? Nevertheless, something attracted Sarah to Joe, and Joe to Sarah, that was arbitrarily akin to a bolt from the benevolent blue. From the moment they first set eyes on each other, they 'clicked' like a couple of coffee cups in a corner café, and linked like lifelong lovers. What was up with that?

In contrast, Jack and Sarah's commitment to each other was more platonic and quixotic, than it was erotic at that point in time, and grew from pluralistic platitudes developed adjacent to their seafaring sojourns, as well as their mutual friendship with Carol Mulhaney. So, when Carol developed a liking for Frank instead of Jack, it was natural for Sarah to pivot over to Jack instead of Frank, in a countervailing flip-flop. Sarah and Jack really were quite fond of each other;

Nevertheless, there was never that 'hit me over the head and drag me away' sort of star-struck attraction like the 'kabooooom' that brought Sarah and Joe to their immediate front and center. Sarah and Joe were smitten from the outset, and were acutely aware of their mutual adjuration. Perhaps it was something in their subconscious that solidified their solitude. Women seem to possess a greater affinity for the subconscious, while men only seem to stumble upon it when it fits their fancy, and/or when they fall in love. Still, there was a 'oneness' between Sarah and Joe that summoned their subconscious spirits and soothed their animus souls.

In any case, upon completing his bartending shift at the grill that afternoon, Seumas hopped into his Toyota RAV4 and rocketed down Highway 307 to Chetumal to meet with his perplexed pals down the Mexican coast. He also packed a black roller bag full of assorted cash from *Guillermo's Grill* to hand to Jack for their later meeting in San Pedro. Chetumal was only a half-day's drive from Cancun, so by the time that Seumas met with Ignacio and Miguel at their waterfront hotel later that evening, the boys were half in the bag, and looked forward to greeting their old boss. No one saw Seumas enter or leave the motel as he made his visit short and sweet. As Seumas slipped down the hallway to their room, he fastened a slick little noise suppressor from his vest pocket onto the barrel of his Bersa Thunder 9mm Kurz, then buried the Bersa in his belt behind his back beneath his shirt. As a bartender, Seumas was quite familiar with the various 'date rape' drugs, 'Mickey Finns', and other anesthetics and pain-killers that people might be inclined to use to incapacitate unsuspecting victims. So, as a precaution, Seumas dropped a couple of 500mg chloral hydrate capsules in his right pocket to slip into his buddy's drinks if an opportunity was afforded him. When Seumas knocked on their door, the thugs cautiously checked to see who was present, then opened the door to let Seumas enter. They greeted each other with a few cursory 'Hola, amigos', then moved to a small round kitchen table to 'catch-up' and reminisce about the good old days as lifetime members of the 'Los Santos' biker gang. Following some casual chit-chat, Seumas asked the two hoods for a clean glass to share in their little celebration, and then poured a small portion of Rum for himself from their bottle with the capsules cupped in his right hand. As Seumas placed the bottle back on the table, and made the sign of the cross, he dropped the capsules into the half-empty bottle of Rum, then made a short toast mentioning something about the 'Los Santos' brotherhood, as the two banditos joined him in communion. The boys were already looking quite tipsy when Seumas asked them how they managed to escape the clutches of Jack and his comrades as the two explained the whole sordid story again about their capture, the leap into the gulf, and the retrieval by a Russian research vessel maneuvering around the reefs, followed by the check-up in Chetumal.

Seumas: "Did you guys mention my name to anyone else, or discuss my involvement with any of our other contacts?" Seumas questioned punctiliously. "Who else knows who we're working with?" he asked.

Miguel: "No, Seumas! We were very careful to keep you out of it! Miguel answered with a minor caveat; … Well, we may have mentioned your name to the skipper of the research boat, … and, that we were meeting you in Chetumal. But only once!" he added.

Seumas: "I understand!" He said. "Anyone else?"

Ignacio: "No. Nobody else" responded Ignacio emphatically. "Well, maybe the nurse", said Ignacio, now slurring his words.

Seumas: "So, what's your next move? Do you plan to get even? He prodded.

Miguel: "Yeah! I'm going to make them pay for putting a bullet in my leg! I'll burn their boat to the waterline while they sleep!" Miguel said. "That'll teach them not to mess with 'Los Santos' hombres", he proudly raged.

Seumas: "Well, that's a pretty bold statement Miguel, and a reply that I didn't really want to hear", Seumas said. "I wouldn't want this situation to get too far out of control", he said as he reached for the Bersa in his back belt.

Seumas quickly stood up and faced them both, planning to pop a cap into each of their foreheads, and two more slugs into each of their chests as they sat drinking their last supper from the half empty bottle of rum. But as he glanced at them again, realizing their pathetic, pitiful little plight, he couldn't bring himself to bring them to their final curtain call. No, it shouldn't be his decision. Besides, as he stood there for a moment pondering his next move, both of the boys did a face plant on the Formica-topped turquoise kitchen table as the effects of the chloral hydrate capsules began to mix their magic. Why waste the bullets, thought Seumas? It wasn't their time, and it wasn't his call. Instead, he would dial in some help. Then, as silently as a sapper, Seumas slipped away from the room leaving the unlocked motel door behind him, and returned to his teased Toyota parked in the adjacent motel lot.

While he cautiously scanned the lot for witnesses, he slithered out the driveway of the waterfront motel and drove to his own hotel near the Chetumal International airport to get a good night's rest. He made a quick phone call to his 'IC' team on the way back to his hotel to request that a 'cleaning crew' be dispatched to the room to quickly extract the two listless bodies. He would park his Toyota in his own hotel lot, then drive the car to the Chetumal airport parking area the next day, and take a cab to the marina for the boat ride to San Pedro the following morning to meet with his good friend Jack.

The cleaning crew arrived at the waterfront motel shortly after Seumas departed and quickly retracted the two thugs using a couple of climbing harnesses, some quick-snap clamps, and a long wire cable with pulleys. They smartly attached the harnesses around each of the victim's waists, and using a large U-bolt welded to a metal plate under the roof of their van, secured the opposite cable end to a bracket at the top inside beam of the second floor window in the hotel room with a spanner bar. With the screen removed, and the cable secured at the two end points, and with the van parked just outside the window in the darkened parking lot below, they fastidiously slid the two harnessed victims into the van, disconnected the cable, closed the back doors, and drove out of the lot within minutes, heading to an undisclosed location elsewhere in the Caribbean (perhaps

Panama or Havana), to be questioned further, learn a new reality, and be dealt with directly.

The following morning, after a nervous night's sleep, Seumas awoke early, showered, put on a fresh change of clothes from his backpack, and grabbed a quick cup of coffee and muffin from the lobby. Back in his room, he grabbed a small towel from the bath to toss into his backpack, then drove to the airport where he parked his car in the long-term lot. With the car parked at the airport, he wrapped the Bersa Thunder .380 in the small towel and placed it back in his backpack. Then, he grabbed his black roller bag from the trunk of his car, as well as a local cab to the Chetumal Marina to buy a water taxi ticket for the first available boat heading out to San Pedro on the *Ambergris Caye*. Although there were quite a few passengers aboard the water taxi that morning heading to the island, no one noticed half way through the trip as Seumas pulled the small towel out of his backpack and, hanging the towel over the side of the boat, quickly let the handgun slide out of the towel into the boat's spray, and down to its final resting place at the bottom of the ocean. And, just like that, the gun was gone. Seumas then used the towel to wipe the grin off his face and placed the towel back in his backpack for the remainder of the boat ride.

AGENTS, AMIGOS, ANGELS, & SAINTS

"We but mirror the world. All the tendencies present in the outer world are to be found in the world of our body. If we could change ourselves, the tendencies in the world would also change. As a man changes his own nature, so does the attitude of the world change towards him. This is the divine mystery supreme. A wonderful thing it is and the source of our happiness. We need not wait to see what others do." – Mahatma Gandhi

While Frank Valero began to lust for a few laps around the *'Jack of Clubs'* with Carol in Topeka, Jack Redhouse began to crave a kosher corned beef sandwich with coleslaw, on rye, ... and a dill pickle on the side. This was something that he could order off the menu in Kansas, but would be a tall order in San Pedro, *Ambergris Caye*, let alone within about a thousand kilometer radius of his current coordinates. Jack understood intuitively that two slices of buttered rye bread stacked with hot, juicy, thickly sliced corned beef, topped with creamy coleslaw, was the closest that he might ever get to heaven on earth, and true happiness. Couple the sandwich with a locally brewed pilsner, or a *Holy Grail Pale Ale*, and one would need to pinch themselves to know whether their feet were still firmly planted on this small blue planet. A large, cold, kosher dill pickle on the side was the pièce de résistance, and was 'to die for'.

Nevertheless, dying was not on Jack's menu just yet. That part would have to wait until the rest of Jack's plan was implemented. As it happened, Jack's history with *Seumas* also went a long way back, and again, there was more to this story than was immediately apparent. Jack's dream of being 'James Bond' began to manifest more magnanimously following his recruitment into covert projects with the CIA while working in the Middle East, many years earlier. Jack now needed to rely on that training to unlock the truth. So, perhaps it was time to make a few phone calls to uncover what was occurring behind the mantle of misdirection. Jack decided that he should probably do that before his meeting with Seumas.

Life is a journey to discover reality, and happiness is directly proportional to the truth. The world was living a lie, and history was replete with false narratives constructed and predicated on faulty premises. Jack's happiness was illusory partly because his own concept of history was false. Of course, that wasn't necessarily Jack's fault; he was merely another casualty of the criminal concoctions contrived by a crass cabal. What did Jack really know, and when did he know it? Those were the questions. *Fly the plane. Be the bird dog. Be the beacon of light that shines on the truth; be the change that you want to see in the world. Love, not hate.*

For that matter, was Aleksandr Isayevich Solzhenitsyn ever really happy in life, or was he just another victim of the long tentacles of satanic dishonesty concealed in a cocoon called yesterday? Is the term 'Bullshit' derived from the word 'Bolshevik'? And in reality, who were the vile 'Bolsheviks' in any case, other than ubiquitous serpentine Khazarians with bulwarks and bastions beyond the Black Sea? Were they in essence responsible for many, if not most malevolent events known to mankind for millenniums? *Muy posiblemente! Muy mucho!*

In reality, much of what we see is innocuously unseen in the underpinnings of political life. Who was it after all, that didn't want Jack to be successful in the *Jack of Clubs* near Forbes field outside of Topeka? Although many of the bikers, banksters, gangs, and apparatchiks had their hands in it, and enjoyed a piece of the pie from a plethora of perspectives, the jealousy, envy, and acrimony from these carnivores was conspicuous relative to Jack's independence, as was their desire to steal Jack's operation for themselves. The forces involved sought to net all business revenue, assets, rent, tax, and profit for those positioned at the top, as the tentacles of the beast extended to the highest levels of the federal state, organized crime, and beyond. Back at *Jack's* place, people had been putting pressure on Jack to relinquish a larger share in the action for well over a year; and in fact, that's why some of his Russian friends, who had earlier 'staked' Jack to set up the club, had visited the bar on numerous occasions to negotiate a larger slice of the cake. Of course Jack had been making regular payouts, or 'distributions', to all of his partners based on a percentage that associates had initially invested in the club. So they all benefited from their close relationship in a 'cash business'. Jack said that he would consider their proposals, but then left town without much notice to get back to his boat in Cancun. From that point forward, everything was left hanging.

So, it was the local 'elite' in the area surrounding the *Jack of Clubs* in Kansas, as well as various political and business interests that were responsible for much of Jack's constant consternation, who were bent on putting Jack down, while Jack struggled to maintain his individual sovereignty and independence. But the actors in the background behind the putsch weren't always 'local', and often had a broader agenda. This was a big deal, … and the conglomerate conversations often came from other continents. So Jack's past was as difficult to escape, as his future was uncertain.

Now, getting back to the story, who actually hired Miguel and Ignacio to kidnap Jack? It wasn't Seumas, since unbeknownst to the others, Jack and Seumas were also both minor partners in *Guillermo's Grill*. Indeed, that was one of the reasons why Jack was in Cancun several weeks earlier in the first place; to discuss setting up the *'Grill'* similar to the *'Jack of Clubs';* with dancers, drinks, and delectable dishes like corned beef sandwiches with coleslaw on rye, and deli dill pickles. Coincidently, in a chess-like stealthy move, Jack had considered offloading much of his operation in Kansas to free up equity, improve cash flow, and dial down the pace of his personal participation, as he looked ahead to his own pullback. He could keep his hand in the *'Jack of Clubs'* on a smaller scale while shifting some of his finer assets closer to Cancun, - and some neighboring islands, - which was one of his objectives, and the main reason he was currently in the Caribbean anyway. Jack liked his solitude, and was quite comfortable with his integral sovereignty, yet still felt closely connected with various friends from the past, which arbitrarily coincided with his compassion for his comrades.

In any case, there were operatives back in Kansas causing trouble, who also believed that Seumas might be able to put pressure on Jack to sell his stake in his properties near Topeka more quickly, since Jack was planning to simplify his life anyway. So, as simplistic as it sounds, they believed that kidnapping Jack might inspire him to get rid of his assets faster, had the plan not been busted up; ... but Frank, Joe, and his other buddies changed all of that when they rescued Jack. Seumas had a sense of the plan from talking with Ignacio and Miguel prior to the abduction, but kept quiet because he didn't know the details from all angles; and yet, there were other 'players' involved that Seumas had had discussions with at the bar in Cancun. Still, when Seumas saw that neither Jack nor the delivery boys had returned to *Guillermo's Grill* after Jack's last visit, he suspected that Miguel and Ignacio were somehow involved in the plot, and were getting payment and instructions from various 'enlightened citizens' that Jack and Seumas knew back in the states. Seumas had also conveyed those thoughts to Sarah when she called. So, without getting too far afield, it was indeed some nefarious business interests back in Kansas that were behind Jack's abduction, working with Russian friends, who weren't actually Russian. These were individuals that had frequented the 'Jack of Clubs', and were likewise interested in expanding the chain of nightclubs throughout the North American continent that extended up, through, and along the I-35 corridor from Cancun to Canada. Nonetheless, they normally spoke Chinese or Spanish, and sometimes French or Italian, but mostly behaved like Khazarians.

    Back at the beach, Jack had now stepped out of his safe space and into the light, as this issue would have to be reconciled with all of the parties involved before Jack would be able to feign his escape. In essence, it was Jack and Seumas that had originally floated the idea of staging a kidnapping to throw the Kansas crowd off his scent, and perhaps fake his disappearance. But then, in accordance with the axioms of Sun Tzu, who wrote <u>*The Art of War,*</u> all war, is based on deception. Having said that, it was a surprise to Jack when his own removal actually happened. Perhaps there was 'mind control' involved, as only Seumas and Jack were aware of their initial chats as far as Jack knew. Frank, Joe, and the other boys weren't briefed on the original plan, so the process became a bit more puzzling when the two punks actually pulled it off. Jack and Seumas would need to regroup. They understood implicitly that 'we are all one', as in the 'WE ARE' embodiment (or perhaps Semper fidelis), yet also desired several degrees of separation as in the 'I AM' mode. Perhaps the idea transcended the subconscious and was somehow ethereally elevated to alien interests!? No, that didn't make sense. Seumas was somehow more intricately involved, and privy to more pertinent information.

When the water taxi arrived at the *Amigo's del Mar* pier in San Pedro, Jack was waiting on the dock in a pair of relaxed fitting pleated slacks and open-toed sandals, with a tropical shirt under a light colored linen jacket. Seumas was all smiles as he reached out to shake his old pal's hand, stepping out of the boat, and onto the dock. He handed his black roller bag over to Jack as he exited the ferry.

The two amigos greeted each other graciously as Jack put one hand on Seumas's shoulder, while pulling the roller bag along behind him, as they both walked down the dock to have a chat at the *Sandy Beach Villa Hotel*. Jack then took the roller bag out to his boat for safekeeping while Seumas checked into his room at the hotel. Back at the bar, Jack ordered a pitcher of Mojo and a couple of clean glasses for himself and Seumas as they grabbed a table out on the covered deck overlooking the beach to catch up on old news. Instead of a corned beef sandwich on rye with coleslaw, he ordered two plates of fish & chips with coleslaw for the two of them. It had been a while since they had last met at *Guillermo's Grill* in Cancun for their previous heart-to-heart talk, and it was good to see his *buen amigo* and ex-*Los Santos* ally again after too many tumultuous weeks. They would work this out together.

While Jack waited for Joe and Sarah to join them down at the bar, the two old friends reconnected as Jack began the conversation by asking Seumas how long it had been since he had last seen the two delivery guys, Miguel and Ignacio? Jack's friend Frank had already departed for the San Pedro airport earlier that same morning to fly back to Kansas and be with Carol; so that just left Jack, Joe, and Sarah to entertain Seumas at the villa bar.

"So, Seumas", began Jack, "this is about the way we left it a few weeks ago when we met at the *Grill*" he said. "Having a cold *cerveza* at the bar. Do you remember our last visit?" He asked.

"Of course I do Jack! And, I thought you'd be back the following day! I was surprised when you didn't show up for our regular afternoon chat. I thought maybe you just needed some 'down time'. In fact, I didn't really suspect that anything was wrong until Sarah called me." Seumas revealed openly.

Jack continued, "I certainly didn't expect that day to end up the way it did! I was headed back down to the boat to take a long nap. I had no idea that your delivery guys were going to try to 'fake' my disappearance the way we had discussed. Lol. Did you happen to discuss our little plan with anyone else?" asked Jack. "Not directly", answered Seumas. "But I did have a few inquiries from some of your regular well-connected customers up in Kansas, as to whether you were making moves to sell the club", he answered.

"Oh, and who might that be?" asked Jack. "Have you seen the delivery guys since we last met? Jack asked curiously.

"Well, Jack, I think you probably already know the answer to that, and perhaps that's why you're asking. I've heard the whole story from the boys themselves, so you probably already know that they made it to shore with a gunshot wound in Miguel's right leg." He said. "I paid them both a visit last night, and now they're gone. They threatened to burn you and your boat to the waterline as you slept, to get back at you. I was going to pop them both at that moment but the drug I gave them caused them to do a face plant on their Formica table while they were drinking their last glass of rum, so I didn't have the heart to waste them. In any case, they're out of the picture. I called a crew to clean the place and move them to a new location. So we won't be seeing either of them again, anytime soon".

"In fact, I believe that the whole stupid little plan may have been their own idea just to gin up some extra cash, after I suggested that we might want to help you disappear", said Seumas. "Or maybe it was just a misunderstanding. Nevertheless, there have been additional inquiries from people to sell your interests in Kansas, and they may have also prompted the boys to act a bit hastily!" Seumas speculated. "As far as who else might be involved in the action in Kansas, you can probably guess that as well. But, there's no need to guess. Some of them are ex-Los Santos guys who would like a bigger 'piece of the pie' than they're currently getting, and the others are mob people backing them; mostly banksters, and gangsters from Asia interested in acquiring real estate in the US and Mexico, as well as Central and South America, to launder their stolen cash from back home. Strip clubs, bars, and restaurants just seem to trip their trigger; plus it might allow them to get some of their gaming and extortion rackets started in the states as well. That pretty much sums it up in a nutshell Jack. Does that surprise you?" Seumas asked. "I think we could also make this work to our advantage, in any case", added Seumas.

"Hahaaa …. No, that doesn't surprise me actually. I kind of expected it. And, yes, I agree. I'm sure that we can make this work to our advantage if we play our cards right!" agreed Jack. "As you know, Seumas, it's good versus evil; and what feeds the dark forces is fear. In other words; F.E.A.R; False Evidence Appearing Real. Or, to say it another way, 'Fake'. As in, … it's all fake! A fake government, run by fake politicians, printing fake money, to prop up a fake economy, reported by fake TV talking heads, paid by the devil himself spewing fake news, about a false reality. Indeed, as I wrote years ago;"

Real-Eyes

Nothing is real;
It's just what we make it.
We're making the motions
While we really just fake it

They feed us the data,
And like fools we take it;
Trying to expand our mind;
Instead we just bake it.

When will it end,
This follow the leader?

"It's pretty apparent that evil forces are encouraging these people to sack the 'Jack of Clubs' and steal my assets in Kansas, Seumas", said Jack. "Wicked forces have been lurking in the background for quite a while. Mucho millennia. The world's religions were ostensibly created through a few fallen angels working with some watchers and seers, that we now call saints; or, *Los Santos*. Fake religion! But it's been Satan in control of the earth for many thousands of years, and that's who's really behind the destruction, decay, and devolution of civilized society. Who really knows the truth, since most of us are fed fake narratives from birth through death, while the average lifespan is only seven or eight decades?! From the time that we're old enough to begin to comprehend what we're being taught, we're fed false information in schools, and on the job, while learning the ways of the world until we expire. Meanwhile, malevolent forces spread disinformation endlessly, hiding behind false paradigms, spewing lies. I think I now understand who may have been behind the abduction, as well as the characters behind the push to control my operations. Organized crime is rampant in the world, and that includes Kansas. However, it's a complex subject with a mixed bag of players and many faces all connected through dark forces. We can turn that corner, but we're up against a tribal mentality. So, now that our immediate problems with Miguel and Ignacio are behind us, I think that we can disregard the coercion for a while and instead just focus on some of the other subjects we discussed. So, to your point, let's make this work to our advantage", conceded Jack.

A moment later, Joe and Sarah emerged from elsewhere in the villa where they were busy discovering each other's finer characteristics. They grinned all smiley-eyed with a hint of mischief and uncomfortable contentment, as they greeted Jack and Seumas at their table overlooking the beach in the warm and breezy open-air bar. They hadn't eaten lunch so they both ordered plates of fish & chips with coleslaw as well. Jack introduced Joe to Seumas, whom Sarah was already acquainted with, as Joe shook his hand and sized him up suspiciously. Then, they all sat around the table to remember, analyze, and assess past events, rehashing the past couple weeks of trouble, and began to plan their island hopping adventures in the weeks ahead. Jack barely noticed the unabashed attraction between Joe and Sarah, and didn't really care. He now had other things on his mind as he began to formulate a more fortuitous future, in the here and now, leaving yesterday behind.

Perhaps Jack's old Navy buddy Sanjo Casagrande could help him sort things out, he thought. He would call Sanjo over the next few days to see whether his old pal could come down from Duluth to join their little party. Sanjo could accompany them to one of the outer islands to help them plan a workable strategy for dissolution and succession management. Sanjo was more of a philosopher than a 'logistics' guy, but he often helped Jack get to the crux of a problem. Jack felt that Sanjo had a circular sort of logic that helped Jack untangle challenging issues. Sanjo had the knack, and the patience to be able to unravel a snarled fishing line from a balled up spinning reel that cut to the core of a conundrum. For instance, he believed that everyone was connected in a universal consciousness, and that there existed some sort of overall justice in life whereby everything eventually comes around full circle towards resolution. Or, as they used to say in the Navy, 'What goes around, … comes around'. It was also Sanjo's theory that when a good life was lost, their soul was often attracted to the life that took it. Or, that the good souls of soldiers and sailors destroyed in battles often became the incarnate children and relatives or friends of those who took their lives. It really didn't make much sense on the face of it, yet it was a way of deliberating that helped Jack to 'think out of the box' and distill the many ingredients into a more homogeneous mix. Sanjo had been taught religion from a variety of sources while growing up in the high desert plains of Albuquerque, attending different religious schools, and living there with his mother, Anita Kelly, before she married Hank; Nevertheless, Sanjo never realized or acknowledged the beliefs that he may have absorbed through osmosis. Or, perhaps it was just the hot high desert sun and clear cold starlit nights that had influenced him most.

Sanjo's wife Marissa (aka *Cassandra*) on the other hand, was Catholic, like many of her Filipina friends and countrymen. Therefore, Sanjo was a bit confused about religion in general, as well as which doctrine and/or dogma that he should embrace. To be honest, Sanjo didn't believe in organized religions anyway. In fact, when wandering in a dream state, Sanjo often found himself merely floating like a feather inside an opaque wall of white-bubbled ambience with nothing below his feet or above his head, or anything around him, wondering what was coming next. In essence, he was waiting to break through a crack in a ubiquitous matrix to experience a majestic universe beyond a barrier that revealed all truth. He often caught a glimpse of unbelievable universal beauty and intricate geometric designs that transcended even Sanjo's vivid imagination, which was essentially ineffable to most. For whatever reason, he also seemed to be visiting otherworldly places in obscure times, both in the past and in the future, having conversations with people that he seemed to know quite well, speaking different languages and singing songs or listening to music in those same languages that he understood completely, as he communicated with others; All very foreign to Sanjo who never remembered being in any of those places previously. Yet it all seemed perfectly natural and was often more real than when he was awake. Both Sanjo, and his wife Marissa believed that they could tap into the ubiquitous universe for anything they desired including strength, health, healing, energy, knowledge, sustenance, and spiritual awareness, among other qualities. Along that same vane, his perception of much of what he believed to be real, was actually false; And, much of what he thought was false, was actually real, which reinforced the riddle. So, it was possible, he postulated, that even angels and saints were real; and, in that case, he felt that we could probably take religious scriptures to the bank. So, what was the truth? Sanjo wasn't really certain whether all of these factors made him a Catholic, a Taoist, a Mormon, or possibly a Presbyterian or Episcopalian. In any case, he was sure that he had previously fought in a few great world battles, and had somehow eclipsed several lifetimes and participated in previous perils on other planets. So in a secular sense, Sanjo was sort of like Superman.

Then again, there was that critical car crash in northern California that had occurred during Sanjo's early days in the Navy that helped him cement his spiritual bonds. He had been the driver of a rental car that hit a telephone pole at about 65 MPH after losing control in a hairpin turn, heading southbound out of Crescent City, California. After the car spun out, the pole smashed the starboard side where his sailor pal had been enjoying the morning cruise, but through the maelstrom, had crushed his crown like a squashed avocado smashing through the passenger-side window. After pulling his pal from the tangled wreck, Sanjo beat on his chest for 10 minutes, praying to God that his sailor friend wouldn't die, when miraculously, the injured sailor gasped for air. Sanjo got juiced on religion during that misty morning miracle, and morphed into a mystic as a result of the mishap. Now, perhaps Sanjo would consider crashing their little party in the Caribbean to help lift Jack, Joe, and Seumas out of another niggling little jam.

"qualche santo provvederà"

DAMAGE CONTROL

"The only real question, as I see it, has two parts: one, 'do I serve truth or deception?' And two, 'how do I best serve truth?" - Dr. Jamisson Neruda, www.wingmakers.com

The October sky heading south from Duluth was overcast, with a sliver of sun shimmering through the morning haze as Sanjo Casagrande headed down I-35 toward Minneapolis. Northbound traffic passed in the opposite direction with headlights on, as Sanjo peered over the hood of his freshly washed black Tahoe SUV, and watched the reflections of oncoming cars driving upside-down in his hood, flowing like raindrops to the port side as he drove; then disappearing over the edge. The images were funny he thought, and entertaining; like watching a movie.

Sanjo had a fondness for Minneapolis from his earlier years spent 'working out' at the downtown Hilton health club where he reconnected with Marissa (aka Cassandra; Sanjo's wife), at the hotel bar. So, he knew his way around the 'Twin Cities' quite well and certainly knew the way to the Minneapolis airport. Sanjo's plan was to catch a flight out of Bloomington to meet with Jack and his buddies down in Belize by evening. He relaxed and let out a deep yawn, comforted by the swinging crucifix dangling from his rear-view mirror as he continued south. He made a sign of the cross, recited a short prayer, asking God, Saint Christopher, and many of the angels and saints for safe travel. It felt good to be on the open road again, looking forward to a new adventure. A grey day, but a good day for driving, he thought.

Untold months had passed since Sanjo had last visited his old Navy buddy Jack Redhouse, so it would be good to reconnect. He felt a bit ambivalent about meeting up with Jack again, initially thinking that it might mean trouble, but then relented to reality. There really was no need for confusion at this juncture in his life. Marissa and he had been all through the semi-surreal social upheavals with Jack and his dysfunctional crew in the past, and those days were conveniently behind them. So, after their countless cruising trips with Jack's mottled crew in the Caribbean, Sanjo and Marissa Casagrande (aka *Cassandra*) found that they were more content to live a more reclusive lifestyle up in Minnesota, while Jack and the girls, as well as his other Navy pals, still preferred the warmer climes below the Mason-Dixie line. That said, there really wasn't all that much happening up in Duluth at that time of year anyway, so he welcomed the break. Sanjo promised himself that he would try to keep his nose clean with Sarah this time around, since Sarah Reid (*Enchanté*) was now dating Jack (but was also interested in Joe Melnik). In any case, he didn't anticipate any distractions from her elegant little end, going forward.

He had a late start after making a few phone calls in response to his morning e-mail. Initially, Sanjo had planned to leave his minimalist Dutch-style bungalow early to allow him to arrive at the Minneapolis airport by noon. Burdened with thoughts about retirement life, as well as family, he was in the habit of mulling over subtle details in his head to deflect problems. Of course, Marissa also felt less stressed whenever Sanjo left town for a few days, so she felt somewhat relieved when he announced that he was leaving on another road trip. It had been well over an hour now since Sanjo left his lakeshore lodging so he needed to make up some time. He turned on the radio to catch up on the local news; He reclined the multidirectional electric driver's seat for more comfort, and adjusted the lumbar support; He then sipped some hot coffee that he had bought just ten minutes earlier while topping off his tank. A gallon of gas was a little over three bucks per gallon (as was a 20 ounce 'bottled water' in some hotels), so he felt better with a full tank of gas. The economy was struggling with high unemployment, and over 45 million Americans were still on food stamps, but Sanjo was retired, and was now collecting a pretty good pension and Social Security. He felt settled, comfortable. Now he could think.

The 'fake news' drifted into the background as he listened to the same old tired stories that often made the American news. Another ball player was accused of murder, another of rape, and there were several more false flag 'terrorist attacks' occurring in major cities around the globe. Another Bishop, as well as a monk admitted that they had sex with a young boy as authorities began arresting pedophiles from government agencies, movie sets, big banks, financial centers, and the Vatican, among other prominent locations worldwide. It was also suggested in various 'alternative news' venues that the previous Pope was an ex-nazi, while Hitler's daughter was running Germany; and apparently Hitler himself had actually escaped to Argentina after World War II where he had survived to a ripe old age with family and friends of like-minded Nazi persuasions. Sanjo also found a photo of Hitler on the internet showing him standing next to his house with his architect near the Villa La Angostura, in Patagonia, Argentina. Additionally, according to some, and to the chagrin of the allies, the Germans had actually won the second world war; but under *'Operation Paperclip'* the ex-Nazi engineers and scientists were given new identities so that the allied countries could develop a secret space program, keeping the technology away from the Russians, while many more Nazis were incorporated into the CIA (from the former OSS) to spread perpetual streams of propaganda and a preponderance of more fake news. In any case, the alternative news media on the world-wide-web allowed individuals to 'snooze or lose', and choose their news, which muddled the mainstream media mayhem all the more. According to 'reliable sources', the 'Khazarian cabal' continued to kill citizens with chemtrails, vaccines, toxic metals, radiation, prescribed pharmaceuticals, pesticides, GMO food, and outright assassinations and yet still, the communists in control along with the fascists in the NSA, CIA, DEA, ICE, ATF, and the FBI had plans to round up about 20 million 'main core' Americans using the DHS to place them into FEMA internment camps and shuttered department stores, for reeducation and/or liquidation. The radio in his SUV played the song 'Dancing Cheek to Cheek' sung by Ella Fitzgerald and Louis Armstrong, as Sanjo headed down the highway to catch a southbound plane to Belize.

https://www.youtube.com/watch?v=GeisCvjwBMo

> "You must understand, the leading Bolsheviks who took over Russia were not Russians. They hated Russians. They hated Christians. Driven by ethnic hatred they tortured and slaughtered millions of Russians without a shred of human remorse. It cannot be overstated. Bolshevism committed the greatest human slaughter of all time. The fact that most of the world is ignorant and uncaring about this enormous crime is proof that the global media is in the hands of the perpetrators." – Alexandr Solzhenitsyn (1918 – 2008)

Meanwhile, back in San Pedro, Jack Redhouse was making plans to move *'Damage Control Central'* further south to the 'Caymans' after a short stop in Roatán (once home to over 5,000 pirates), off the coast of Honduras. They would put in at Coxen Hole for a couple of days (remaining aboard the boat mostly), stock up on some supplies, then prepare for a longer trip eastward to the Cayman islands for an extended stay. Prior to that though, Jack would meet Sanjo at the Belize airport for an overnight stopover, and maybe visit a couple of the local gin joints, then take the boat back to San Pedro the following morning to meet with the others. Logistically, the Cayman Islands were more central to Jack's overall plan with a large airport that could be used as backup if needed, with all of the amenities that Jack and his crew desired. Jack preferred the area around 'Bodden Town' on the southern side of Grand Cayman with its coastal 'Pirate Dens', rather than the more popular resort areas on either end of the island. However, his eventual plan might land him in Havana.

A quick search on 'Airbnb' revealed numerous villas for rent that offered seaside relaxation, as well as entertainment and good dining options. A number of hotels and resorts were also available. Then again, they could all just spend the nights aboard the boat while lounging around the bars and beeches during the day. Be that as it may, the extended weather forecast was showing overcast skies with higher temperatures in the Caribbean for that time of year, and they were still in 'hurricane season' as well. Jack also had to find a way to take on more diesel fuel for the trip, so he began to investigate his options. He discovered that diesel was not readily available in San Pedro, so he would take the boat down to the bigger city of Belize to greet Sanjo, and try to refuel at a marina while he was in that neighborhood. Then, he would try to top off his tanks again in Coxen Hole, if practical. In any case, the distance from San Pedro down to Coxen Hole, and the islands of Utila, Roátan, and Guajana, was only about 150 miles, and well within his boat's range since it could easily cruise for up to 1,800 nautical miles at a steady 12 plus knots (with the modifications that Jack, Frank, and their friend Gino had made) for five days without refueling. The distance from Coxen Hole to the Caymans was only about 300 miles, so was also well within range.

Seumas, for his part, would return to Cancun to work his bar shifts at *Guillermo's Grill*. So, Jack and Seumas had a few more discussions about their plans to set up the '*Grill*' like the 'Jack of Clubs' with dancing girls delivering deli dishes and drinks, … and other delightful diversions to develop more sales. They also discussed their plans for adding assets in the Cayman Islands, and perhaps Havana, to further expand their operation(s). The roller bag full of cash from *Guillermo's Grill* would be mostly converted to precious metals and cryptocurrencies for later transactions, with a portion of the funds returned to Seumas. If possible

Jack was also going to look into the prospect of buying an older stylish, chic hotel in Havana, and perhaps start another restaurant, club, and casino if he could make the right connections. A *'Nuevo Hotel Nacional'* perhaps, like in the '50's thought Jack. For now though, it was just a passing fantasy. Discussions about the earlier abduction, and the perps behind the assault, would be tabled for the time being. It was probably the mob behind the mess in any case, so Jack preferred to back away for the moment. Be that as it may, there were still some cryptic questions remaining in the bulkheads of their obdurate brains that would need to be brought back to the boards. Jack needed to know 'Who Dunnit', in an effort to put the incident behind him, ... and/or maybe take a few of them out. Seumas might be able to help him with that little task also.

It should also be said that, although Jack and Seumus were good friends, and were somewhat familiar with each other's backgrounds, their relationship was a bit tentative, since there were facts about each other that they didn't really want to know. For example, Seamus didn't want to know more details about Jack's relationships with Sarah and his Navy buddies to any great extent, and conversely Jack didn't want additional information about Seamus's biker gang buddies and 'agency contacts'. However, beyond that, Jack also knew that Seamus had deeper ties to an underground, shadowy underworld, that had strong covert ties to agents in 'third world' governments, black ops, and 'deep state' projects, that actually had financial control over 'legitimate' governments in the eastern and western worlds. Seamus also had closer ties with Miguel, Ignacio, and other gang members like them, than he was letting on, and they were both aware of the anomaly. Nevertheless, they also knew that these ties often come in handy when some 'out-of-the-box' thinking became necessary. All of that could prove to be beneficial later in the game as Jack began to transition from his current situation. As Woodrow Wilson indicated to the world in 1913;

"Since I entered politics, I have chiefly had men's views confided to me privately. Some of the biggest men in the United States, in the field of commerce and manufacture, are afraid of something. They know that there is a power somewhere so organized, so subtle, so watchful, so interlocked, so complete, so

pervasive, that they better not speak above their breath when they speak in condemnation of it."

— <u>Woodrow Wilson</u>, <u>The New Freedom</u>

But Jack, conversely, was already beginning to disappear, to transition, evolve, transform, and turn the page to a new chapter in a higher plane. He had already made the move in his own mind, so it was just a matter of following through. In fact, his dreams were becoming more vivid, detailed, and distinct with variegated visions of vivacious variants of red, yellow, violet, and blue, as well as a multitude of pastels and Italian hues, combined with immeasurable amounts of complicated geometric patterns that were new to Jack. He knew innately where he needed to be; but had to follow his heart and the truth to get there. "I'll reconnect with you as we move forward', Jack said to Seumas. "Let's touch base every couple of weeks or so until we can set up shop. You can contact your comrades to keep them apprised until we make the transition." he instructed.

Jack also began to realize that it was 'The Truth' that might make him happiest in life; that, if he could just discover the truth, instead of trying to process all of the lies that had been shoveled to him throughout his entire existence, 'Truth' would set him free, … since truth seemed to be a core element of his happiness. Jack knew the truth intuitively, and truth knew Jack intimately, which was why Jack questioned so many of the things that he had been taught - which rarely made much sense - as people reinforced the same lies over and over, stacked like Paul Bunyan flapjacks being flipped and fed to a big blue ox his whole life. Jack also realized that he needed a mission, a purpose, a plan; something that he could 'sink his teeth into' that might keep him engaged and interested, and that he might follow to a successful conclusion. For Jack, that void was currently filled via the '*Redhouse Ranch*', the '*Jack of Clubs*', and his blue and white Cessna 170 'tail-dragger' airplane stowed in his Quonset hut hangar back at Forbes Field in Topeka, Kansas; but Jack was anxious to turn the page, push the throttle forward, and start a new chapter in his life while he kept one eye on the altimeter, and the other on the carburetor heat. He just didn't yet know what that project might entail. Maybe, the answers were in Havana.

Jack understood that he needed to be more grounded with both the earth, and the truth; That, it was the earth that had helped energize his life, just as it was truth which strengthened and nourished him; and the combination of truth and grounding allowed greater gratification ostensibly. As a result of listening to this new stream of internal consciousness, he began to feel less stressed and more satisfied. Indeed, Jack discovered that he was beginning to realize more strength, energy, and sustenance from the good vibrations within the earth, than he was from the products upon the earth. If he just let the vibrations course through his body, he discovered that he needed less from the outside world. He discovered a source of power beneath his feet that had always been there, and it came from within the earth. Perhaps it was the Vril, or electromagnetic power of a spinning earth that cut through the lines of flux and regenerated the cells of his mind and body. 'Just add water' he thought, as he let the vibrations do their work.

There was so much bullshit in the world that had been fastidiously fed to Jack and others for so long, that many minds were turning to mush, resulting in angst, sadness, and confusion. The phenomena had greatly increased since the 9/11 events in the states, to the point where more people questioned the status quo, and began to awaken to the enormous evils thrust upon them by TPTB. And, as more facts came to light, more and more people began to realize that '9/11' was just another false flag event perpetrated by their own government and a 'new world order' to advance an agenda of endless war, pain, and suffering. Until those responsible for their crimes were held accountable, and brought to justice,

… peace, joy, truth, and happiness would be elusive, as hope and change evaporated. Therefore, truth had to be exposed to show that America's own government, along with other governments and associated enemy accomplices, had been behind the 9/11 attacks, and could not be trusted.

Indeed, it was pretty well understood by many astute observers that a rocket had hit the Pentagon on September 11, 2001 (not a plane), in an area where a Naval Intelligence team had been investigating the administration for serious crimes, as building #7 also disintegrated into it's own pernicious footprint after no plane hit it. Authorities had even found a jet engine from an arbitrary airplane at the base of one of the twin towers in New York City after the buildings were pulverized into powder, and also 'just happened to find' a perfect passport from one of the alleged 'terrorists' sitting in the dust from the disintegrated buildings, as molten steel ran continuously for several weeks after the event, and they tried to clean up the mess and hide the facts. That caused other knowledgeable observers to speculate that a thermonuclear device had been planted at the base of the buildings, long before the 9/11 events, which pulverized and collapsed all three buildings on the same day, as all credible evidence seemed to vanish. On top of that, it was revealed by some, that the alleged terrorists had all turned up alive elsewhere in the world at later dates, … so the whole event was apparently staged. The real story was obscured, and the facts were buried along with the bodies and the truth, as more wars were started, and as the 'fake news' press belched endless bullshit. Hope and change was needed, but none followed in the years after the 9/11 events. Again, Jack and the others really wanted to know 'Who dunnit', and wouldn't rest until they knew the truth.

The dirty little secret was that after the American Civil War (1861 to 1865), the Federal Government along with Congress, and other criminals residing in Washington DC, created a fake government that was separate from 'the American people' residing in the real 'United States' and the original 'Republic'. Indeed, the situation changed officially with the 'Act of 1871' when the 'UNITED STATES' became a separate corporation (after Lincoln placed the Grand Army of the Republic in charge, and issued the Lieber Code in 1863. The Army then controlled the Territorial United States, and the Municipal United States was run by the Congress, to continue the charade), intent upon stealing the wealth from the American people to create their own corrupt, criminal, collusional empire, with more crooks, congress, and banksters finally setting up the Federal Reserve bank ponzi scheme in 1913.

Read; http://12160.info/profiles/blogs/the-act-of-1871-formed-the-corporation-called-the-united-states

View; https://www.youtube.com/watch?v=yikOoysUGIY https://www.youtube.com/watch?v=V8PblX_Qaf0

As Jack retreated into himself and attempted to implement personal life changes, he began to walk barefoot on the beach again, barefoot through the sand, and was delighted to feel his tingling toes brushing through the grass, while walking barefoot on freshly cut tropical lawns; and barefoot on the wooden docks in the morning mist, as he felt more grounded and connected to the good vibrations of the earth, air, sun, and water. These actions also allowed Jack to partially cleanse himself of toxins from the chemtrails in the air, the fluorides in the water, and the GMO contaminants in the soil and foods, although he believed it was difficult to remove all traces of toxins from his body. As he advanced in years, his body began to experience more aches and pains, so that grounding with the earth verily relieved his quickening aches and pains. Jack also discovered that he needed more water as he aged for both his brain and his joints. As he ached more in the morning, he found that just having a hot cup of tea and drinking more water helped him lubricate his joints so that his body healed, and he didn't need to steal water from other areas of his body to satisfy his under-hydrated brain. A little lemon and honey also helped, as did a few tabs of Organic Curcumin and Licorice Root.

In any case, Jack knew that he would have to move to higher ground to position himself for future events, especially with upcoming planetary changes. He also knew that his moves would be independent since he didn't expect much help from others. 'Friends want two things, ... your money or your time', Crazy Joe used to say. And, that was the way that Jack looked at most situations as well. Jack, Joe, Frank, and Sanjo were mostly in agreement on that belief.

Back in Belize, Sanjo Casagrande's flight from Minneapolis landed pretty much on time as Jack Redhouse greeted his old Navy buddy at that Central American airport. They flagged down a cab outside of baggage claim, and then headed down the coast a bit to 'Old Belize' near Kukumba Beach, just south of the main city of Belize, where Jack's boat was berthed at a Marina there. They took in a couple of waterfront calypso joints for dinner and drinks before heading back to the boat for the trip back to San Pedro the following morning. As was often the case after a few stiff drinks, Jack and Sanjo entered into a variety of conversations from rehashing their old Navy days, to discussions about religion, philosophy, and fantasies, as well as talk about exotic dreams in far off places, and a little bit about Superman. They also began to strategize as they entered into discussions about MK Ultra mind control, 'Predictive Programming', secret government projects, agency spying programs, and how they might try a few magic tricks of their own design to reverse events and take back the high ground.

Jack: "Well, yes, Sanjo, as we've discussed in the past, you and I agree on that one. I call it the 'Know' where we seem to know telepathically what others are thinking. Women are better at it than men, I think. So, if we can determine what people are thinking, can we redirect that thinking to effect the actions of others? Is it a two-way street? Can the mind be used as a tool or weapon? When our thoughts are lucid, are others thinking the same things that we are, at the same time, through some universal subconsciousness? That's one thing; and secondly, can we access a higher power to increase physical strength, quicken reactions, and sharpen our minds to defeat our adversaries? I guess I'm talking about an ability to develop super-human traits like the action heroes in comic books that we used to read about as kids. On top of that, what do we really know about repairing wounds and removing toxins that are not normally practiced today?" Jack queried.

Sanjo; "So, sure Jack. In fact, I think that the military is way ahead of us on those subjects. In some ways we may be talking about 'AI' or 'Artificial Intelligence' where scientists have been experimenting with various computer based electronics and machines like robots to make them react more quickly than humans can, for any given situation. We already see this in cars, where computers can react more quickly than humans, to apply brakes electronically, control skidding on slippery roads, avoid collisions, and drive automatically to locations using GPS. We're also seeing smart technologies in manufacturing plants, financial markets, and even retail stores to track customer decisions, predict responses, establish price points and more, to increase market share and boost sales. All of this, combined with blockchain technologies to replace money, eliminate banks, and other artificial intermediaries, will change the face of business in general, and move the world into a new renaissance and age of enlightenment in the coming years, I think. In fact, there are those that suggest that we may be living in one of the last ages of 'humanity', and that future generations will be much more 'AI oriented', where thoughts and actions will be directed by artificial intelligence and humanity will go missing. So the 'human element' may vanish. That prospect frightens some people, while others are encouraged by it. There's also that 'traceability' thing where using barcodes, UPC's (Universal Product Codes), and 3D barcodes, whereby companies can track products from the material and manufacturing sources, to the store and on to the consumer, to determine who is buying what, when, and how, to gather accurate, current, and continuous sales and marketing information."

Jack: "That's a pretty prescient summary, Sanjo! You seem to have a good handle on our changing world", Jack continued. "But getting back to 'superhuman' feats and how we might use that energy to improve our more immediate predicament, I read about a karate master in Japan named *Mas Oyama* who could kill bulls with his bare hands and could fight a hundred guys at once. Then there was another Kung Fu master in China named 'Zhou' who could heat things with his bare hands, and even bring water to a boil, as well as heal wounds and cure tumors. There was also a girl in Russia named 'Natasha' that had x-ray eyes and could see into people's bodies to locate tumors and other abnormalities. Another guy I read about could shoot lightning bolts and stop a bullet coming at him in mid-air by just pointing his finger or hand. Others have super strength and super endurance. So, there's that."

Sanjo: "Wow, maybe I just need another gin and tonic! That's all well and good Jack, but if I could just get my prostate problems to go away so that I don't have to get up ten times a night to take a leak, I'd be satisfied enough with that. Nevertheless, I'm sure that there are ways to tap into a greater power and access more strength. Perhaps a steroid like 'Prednisone' would help. Still, I think we're a long way from being 'more powerful than a locomotive, leaping tall buildings in a single bound, or flying faster than a speeding bullet'." "Look, up in the sky, … it's Superman", he mused.

Jack: "Well yeah, we're getting a bit off topic. The other thing that I'm a bit unsure of is whether or not there are unseen nefarious forces that continually influence our thinking from the outside, that prevent us from knowing the truth. What I was talking about was something more like 'predictive programming' where people might control or modify behavior just by concentrating thoughts. Maybe that means tapping into the subconscious of multiple individuals to alter their actions or modify events. I think that would be a powerful tool, in and of itself. Still, we'll need to hash all of this out with the others and decide how we're going take care of our immediate problems, and get to the bottom of who may have been behind trying to take me out, and how to counteract that. I have some ideas along those lines that I'd like to toss around with Sarah and the others when we get together in San Pedro tomorrow." Jack added.

Sanjo: "Yes. That should be fun. I'd like to toss a few things around with Sarah again myself!" he smiled.

Jack just grinned, knowing the history of Sanjo and Sarah's relationship when they last hooked up back at the '*Redhouse Ranch*', as he recalled with affectionate detail Sarah performing her well executed cowgirl strip routine as she seductively removed every morsel of intimate apparel in Jack's living room at the ranch after kicking off her cowgirl boots. Hopefully, Jack could keep the two of them separated this time. Then he asked how Sanjo and Marissa were getting along, and whether they were content with their lifestyle up in Duluth now that Sanjo had pretty much retired and was enjoying his golden years.

Sanjo: "It's all good Jack. In fact, I was a little hesitant about making this trip, since I've tried to put all of that hanky-panky behind us. Married life is peaceful and we've settled into a very nice little routine. We live in a very cozy little Dutch bungalow right on Lake Superior on a peninsula that juts out from all of the action in downtown Duluth. So it's cozy and convenient. Marissa is close to shopping and I'm close to the outdoors. We have a nice 'Master Room' with a fireplace and wood-beamed ceilings, and a big thermo-pane window overlooking the lake, with a couple of European style 'tilt and turn' windows on both sides to listen to the water, and feel the fresh lake air. So, it's all good. Regarding marriage, things are not always what they're cracked up to be in any relationship between the sexes, as far as I can see. But Marissa and I go way back as you know, and we enjoy each other's company. In fact, at times it can be kind of priestly. There's some celibacy involved as you advance in years, I think. But at some point, you have to just make your bed and lay in it. Actually, I believe that some people might argue that a long distance relationship often works better for some couples. How about you Jack, why haven't you ever settled down and taken your cards off the table, so to speak? Have you ever actually been in love?"

Jack: "Well, that's a good question Sanjo, I guess I'm just having too much fun meeting sexy little *chiquitas* and developing fresh new relationships. The water becomes a bit like a stagnant pond if you aren't constantly moving the water around. But, your analogy about taking cards off the table is a good one. The way I see it, marriage is a lot like blackjack; you can always change tables, but the game remains the same. You can switch dealers too, but in the end, the game is still '21'. And, I guess I just like playing the game. As far as ever actually being in love, … Maybe I've been close a couple of times. Define love. And, is it better to love, or to be loved? Do some people actually have it both ways?"

Sanjo; "Capisco, Jack. I understand; and that sounds like a healthy perspective from my point of view. Do you believe in mermaids?" He asked with a chuckle.

Jack: Yes, there's a lot that we don't know, … but I'm not sure that mermaids are of the surface world. Perhaps they actually originate and reside in the inner world of Agharta, in a different ocean beneath us, along with giants, and the Nordic Gods."

With their conversation beginning to get a bit muddled after multiple mixed drinks, the two of them ordered a good dinner to help settle their stomachs before heading back to the boat for the evening. They would rest up, then get underway for San Pedro early the next day to meet up with the rest of the crew. Back on the boat the two of them talked a bit more, then Jack offered Sanjo one of the better sleeping quarters, and the two of them retired for the evening.

The following morning, the two ex-sailors awakened early from a nightlong snooze aboard *Victory Liner 504*, berthed at the little marina in Belize. Although, Sanjo's head felt a bit fried, as if he had weathered a hard night on the beach like those of his past Navy days. They showered and shaved, flossed between their teeth, dried between their toes, dressed, then met in the galley to enjoy a hearty breakfast of oatmeal, grapefruit juice, English muffin, and melon. Shortly after breakfast a diesel fuel truck from the airport pulled up to the pier to top off the boat's tanks. Jack had contacted them the night before and had arranged for the truck to be there in the morning before they got underway, so it was one more little detail out of the way for their next island hopping adventure. Jack also picked up a couple of old orange and white flotation rings that he found at the marina to replace the two that he had lost along the coast of *Quintana Roo*, near *Banco Chinchorro*, and stowed the rings on the back deck. They poured a couple more cups of coffee from the galley then headed up to the bridge to get the boat underway for San Pedro. Jack and Sanjo then continued their conversations from the previous evening as they headed out of port towards the *Ambergris Caye* and San Pedro.

Jack: "Following our conversation last night Sanjo, the whole reason that I was looking for ways to strengthen our perimeters is because I'm afraid that these clowns back in Kansas might try to take another run at me," said Jack.

Sanjo: "Haha, fear. I think you just pressed another one of my 'Hot' buttons, Jack. 'Fear', it's a great driving force, and the best 'sales tool' used for as long as man has been on this small blue planet. It's what makes the world go 'round, and what drives the world economy" he continued. "It's the best sales tool that TPTB have, so they try to keep it juiced. What kind of economy would we have without enormous daily doses of FEAR? If it weren't for fear, there would be a lot fewer jobs, wouldn't there? Without fear, why would we need so many cops and firemen, or doctors, lawyers, and insurance scams? Without fear, we wouldn't need a stronger military with over 500 military bases in countless different foreign countries. Without the fear of cancer, how would doctor's salaries continue to go through the roof? Without big universities and corrupt staffs to feed our brains with their 'educated' bullshit, why would schools be so expensive, and yet the truth kept hidden? The government is in the business of spreading fear to steal more money in the form of taxes and other outright scams, all to allay people's many fears. As Roosevelt said before the start of World War II, when the USA attacked Germany after the Japanese bombed Pearl Harbor. By the way, what was up with that? Roosevelt said in a radio broadcast that; "there is nothing to fear, but fear itself". Hahaa; I think that he probably had a lot of inside information before demanding that everyone give up their gold to the government, then getting us into a world war, don't you? After all, the world's governments had been building their war machines and boosting factory output for several years prior to announcing that we were going to fight the Germans; all because the Japs bombed Pearl Harbor! Think about it Jack! The CDC creates diseases so that they have more diseases to fight. The US government makes up a story about terrorists, so that they can hire 50,000 TSA thugs under the cloak of the DHS to comb through luggage in airports, while herding them like cattle through their screening lines, all to combat 'terrorism'. For God's sake Jack, THEY are the terrorists! In the many years since the

9/11 event in New York, have they ever actually found a terrorist going through their screening lines at an airport? Without crimes and divorces, there would be no cops or lawyers; without fires, there would be no firemen, without tainted GMO food, chemtrails, and fluoride in the water, attempted mandatory vaccines with rat poison and toxic metals, and other fear porn paraphernalia, there would be fewer obese hacking people with parasites, or dentists to fix their teeth, and we would all be thinking more clearly with decalcified pineal glands, … not to mention, an opportunity to string up more of the bad actors."

Jack: "So, you think that I shouldn't be so fearful?" asked Jack.

Sanjo: "Exactly! Their magic is all in the mojo, but it's generally negative. Negativity is where they get their power. You need to be more positive, Jack. Or, like the song says, ♪♪♪ ♪ 'we better, accentuate the positive; Eliminate the negative, Latch on to the affirmative, and don't mess with Mister In-Between'. ♪ ♪♪ ♪ It could all be in your head, Jack. You need to move on, get past the bad vibes."

Jack: "You know, you may have something there, Sanjo. I knew there was a good reason why I asked you to join us down here. Maybe you're right! Maybe I'm just being too negative! Maybe I need to move on."

Sanjo: "Well, maybe you should at least consider a few other scenarios, Jack. Like, maybe the people in Kansas aren't really after your ranch, assets, and the club. And, maybe they're not even really after YOU! Maybe your pals up north don't actually want to cut you out, … maybe they want to INCLUDE you in their operations. Maybe that's how you should look at it! I mean, you know a lot Jack, so perhaps they want your expertise. Maybe you're being a little paranoid due to what happened, and the two clowns that kidnapped you were just out to get a little action on the side. So, it's possible that something else is driving these events. Accentuate the positive."

Jack: "You're right, Sanjo. I need to be more positive and try to think this thing through."

Sanjo: "Sure. Have you ever considered that this might all be about oil, or water, or maybe money? Look what's going on in Venezuela. Maybe things are beginning to pop with Garry and Zak in the water and oil businesses, and someone needs your knowledge to bring in more oil, gas, and water projects. Also, along the lines of that 'magic' that you were talking about earlier, perhaps we should be locating the 'Ley Lines' down this way, and tapping into the electromagnetic energy from the earth to energize and strengthen our positions', said Sanjo. Do we know where the Ley Lines sit down here by the equator? Wherever they are, I'll bet the mermaids aren't far behind."

Jack appreciated Sanjo's perspective and was glad that he could join the group for a short spell. He liked the way that Sanjo's mind worked, - even though his thinking was often a bit off center, *or maybe because* his thinking was more 'out of the box' - and decided that he should listen to Sanjo more, as well as his own inner voice. There was a lot of external static coming from other directions in his life; 'just a lotta, yada, yada, yada', so Jack needed to be a bit more introspective at that juncture. With that said, Sanjo made sure that the mooring lines were free of the pier as Jack pushed the throttle forward and got underway. He felt the breeze blowing through his bristled beard as the diesels began to unwind, and set a course for the *Ambergris Caye* and San Pedro, putting Old Belize and the Sibun Bight behind them.

The ride went quickly for Sanjo and Jack, as *Victory Liner 504* soon pulled into the dock near the Beach Villa hotel in San Pedro after about an hour-long ride from Old Belize. Sanjo truly enjoyed the crossing, as it had been quite a while since he had traveled on the old patrol craft with Jack, Cassandra, and the others. So, it 'took him back' to their many past crusades, as well as his old Navy days with Jack, Frank, and 'Crazy Joe' 'hitting the beach' in the South China Seas, with their own unique variety of Asian pubs and clubs.

Sarah and the 'boys' were all sitting in the hotel bar as Jack and Sanjo walked up the beach to greet them, while Sarah revealed a combined look of both shock and glee at seeing Sanjo's strong stance, square shoulders, and confident saunter once again. Sanjo felt the same rush of excitement, as their eyes caught a glimpse of each other's aura. '*This could be a tough trip after all; I may need to initiate some damage control of my own before this little tryst is over*', thought Sanjo.

ISLAND HOPPING TO 'HABANA'

"History is a pack of lies about events that never happened told by people who weren't there." - George Santayana

Havana, Cuba had long been considered a central hub for CIA money laundering operations used by the 'deep state' mob that ran world governments. Akin to that, Jack had listened to many vibrant stories in his youth from his Irish uncle in Detroit, who had frequented the famous clubs and casinos in Cuba during the fabulous '50's, and rubbed elbows with some pretty big names in his day.

Movie stars, dancing girls, dinner and drinks, along with famous celebrities like Frank Sinatra, Marlon Brando, Nat King Cole, Ernest Hemingway, and other great names, made their presence known in Havana in the 'early '50's. Jack had also read a book entitled *Havana Nocturne* written by *T. J. English* that described in detail how Havana had 'really rocked' in the late 1940's and early 1950's when Meyer Lansky, 'Lucky' Luciano, Santo Trafficante, and a gaggle of other gregarious gangsters ran the clubs, casinos, racetracks, and hotels in collusion with the Cuban government. It was also a time when Dámaso Pérez Prado made the 'mambo' a household hit, which Jack remembered from his youth. He remembered his mother singing along to tunes like *Papa Loves Mambo* by Dean Martin or Perry Como, as the song played on the radio while she ironed clothes in the kitchen when Jack was growing up. The 'Razzle Dazzle' ended in the late '50's when Fidel Castro led the Cuban Revolution, and temporarily expunged the mob's dreams of running a criminal island country, as Meyer Lansky and 'Lucky' Luciano exited stage left. That left the CIA along with a Navy base in Guantanamo (established in 1898) to entertain US government interests. Perhaps his uncle's apologues recounting those earlier years in Cuba created the kindling that ignited Jack's passion to open the 'Jack of Clubs' in Kansas, after making his mark in the Middle East. But that was then, and this was now. Jack was nevertheless bent on replicating and rebooting the 'Habana' program through his own vision, with his own capital, through his own action, while trying to keep his money transfer business, restaurant, and strip club activities above board and legal, … or at least away from obtrusive eyes. That would certainly require some fancy footwork, finesse, and refinement on Jack's part. So, a plan was coming together, but 'Habana' was still a wet dream, while Coxen Hole lay dead ahead.

Back at the Beach Villa Hotel in San Pedro, Jack made preparations for the upcoming island hopping adventure with his new brew crew (Joe, Sanjo, and Sarah). They all agreed that Coxen Hole would be just a brief stopover on their way to the Caymans, with the ultimate goal of eventually landing in Havana, Cuba. Coxen Hole was simply not very compatible with their immediate pursuits to spend much time there. Jack had a few friends in Coxen Hole as well as some business to conduct, but otherwise they would just be taking on more supplies as well as topping off the diesel fuel tanks for the further trek eastward. The five of them agreed that they had enjoyed San Pedro as much as they could stand, and decided that it was time to move on to a new party port for more fun in the sun. They would pull up stakes in just two days time. That would give them a chance to get their personal gear in order for the proposed trip.

Jack also had a black roller bag suitcase full of cash from Seumas that he needed to keep safe and eventually unload. The cash was denominated in US Dollar Federal Reserve notes that had been converted by Seumas from Mexican Pesos, as well as a few other currencies that Jack could easily exchange throughout his travels. He would need the funds later for investments in either the Caymans or Cuba, or both. He had contacts in Coxen Hole and the Caymans that could help him convert cash to cryptocurrencies like 'estcoin' or 'ethereum', and could also be used as a medium of exchange for later transactions.

His immediate plan was to wait until they landed in the Caymans to convert much of the cash to either T-bills, bonds, or some other payment scheme, but that could change. For now, he would deposit some of the cash in a bank in Belize, and use the new account number to send a portion of the funds to either his 'PayPal' account, or a cryptocurrency of his choosing. He wanted to have crytocurrencies in his 'portfolio' in case the US dollar crashed and the US Federal Reserve went belly up. The PayPal account would help him with current business expenses as he traveled, but could also be used to buy various other cryptocurrencies at a later date. He kept some of the cash stowed in a safe place aboard his boat for various business transactions along the way. Nevertheless, almost everyone that Jack knew still preferred to hold cold hard cash in one form or another. US Dollars and 'Euros" were common, as was Canadian currency, and were typically all accepted where he traveled most. The well capitalized Hong Kong dollar was not as common, however it was probably the most stable of all fiat currencies at the time, and was also pegged to the US dollar at the very stable rate of about 7.8:1. In addition, Hong Kong had virtually zero debt, and nearly $1 trillion Hong Kong dollars ($126 billion) in net foreign reserves. Be that as it may, under the prevailing geopolitical conditions in the world he faced, changes were happening quickly, and Jack needed to remain flexible. There was a lot of talk by big governments and big banks about limiting, and possibly eliminating cash in the future, so Jack needed to be prepared for any eventual outcome.

Foreign exchange rates were a bit of a digital mystery to Jack in any case. Were they somehow actually a tax? For example, why was it that a British Pound was worth 1.32 times more than a US Dollar, or that it took 17.661 Mexican Pesos to equal a US buck? Or, that it took 57.625 Russian Rubles to equal a US Dollar? Who decided, since they were all fiat and could be printed on a whim? *Cui bono?* Did countries adjust their exchange rates, after winning a war or some other geopolitical event, as a hidden tax? Many world currencies appeared to be just printed counterfeit paper anyway, manipulated by the big banks and the BIS (Bank for International Settlements based in Basel, Switzerland) which were owned by the Central Banks, and which were effectively counterfeit currencies themselves, if nothing backed them up but digits.

The US Constitution in Article I, section 10 indicated that "No state shall… coin money, emit bills of credit, make any thing but gold and silver a tender in payment of debts…". So, why was it that the 'Federal Reserve' printed notes (IOU's) and lent them to the US Treasury in the first place? The funny business appeared to have begun around the year 1862 (during the American Civil War) when the US Congress declared that Treasury notes were 'lawful money'. But later on, they shot Lincoln. With regards to the US Dollar, the underlying confusion seemed to be in determining what was 'lawful money' versus what was 'legal tender' (money that could be used to pay taxes). According to one source, 'the annoying part …, [was] that Congress never stated exactly what lawful money was supposed to be.' In any case, the US Federal debt was pushing upwards of $20 trillion dollars at last glance, with 'unfunded liabilities' (money owed to pensioners, etc.) pushing north of an estimated $200 Trillion, yet the USA went off the gold standard in 1971 under President Richard Nixon's watch, prior to his resignation. Since then, the 'Federal Reserve' (a nefarious, nebulous, mysterious, and illegal foreign entity in and of itself, according to historical accounts), which lent 'Notes' (debt) to the US Treasury for use as 'lawful money', wasn't really backed by much more than the US military, and the 'full faith and credit' of the 'Federal Government'. Plus, the USD was coincidently a digital medium of exchange, and central banks just kept adding more digits *ad infinitum*. Smoke and mirrors. But, who was the 'Federal Government' really? And, shouldn't the 'States' have been making their own decisions? Having asked those questions, another question might have been; 'if printed currencies were backed by nothing more than the *full faith and credit* of their governments' (with little confidence in who might be pulling strings), why did it cost 17.661 times more money to lay a brick in Mexico than it did for the same labor in the US? Or, why did it cost 57.625 times more for an hour of labor in Russia, compared with the same hour of labor in the US? One might argue that 'it didn't', because labor rates varied throughout the world as well. Still, the question remained 'where was the market'? And, did the price of anything really make a difference if there was little reference to the actual value of goods and services such as a fixed quantity of Gold or Silver backing the currency (i.e., no price discovery)? Or, did oil also count as a commodity backing a currency? Likewise, what would happen if countries like Russia, China, Brazil, or Venezuela all of a sudden stopped accepting US dollars in exchange for US oil? So that, was the concurrent conundrum, … yet it was also where the world was headed at the time. Consequently, the questions and related facts remained a bit muddled to guys like Jack.

Upon closer analysis, why did a 'Federal Government' need to exist in the first place, since a 'Republic' should be able to function without a 'central authority' command center telling individual states how to behave? Perhaps it all started with the passage of the 'District of Columbia Organic Act of 1871' handing power over to DC;

https://en.wikipedia.org/wiki/District_of_Columbia_Organic_Act_of_1871

Moreover, why were so many 'alphabet soup agencies' aligned with the 'Federal' government corporation, and what were their actual functions? It seemed to Jack, Sanjo, Frank, and Joe that the CIA, FBI and the ATF among others, had actually been responsible for more criminal acts throughout American history than were generally known. There were many unanswered and questionable events such as the 'Oklahoma City Bombing', 'Ruby Ridge', and the 'Waco Texas' incident at the Branch Davidian complex for starters. There were also numerous 'Operations' and 'Projects', such as 'Operation Paperclip', 'Operation Highjump', 'Operation Northwoods', 'Operation Mockingbird', 'Operation Mongoose', 'Project MKUltra', 'Project Artichoke', 'Project Rainbow', 'Montauk Project','Project Blue Book', and other nefarious dark ops too numerous to mention (yet a quick computer search would reveal many of them). More recently, there were the 'Sandy Hook' and 'Boston Marathon' false flags where key witnesses were allegedly assassinated after being interviewed by FBI agents. Then there was the standoff at the 'Bundy Ranch' in Nevada and the 'Hammond Ranch' in Oregon where the BLM was allegedly stealing ranch land from the 'Bundys' and/or the 'Hammonds' to hand it over to Chinese or Russian interests. Subsequent to that, Robert LaVoy Finicum was ambushed by the Oregon State Police and the FBI, then shot and killed. Figuratively speaking, more than one Federal Senator and/or government representative ended up with a black eye in that event. So, in retrospect, what really happened on 9/11? Who, and/or what was really behind that event? For that matter, what really happened, and who was involved in the sinking of the USS Liberty by the Israelis? Or, what was up with the sinking of the RMS Lusitania prior to WWI; or the attack on the US Navy fleet sitting in Pearl Harbor, Hawaii prior to WWII (who really won that war?); or the Gulf of Tonkin incident with the USS Maddox prior to the escalation of the Viet Nam war? Rather than investigating major national crimes, it appeared to many Americans that the FBI and/or the ATF, DEA, DHS, CIA, NSA, CFR, USSS, DIA, and other feral [sic] agencies had been complicit in numerous heinous crimes and assassinations, which afterwards were covered up. Was the DEA actually involved in drug busts, or was it running drugs; was the ATF involved in fast and furious gun running; was the CIA run by the Russian and/or Khazarian/Israeli Mafias? Did the CDC actually eradicate diseases, or were they the 'Center for Disease Creation'? Who was WHO really? Or, the IMF and/or the DHS, FEMA, and the TSA? WTF was really going on in Afghanistan? Was NASA actually responsible for space exploration, or were they a covert deep state operation involved in a 'Secret Space Program' to weaponize space? Why was a 'Federal Tax' system needed in the first place, since it was mainly responsible for inflating government programs and encouraging a less effective, less efficient, corrupt governing system? Why not let the states decide how best to allocate funds, and let the states support a centralized taxing system if a tax system was indeed even necessary in the first place. Better yet, why not run a surplus and eliminate, or at least reduce the incompetence typically associated with bloated government programs? Shouldn't the goal have been to improve the quality of life, through effective and efficient programs rather than to encourage waste, fraud, and abuse? In any case, the government shouldn't have been taxing people's wages since wages were their 'property', and 'income' was profit from a 'producing asset' as in, sales minus cost of sales equals profit. So, the whole system needed to be dismantled and reconstructed. It has been said that Al Capone was sent to prison on trumped up charges of tax evasion, as if that were actually a real crime at the time. Where were the real heroes like Frank and Jesse James, and the 'Outlaw Josey Wales' (aka Bushwhacker Bill Wilson?) when they were needed? Who were the actual 'outlaws'? The answers, of course, depended upon one's historical perspective.

http://www.zerohedge.com/news/2017-10-09/unsealed-cia-memos-provide- shocking-salt-pit-black-site-details http://www.whatdoesitmean.com/index2459.htm http://www.nukepro.net/2017/10/ashkenazi-jews-and-nwo-creation-of.html

So, what did central governments truly accomplish? Who benefited? *Cui bono?* In essence, how did they actually contribute to a healthy and wholesome economy? It appeared that many of their projects and operations were abject failures in the long run. Consequently, inquiring minds wanted answers. Subjectively, was central government actually just a collection of contrived agencies in a corrupt and criminal incompetent cabalist corporation that controlled collective communities inclined towards criminality, contradiction, conflict, chaos, and confusion? The list of 'alphabet soup' agencies didn't even include the numerous NGO's, lobbyists, and 'integrators' that often resided on 'K Street', or the numerous other spy agencies on the least and left coasts. Who were these guys? Could the list at least be consolidated and/or standardized to control the numerous overlapping functions? Perhaps they needed an engineer, or maybe a modest marine mechanic to sort out the mess, rather than a bunch of political high school hacks. And, why were they all so heavily armed?

AHCPR	Agency for Health Care Policy and Research
AOA	Administration on Aging
AOC	Architect of the Capitol
ATF	Bureau of Alcohol, Tobacco and Firearms
ATSDR	Agency for Toxic Substances and Disease Registry
BEA	Bureau of Economic Analysis
BIA	Bureau of Indian Affairs
BLS	Bureau of Labor Statistics
BLM	Bureau of Land Management
BOP	Bureau of Prisons
BTS	Bureau of Transportation Statistics
CBO	Congressional Budget Office
CDC	Centers for Disease Control and Prevention
CFTC	Commodity Futures Trading Commission
CIA	Central Intelligence Agency
CNS	Corporation for National and Community Service

CPSC	Consumer Product Safety Commission
CSREES	Cooperative State Research, Education, and Extension
DATT	Defense Attache (Embassy)
DCD	Domestic Collections Division (CIA)
DCSOPS	Deputy Chief of State for Operations and Plans (Air Force)
DEA	Drug Enforcement Administration
DLA	Defense Logistics Agency
DIA	Defense Intelligence Agency
DIS	Defense Security Service
DISA	Defense Information Systems Agency
DNFSB	Defense Nuclear Facilities Safety Board
DOC	Department of Commerce
DOD	Department of Defense
DOE	Department of Energy
DOI	Department of the Interior
DOJ	Department of Justice
DOL	Department of Labor
DOT	Department of Transportation
DSCA	Defense Security Cooperation Agency
EDA	Economic Development Administration
EEOC	Equal Employment Opportunity Commission
EPA	Environmental Protection Agency
ESA	Employment Standards Administration
ESA	The Economic and Statistics Administration
EXIM	Export-Import Bank of the United States
FAA	Federal Aviation Administration
FBI	Federal Bureau of Investigation
FCA	Farm Credit Administration
FCC	Federal Communications Commission
FDA	Food and Drug Administration
FDIC	Federal Deposit Insurance Corporation

FEC	Federal Election Commission
FEMA	Federal Emergency Management Agency
FERC	Federal Energy Regulatory Commission
FHFB	Federal Housing Finance Board
FLRA	Federal Labor Relations Authority
FMC	Federal Maritime Commission
FMCS	Federal Mediation and Conciliation Service
FMS	Financial Management Service
FMSHRC	Federal Mine Safety and Health Review Commission
FNS	Food and Nutrition Service
FRA	Federal Railroad Administration
FSA	Farm Service Agency
FTA	Federal Transit Administration
TC	Federal Trade Commission
FWS	United States Fish and Wildlife Service
GAO	General Accounting Office
GPO	Government Printing Office
GSA	General Services Administration
HCFA	Health Care Financing Administration
HHS	Department of Health and Human Services
HRSA	Health Resources and Services Administration
IMLS	Institute of Museum and Library Services
INS	Immigration and Naturalization Service
IHS	Indian Health Service
IRS	Internal Revenue Service
ITA	International Trade Administration
JCS	Joint Chiefs of Staff
LOC	Library of Congress
LSC	Legal Services Corporation
MARAD	Maritime Administration
MBDA	Minority Business Development Agency
MMS	Minerals Management Service

MSHA	Mine Safety and Health Administration
MSPB	Merit Systems Protection Board
NARA	National Archives and Records Administration
NASA	National Aeronautics and Space Administration
NCPC	National Capital Planning Commission
NCUA	National Credit Union Administration
NEH	National Endowment for the Humanities
NIMA	National Imagery and Mapping Agency
NIST	National Institute of Standards and Technology
NIH	National Institutes of Health
NLRB	National Labor Relations Board
NOAA	National Oceanic and Atmospheric Administration
NRC	Nuclear Regulatory Commission
NPS	National Park Service
NRCS	Natural Resources Conservation Service
NSA	National Security Agency/Central Security Service
NSF	National Science Foundation
NTIS	National Technical Information Service
NTIA	National Telecommunications and Information Administration
NTSB	National Transportation Safety Board
OCC	Comptroller of the Currency
OPIC	Overseas Private Investment Corporation
OPM	Office of Personnel Management
OSC	Office of Special Counsel
OSHA	Occupational Safety and Health Administration
OSHRC	Occupational Safety and Health Review Commission
OSM	Office of Surface Mining Reclamation and Enforcement
OTS	Office of Thrift Supervision

PBGC	Pension Benefit Guaranty Corporation
PRC	Postal Rate Commission
PSC	Program Support Center
PTO	Patent and Trademark Office
PWBA	Pension and Welfare Benefit Administration
SLSDC	Saint Lawrence Seaway Development Corporation
SAMHSA	Substance Abuse and Mental Health Services Administration
SBA	Small Business Administration
SEC	Securities and Exchange Commission
SI	Smithsonian Institution
SJI	State Justice Institute
SSA	Social Security Administration
STB	Surface Transportation Board
TDA	Trade and Development Agency
USA	Department of the Army
USAID	Agency for International Development
USBR	Bureau of Reclamation
USCG	United States Coast Guard
USDA	Department of Agriculture
USFS	Forest Service
USIA	United States Information Agency
USIP	United States Institute of Peace
USITC	United States International Trade Commission
USN	Department of the Navy
USGS	United States Geological Survey
USOGE	Office of Government Ethics
USPC	United States Parole Commission
USPS	United States Postal Service
USSS	United States Secret Service
VA	Department of Veterans Affairs

Meanwhile, as the group pondered the past and planned their next adventure at the Beach Villa Hotel, Jack's crew faced several headwinds. Where to go, what to take, how to handle the expenses, places to stay, when to depart, and of course, who would spend more time with Sarah? The dynamics were getting interesting, … almost entertaining. For one thing, they now had three ex-sailors aboard a boat bound for bedlam that were all attracted to the same little sexy woman as they faced churning seas, unexpected maintenance aboard the boat, arduous hours on the water, and sundry other external forces, while they languished in their own little pack of problems. So it was 'man versus man', 'man versus woman', 'man versus himself', and 'man versus his environment',

… all classical clinical conundrums.

One thing that Jack's quiet little crew didn't quite comprehend at the time of their quaint little beach get-together was that, when Seumas Santaña needed to extract Miguel Parás and Ignacio Escondido from the waterfront motel in Chetumal a couple of weeks earlier, Seumas had again contacted Jack's old Russian pals, Garry Odonavich and Zakhar Maxikov down in Panama to do the heavy lifting. Garry and Zak had other plans for Miguel and Ignacio at the time, and decided that rather than expunge the two of them, it might be more efficient and effective to use their talents in another project that they were planning dubbed 'Operation Highjack', which was about to take place in Cuba during the approaching hurricane season. Therefore, after questioning the two men, and ascertaining their loyalties, they shipped the two off to Havana to await further guidance. Under the circumstances, in a changing world that appeared to be in a constant state of flux, Miguel and Ignacio were once again more than happy to oblige.

Adding to the suspense, Jack and his crew also began to question where the world was headed. Was war on the horizon? If there was a World War, where would they wander, they wondered? Although their future was uncertain, the group seemed to have several options available to them, with a reasonable means of travel (a boat), and many connections around the world, with pretty good intelligence. They merely needed to get underway and decide the appropriate direction later. So the following Sunday morning under good weather conditions, as they looked to the sky and began their journey east, they gathered up their belongings and set out in the direction of Coxen Hole.

The morning of their departure found them all aboard *Victory Liner 504* with calm seas and pleasant weather. However, the weather would later turn a bit rougher as forecasts reported hurricanes already forming in the southeast Atlantic. Sarah debunked one of the more dodgy questions by announcing that, since she had flown down to Belize from Kansas to be with Jack, she would be bunking with him in the more comfortable and luxurious Captain's quarters. That decision relieved some of the tension aboard the boat since they all then understood their place and how to behave going forward. Besides, Sarah really liked Jack and thought she owed him as much. It would also be more cozy for Sarah since the skipper's quarters had a large king size bed, it's own shower, and refreshing amenities in the boat's otherwise close quarters. Jack also had a lot on his mind though, and was looking forward to spending more time with Sarah and enjoying her dance moves for at least one or two legs of the cruise, as well as getting some well-needed relaxation. As it turned out, Jack spent much of the next couple of days napping with Sarah, or just sleeping alone to catch up on his rest. When Sarah wasn't spending time with Jack, she was usually up on the bridge flirting with Sanjo and Joe as they retold sea stories, drank a bunch of coffee (and maybe an occasional brandy), laughed and chuckled, and made their way toward the islands. When things began to get a little slow out on the water, Sanjo would put on some calypso music and Sarah would do a little dance for them just to break the monotony. Still, out on the open water, they had to remain vigilant and keep an eye out for traffic and weather, since things always seemed to happen when they least expected them.

Space weather events raised additional questions as the ocean waters warmed and hurricanes became more intense, ominous, and numerous in the proposed path. Was the weather due to a rogue and relatively unknown incoming large dark planet like Nibiru, or was it otherwise geo-engineered by pernicious aphotic forces? They recognized and appreciated the fact that their crew included three experienced ex-sailors who understood the importance of 'watertight integrity', as well as the significance of being 'sound and secure' as they powered their craft towards the *Islas de la Bahia*, north of the Spanish Honduras. Perhaps Jack should have consulted the Norse gods Odin, Thor, and Freyja for answers to the questions he pondered, rather than relying on some fake news that was forever lambasting their consciousness. Then again, it may have actually been a form of 'weaponized weather' developed by a deep state shadow government that was causing them some concern. Who knew? Still, Roatán, the Caymans, and Cuba called to them as they continued their adventure through a cryptic shroud toward their ultimate destinies.

The first leg of the trip went rather quickly and the distance was relatively short, since on the following Tuesday they altered their original plan, and instead of pulling into Coxen Hole, steered the craft alongside a pier in French Harbor on Roatán without incident, and headed over to Gino's for a late afternoon meal and a beer.

Gino Giovanni was the proprietor, headwaiter, and chief cook and bottle washer at '*Gino's Reef Lounge*' located just down the road from a group of docks in French Harbor. He had been an old friend of both Frank and Jack when he worked with Frank many years earlier in the Louisiana shipyards, … when Frank was married to Yolanda. Frank and Jack also included Gino when they were refurbishing *Victory Liner 504* down on the Gulf coast years earlier since Gino was an excellent welder and marine mechanic, and therefore helped with some of the early 'modernizations' to the boat. Their yacht was actually an older 'mothballed' US Navy 'Yard Patrol Craft' with hull number 'YP-504' that Frank had found down in the bayou near New Orleans. Jack had wanted to 'upgrade' the boat so, in accordance with Jack's suggestions, Gino helped with the conversions at a local shipbuilder near Mobile, Alabama. Working with some local Marine Architects, Engineers, and Designers they made several interior modifications to the boat to improve the quality and comfort level in the berthing areas, as well as upgrade components and equipment. They also replaced the four older 6-71N Detroit Diesel, 165 shaft horsepower engines with two newer more powerful 12V-71N Detroit Diesel engines, with 437 shaft horsepower each, like those used in a newer generation of yard patrol craft. The engine selection was based upon their power-to-weight ratio, which provided the boat with greater power while taking up less space and controlling the weight of the propulsion system in general. In addition to replacing the four diesel engines with two more powerful engines, they installed a new 'common rail diesel fuel injection' system to improve engine performance and power, reduce overall fuel consumption, as well lower their maintenance requirements. They also modified the gearing to allow the boat to run on one diesel engine, or both, depending on load requirements, so they maintained the reliability and redundancy of components while reducing overall weight and improving readiness. The total package of ship enhancements provided more space in the engine room and other shipboard spaces in the yacht's interior, while also enhancing the overall performance and efficiency of the boat. They changed out the two propellers (screws) to a newer more efficient design to also increase power and performance, and initiated some electrical upgrades as well. They had renamed the patrol boat 'Victory Liner' in honor of a bus company that operated between Subic Bay and Manila in the Philippines during their Navy days, and the whole crew fondly referred to her as 'Victory Liner 504'. After the modifications were completed, and since the modified motor yacht was no longer a US Navy vessel and had its armament removed, Jack had the hull painted blue and grey, with the new aluminum superstructure painted white, to show that the boat had then been converted to a modern seagoing vessel and was then a proud member of the 'civilian' fleet. Following the refurbishment, Jack and his crew used their redesigned 'motor yacht' for their many special getaways as they plied their way from Cancun to the Caymans, and on to Panama, and back. It had plenty of berthing space for the crew, plus room for a few more, as well as a welcoming rear deck for late night parties where they could combine rum and coke with calypso music and watch the romantic moon rise over the beguiling waters of the Caribbean, as they scanned the skies for the occasional UFO.

Original specifications for the Navy Yard Patrol Craft (YP) were as follows;

- Propulsion: Four 6-71N Detroit diesel engines 165 HP each @ 1800 rpm, 2 propellers; (replaced with Two 12V-71N Detroit diesel engines 437 HP each @ 2,100 rpm, 2 props)
- Length: Overall: 81 ft., 24 meters; Waterline Length: 77 ft., 23.47 meters.
- Beam: 18 ft., 5.5 meters.
- Displacement: 66 tons full load, 67 metric tons; Dead Weight: 11 tons.

- Draft: 6 ft., 1.8 meters.
- Speed: 12 knots (22 km/h), 19.6 km/h.
- Range: 1800 NM, 3300 km. (over 2,000 NM with the upgrades)
- Hull Material: Wood hull, aluminum superstructure.
- Crew: Officers: 2 Enlisted: 8; Safe capacity: 50 people.

With Gino's Cajun and Italian heritage, classic aquiline nose, and ruddy complexion, he had worn his hair closely cropped back in the bayou, but was now wearing it pulled back in a ponytail under a rubber band, with single strands of grey hair springing out through the curly black parts. Jack was a bit unsure of Gino's earlier background, but knew that he was a damn good welder and mechanic, and a good worker in the yards. Frank and Gino had worked together in some side businesses too, since they were both good with money and had operated their own 'slush funds' back in the yards in their day. Gino's girlfriend 'Gabriela' was a cute little Honduran native gal from the mainland whom Gino had met years before at a bar in the French Quarter section of New Orleans during her travels there, and now also worked with Gino as a waitress and hostess at the lounge. They both enjoyed their laid-back 'Key Largo island lifestyle' in Roatán, along with the amenities and income from the '*Reef Lounge*', as well as their slower paced coexistence.

The two of them, Gino and Gabriela both greeted Jack and his shipmates, - Sarah, Joe, and Sanjo - with big wide grins as they approached the front entrance to *Gino's Reef Lounge* in French Harbor. Frank would have enjoyed seeing Gino as well, but was now back up in Kansas with Carol Mulhaney (aka *Pernicious*) at the '*Jack of Clubs*' helping to run the place. Frank's return to Topeka allowed Carol to dance more, as well as wait on tables for tips, while Frank tended bar and helped out with the chores. So Jack would have to do all of the 'catching up' with their old friend Gino, without Frank. Jack had called the restaurant beforehand to let them know that they would be stopping over at the lounge for dinner and drinks, so Gino and Gabriela were anxiously looking forward to welcoming their old 'Louisiana pal' Jack Redhouse again, as well as meeting Joe, Sanjo, and Sarah, to reflect on the past as well as plan a tentative future.

GINO'S LOUNGE

"Too few people understand a really good sandwich."
~ James Beard

Gino and Gabriela greeted Jack and his friends with open arms as they approached the bright green double-door front entrance to the lounge, with big wooden red lobster handles attached to each of the doors, and entered the restaurant and bar. They pulled up some chairs at a center table, said a few more 'hellos', then ordered a round of drinks and some sandwiches - or fish & chips according to their individual tastes - while Gabriela continued to wait on a couple of remaining customers that were still seated out on the back deck. Gino brought the crew their drinks then returned to the kitchen to quickly prepare their meals. Gino had the place looking very cozy with plenty of windows, a long wooden bar with one end curved around a corner, an open terrace sitting area with milled wood railings and tables overlooking the water, and wood-beamed ceilings with fans to give the place a warm, yet 'outback' ambience, allowing them all to take a deep breath and relax. The bar also had some overhead netting under the wooden beams in various places with sundry beach type paraphernalia sitting in the netting, or placed on surrounding walls, to give the place a more 'tropical' feel. In short order, Gino brought their dinners back to where they were all seated then joined Jack and his friends while they ate their meals.

"Your place is looking good, Gino" said Jack, as he looked around the lounge.

"How long have you two been down here now in Roátan?" he asked. "Are you loving it?"

"Time flies", answered Gino, "But it's been over ten years now for sure, maybe more", and "yes, we like it here. We lost just about everything during Hurricane Katrina, so rather than start over in New Orleans, we just packed our bags and moved down here to the island. We had spent some holidays here a couple of times in the past so we knew the area fairly well. We bought this old place with some insurance money from the damage up north and started over. It's worked out pretty well for us, so far", said Gino. "No complaints."

Jack just nodded like he understood, then blurted out "When are the two of you getting married?" as he sipped his cocktail and took a bite of his sandwich, knowing that he could probably get away with that kind of question with his old pal Gino.

"What's the point?" asked Gino. "It's not like the two of us are going anywhere soon, and we both like things just the way they are." He said with a grin. "When are you getting hitched Jack, or don't the girls hang around you long enough for you to even have to consider that kind of question?' Gino shot back. Joe and Sanjo just laughed at Gino's sharp response, as well as the thought of Jack actually getting 'hitched'. Sarah wasn't so sure. "It probably only works well, if both parties benefit", she added, reflecting on her own personal considerations.

"Well, yes, actually, Sanjo just recently asked me the same thing, just the other day in fact", Jack stammered, knowing that Sarah was listening intently, ... so he'd have to be a little careful. "So, I'll give you the same answer that I gave him. I guess I'm just having too much fun meeting interesting new people and developing fresh relationships", he said succinctly. Then he finished by adding, "Relationships are a lot like blackjack; You can always change tables, but the game remains the same. You can switch dealers too, but in the end, the game is still 21, and I guess I just like playing the game", he said, not really knowing how the last two sentences actually fit together. "A lot depends on the individuals".

"Well then, ... I guess that means we're in agreement on that point." said Gino. "The fact is that, it's a relationship, and you're either going to make it work, or you're not. It's just that simple. No signed contracts are really necessary under those circumstances. That is, unless you like working with greedy lawyers at some point, which I've rarely found to be a pleasant experience."

"Right. Marriage is a good institution, but who wants to live in an institution?" Jack chuckled, again knowing the type of response that he would get. To switch gears, Jack then just followed up with the mantra "The important thing is the 'family unit'. As long as you have two loving parents raising the children, it's possible to have peace and harmony in your own little world.", he said thinking about his Minnesota upbringing. Sanjo just looked at Jack a little funny thinking about his own childhood and the way he was raised in different religious schools around the southwest desert, with his mother Anita Kelley dating or marrying different guys throughout his childhood, and wondered how Jack continued to come up with such bullshit. Then Joe chimed in with, "Well, maybe it's possible for two people to stay together for at least 5 years", then added, "of course, without alcohol added to the mix, there would be a lot fewer relationships, let alone fewer marriages", then dropped the subject while taking another sip of his beer.

"I think Gino's got it right", said Sanjo, again reflecting on his younger years attending sundry different religious schools scattered throughout the southwest desert where he had been made to listen to a variety of religious doctrines regurgitated by questionable 'scholars' and religious laymen. "People seem to pick up beliefs fairly easily from an early age, passed down from generation to generation, based on some ancient writings, or some old wives' tales that were written thousands of years ago, many of which may be utterly false. There sure are a lot of different religions, and they can't all be correct, can they? In fact, religions may just be another form of government predictive programming or a control mechanism put into place and practice by 'the powers that be' to keep people in line. I tend to believe that some of the older religions, and/or the teachings told by tribal elders in some of the North American Indian tribes like the Navajo, Apache, Arapaho, and Crow, where they may have worshiped some strange Gods or a central sun long ago, might be closer to the truth" Sanjo added.

From Wikipedia under 'Crow Religion';

"Crows will often use 'Grandmother Earth' as a way of expressing the physical things that God created, as God, although part of the physical world, transcends the first world. Because of this God is often referred to hierarchically as being 'Above,' as in superior, rather than physically in the heavens.[5] As God created everything Crows believe that the power of the Creator is in all things, and therefore, all things in nature are sacred.[6] As God created everything and is therefore omnipresent, Crows are in contact with God during every aspect of their daily lives. It is because of this omnipresence and omnipotence that Crows are religiously tolerant. One example of this tolerance is the overview of the world's religions provided by Thomas Yellowtail, a Crow medicine man and Sun Dance chief. Yellowtail used the metaphor of a wagon wheel to describe religious belief, noting that, each spoke represented a unique people and religion. If one spoke was removed, the wheel would not work, meaning all spokes must be present to form the circle of life. All spokes however are connected to the central beam, the Creator. Therefore, all religions and peoples are connected to God, and all equally valid as ways of establishing a spiritual relationship. As a result, Crows can participate in multiple religions, it is up to individuals to decide which methods they believe to be most effective.[7] What is now considered traditional Crow religious practices were most likely developed sometime between 1725-1770, at a time of great cultural change after the Crow acquired their first horses from the Comanche tribe during the 1730s.[8]"
https://en.wikipedia.org/wiki/Crow_religion

Jack seemed to think that the Vikings probably had it correct and were closer to the truth when they paid their respects to the Gods, Odin, Thor, Freyja, and others, although he really had no idea of what the actual Nordic religious beliefs entailed. Still, Jack believed that the 'family unit' was central to a well- structured, civilized society supporting strong family values. "Well Sanjo, perhaps man hasn't been around as long as many people claim, and perhaps religions stem from a variety of assorted and/or combined beliefs developed by man but extended from alien cultures long forgotten and unknown to mankind now. Or maybe, man originated in the inner earth and worshiped a central sun and we're all actually just hybrids of beings that came many years before us, and maybe everyone is both right *and* wrong about the past", Jack embellished. Gabriela overheard Jack's pronouncement and just laughed as she waited on the other tables.

One of the tables included two other gals that Gabriela knew from elsewhere (or perhaps she just knew their families), but nevertheless, one gal was named 'Elena' who was visiting from Las Vegas, and who had recently decided to leave 'Sin City' to find herself, and a young lady friend of hers by the name of 'Estee' who was visiting her from Belgium. Both gals were in their early to mid- 30's and were essentially just passing through the islands on a holiday trying to figure out where they would be heading to next. When Gabriela laughed, the two women asked her what the others were discussing? Gabriela responded saying, "The 'gist of it' seems to be mostly about religion, aliens, and Indians." The conversation intrigued them since they had both read about various occult religions, knew some folklore about Indians, and had surprisingly even read some stories about Helena Blavatsky's 'Theosophical' society in school. Plus, they were looking to engage in some additional adult conversation rather than just talking about their shopping sprees, friends, and families. They were also interested in learning more about the curious cast of characters that had just 'parachuted' into their island backyard in French Harbor from their own boat, and who also seemed to be 'just passing through' towards places yet unknown. Since the two gals were finished with their meals, they asked Gabriela whether they might be able to join the group, to which Gabriela responded "I'm sure that it would be OK", and then walked over to the crew's table with her two friends to introduce them to Gino, Jack, Sanjo, Joe, and Sarah.

Elena was the most forthright as she held out her petite little paw to shake Sanjo's hand, who was seated closest to her at the table, and just said "Hi, my name is Elena, but my friends call me 'Laney', how are you?" Then she introduced herself to the others seated around the table. Estee followed suit, doing the same thing as Laney, which was followed by the names of all of the shipmates seated in the circle. Laney had been a cocktail waitress at a hotel in Las Vegas, whose family origins were mainly Cuban and Italian. Her parents were from New Jersey (but later from New Orleans), which is how Gabriela happened to know her. You really wouldn't know that she was Cuban/Italian by looking at her since she was rather slender with long dishwater blond hair down around her shoulders; however, upon closer inspection one could see the more 'latina' appearance in her face, as well as some other interesting curves. Her friend Estee was also a blonde and had a similar build to Laney, but appeared to be more Nordic or northern European; so one could see how the two women might identify with one another and be good friends. Apparently they had been close amigos since college, had kept in touch with one another since their sorority days, and had traveled together quite a few times in the past. Laney Minetti had studied 'Communications' in school so had a harder time finding work that satisfied her curriculum, thus mainly worked as a cocktail waitress after graduation. Estee Snyder, on the other hand, had studied 'Classical Architecture' and other building design, so was still searching for a career that would satisfy her many interests. They were both single, with an eye toward adventure, so seemed to fit in rather well with the little group.

"So, we understand that y'all have an in-depth understanding of the various taboo subjects like sex, religion, and politics, and like to debate those issues" Laney declared with a confident southern drawl to break the ice. Estee just smiled at Laney's boldness but greatly appreciated her opening salvo. Estee then asked Gino if they could perhaps order a couple more margaritas for the two of them, so that they could more comfortably engage in the anticipated conversation, then turned to Jack and said, "Well sir, my 'ex' always used to say that to figure these things out, you just have to follow the money. Do you think that's correct?' she asked. To which Jack just replied "Well, ma'am', that may be true, since others have said that 'Marriage is an institution invented by women, but supported by man'. But as I mentioned a few minutes ago, who wants to live in an institution?" Jack's comment got a little laugh from everyone as they all jumped into the fray and attacked Jack for his 'unacceptable' response, which led to a whole host of reckless comments related to sex, religion, and politics well into the evening hours as they ordered several more rounds of drinks from Gino.

In a follow up to Estee's remark that 'one should follow the money', Jack responded by saying that, 'in that case, there may be less incentive to getting hitched at all, since men in the middle class were making less and less, and couldn't afford to get married in the first place'. Following that, he questioned whether women would even be attracted to men earning less and less. He also opined that if people were to 'follow the money', the people hurt most might be doctors, lawyers, bankers, hookers, insurance companies, hollyweird actors, and people in government, since they might feel the squeeze more profoundly. Estee replied to Jack saying that 'if they're not making it, we're not taking it' implying that they were mainly in the relationship for the money in any case. And, on and on it went. Regarding religion, they spent about an hour talking about Indian rituals and ancient beliefs, Catholicism, Presbyterians, the Jesuits, Communism, Socialism, Vikings, Nazi's, Bolsheviks, Genghis Khan and Caucasians, the Chinese and Russians, and even touched on Helena Blavatsky's 'Theosophical' beliefs. Intertwined in many of the related exchanges were numerous references to politics and 'left wing, versus right wing leanings' so that in the end, not much was really said. Which was why the various topics related to sex, religion, and politics were considered 'taboo' in the first place, and very little was ever resolved or accomplished in those types of conversations. In the end, people typically just got drunk and had sex until most of the detail was forgotten; Which, be that as it may, was why they all ended up later walking back to Jack's boat, *Victory Liner 504*, tied up at the dock in French Harbor, to have one more nightcap and retire for the evening.

At some point during the evening, Laney asked them all what they did for a living to which Jack replied succinctly, "We're pirates". His response got a big chuckle from everyone in the group, while Laney waited for a better answer. Then Joe just said, "Well Laney, the short answer is that we were all sailors together in the Navy a long time ago. Jack and I were 'Snipes' and Sanjo was a 'Deck Ape'. After we were discharged, Jack pursued a career in engineering, while Sanjo got into business, and I worked for the government. Now, we're all retired from those jobs and every once in a while, we just get together to party", he said. Jack then added, "Well, I also operate a small ranch up in Kansas where I keep a small plane, and produce food and beverages for a few clubs and restaurants that I own", said Jack, "so it keeps us all busy so that we don't get bored or into too much trouble. Although, I'm still searching for ultimate truth, happiness, and the American way", he added. Estee then asked, "What's a 'snipe'? To which Sanjo replied, "That's a good question Estee! In the Navy, 'Snipes' were sailors that worked in the 'Engineering division', or the guys that worked mainly below deck in the engine room and elsewhere to keep the machinery running. Snipes were typically Machinist Mates, or Electricians, Enginemen, Hull Technicians and such that worked in propulsion or other technical areas. Whereas, 'Deck Apes' were the guys that worked on the main deck and above and were typically Boatswain's Mates, Gunners Mates, Hospital Corpsmen, supply clerks, yeomen, and other seamen that were good at tying knots. There was also a group called the 'Airdales' that worked in aviation related jobs to keep the 'Helos' and aircraft in good working order. Together, they made up the 'enlisted' group of sailors that worked on a ship. "OK, I think I get it", said Laney. "So, y'all sailed the ocean blue, then got out, and did it too! So, what brings you down here to Roátan now? she asked. "Well, we come down here every once in awhile just to escape the rat race up north and do some drinking, and try to get a little sun", said Jack. "But also, we're always keeping an eye out for any new business opportunities, just to keep things interesting", he said. The boys didn't see any point in providing any greater detail about their trip beyond what they had already revealed to their new friends. Also, as they all had plenty to drink up to that point in the evening, the answers seemed to be sufficient enough to satisfy their curiosity for all of them to feel more comfortable in each other's company. At least the girls knew that Jack and his crew weren't part of any mob, or so they believed. So later that night, Estee Snyder somehow ended up with Jack in the Captain's quarters, while Sarah spent the night with Joe Melnik, and Laney Minetti shacked up with Sanjo, as they all adjusted to the new surroundings, and got to know each other just a little bit better.

Pursuant to 'Crazy Joe's' earlier statement that 'of course, without alcohol added to the mix, there would be a lot fewer relationships, let alone fewer marriages', they all seemed to agree on that one salient point. They were all adults, and at that point in their lives realized that many relationships often became rather dysfunctional, or complicated, or conflicted, or confused in any case. Row, row, row your boat gently down the stream; merrily, merrily, merrily, merrily, life was but a dream. Sanjo, for his part, believed that the whole group had somehow 'quantum jumped' to a new reality as he felt the strong love vibrations at 528 Hertz again, and awoke the following morning next to Laney Minetti with another serious hangover and the unfortunate realization that he had once again, metaphorically speaking, taken a wrong turn, and fallen in the drink.

The day after their little meet-and-greet, Jack emerged all bright-eyed and bushy tailed to take care of a few chores around the boat before the rest of the crew slowly made their way topside to enjoy some breakfast. Jack then announced that he would be taking the boat over to Coxen Hole for a few hours to pick up some needed supplies as well as refuel and would return later that afternoon. Joe volunteered to go with Jack to assist him, which left Sanjo with the three lady friends to entertain for the remainder of the day until Jack and Joe returned. The arrangement seemed to work well enough for all of them, so they all agreed to meet up at Gino's again for dinner later that same evening for one more go-around, and perhaps patch up a few open wounds. The good news was that there were no longer three ex-sailors chasing after the same skirt since they were now more evenly paired up with the two new girlfriends. The difficulty was that Sarah needed to decide which of the three sailors she liked the best, and Sanjo would need to once again make amends back home, or more poignantly, just forget that the whole thing had ever happened, and try not to let it happen again.

Around noon, Joe released the mooring lines and stowed the side bumpers to allow the boat to float free, then hopped on board the main deck as Jack lit up the diesel engines and backed the boat away from the dock; then headed out to sea toward Coxen Hole, located just ten miles down the coast to the southwest. Jack and Joe felt relieved to escape the fray, take themselves out of the mix for a spell, and hoped that things would normalize by the time they returned to port a few hours later. They all felt a bit muddled about the previous night's events and were trying to wrap their heads around what had just happened, as the cobwebs in their craniums cleared.

A short time later they pulled into the Port of Roátan near where the big cruise liners tie up just off the tip of Runway '07' near the local airport, then topped off the tanks with diesel fuel. When the tanks were full they turned the boat around and cruised across the small bay and tied up again near the local 'Supermercado' to pick up a few food supplies and other utensils before heading back to the boat. They talked about stopping for a beer, but decided against it since they had had their fill the night before and didn't really want to spend a lot of time in the main port. Instead, they just returned to the boat where Jack retrieved his old Model 64 Smith & Wesson .38 Special revolver from under his mattress and stuck it in his trousers in the small of his back under his shirt, then grabbed the black roller bag suitcase with cash that he had gotten from Seumas a few days earlier in San Pedro, and headed up to the main deck to meet Crazy Joe. Likewise, Joe retrieved the small 'concealed carry' Taurus model 180 Curve .380 ACP that had been loaned to him by their Panamanian pals up in Cancun, secured it to his left side belt under his shirt with the grip facing forward, and headed up to the main deck to meet Jack. Together they walked back off the boat, onto the pier and into the supermarket with the roller bag in tow, then out onto 'Main Street' and down the road about 100 meters to the local branch of a big name London bank located prominently on the main drag.

The two pals entered the bank and asked to see the manager, whom Jack knew from prior visits to the same bank. When the manager appeared in the lobby and recognized Jack he said 'Hello' then signaled the two shipmates to move to a private room in the back where they could count the cash and deposit the money according to Jack's wishes. The manager also received a stack of 'notes' for his own personal stash for his troubles. Jack had some of the money placed into a personal account at the bank, as well as a good chunk wired to a PayPal account, with most of the remaining cash, also a large amount, deposited into blockchain currencies, mainly Bitcoin and Ethereum through BitMEX (Bitcoin mercantile exchange; - more for speculation than anything else), that was associated with an offshore trust account that Jack had previously set up. He could later parlay some of the funds into precious metals, or buy real estate assets with the currency if it suddenly appeared that geopolitical events were heading south. He also picked up some 'CUC's' or Cuban Convertible Peso's while he was at the bank since he would need them when they landed in Havana. He could also exchange US dollars but they would charge a hefty premium for them in Cuba, so he was better off with CUC's, Euro's, or British Pounds for currencies there. Jack deposited the rest of the cash in a safe deposit box located at the bank for later use. When the transactions were completed, Jack and Joe left the black roller bag behind with the manager and exited the bank the same way they had entered onto the main street, and casually walked back to the boat as if nothing had happened; feeling satisfied to have successfully completed the transaction. They slowly sauntered back to the boat, thought again about stopping for a beer, but then agreed to 'blow it off' for the time being, and just continued on their way. Back at the boat, they stowed the remainder of the supplies that they had recently purchased, stashed their handguns back where they belonged, then got underway again back up the coast to French Harbor, opting to have a short 'hair of the of the dog that bit ya' Blackberry Brandy on the way back to French Harbor to help relieve their slight hangovers. When they tied up again in French Harbor the two of them remained on board the boat for a while to store more of their wares, tidy up a bit, perform some general maintenance around the boat, talk a bit more about their current situation, shower and clean up, and just generally relax.

Later that same afternoon (or early evening), around 6:30 PM, Jack and Joe walked over to Gino's Lounge where Sanjo, with his square shoulders and lanky frame was leaning back on a chair out on the back terrace overlooking the ocean with their three women friends Sarah, Laney, and Estee all sipping cocktails and enjoying the early evening ocean air, while Sanjo enjoyed a beer. The sky was exquisite, with a slight ocean breeze and effulgent moon sitting over the horizon in the azure twilight, as Jack and Joe approached, thereby adding a raw awkward ambience to the salient sea salt air as the group momentarily halted their conversations to greet one another.

They settled in as more drinks were ordered, sizing up the situation, and squirming restlessly in their seats. It was a winsome autumn evening by the sea as they discussed the various events of their day. Sanjo was seated with his back to one of the railings and pulling on a toothpick, with Laney on the left of him and Sarah on his right. By then, Sanjo had found his ring again and placed it back on his left ring finger. Joe took the empty seat next to Sarah while Jack pulled up a chair next to Estee to continue their little chat. Then Jack, as was often the case, just blurted out "So, what happened last night?", as the others sort of stared at him with their jaws ajar in some sort of suspended animation. Sanjo was quick to comment saying jokingly, "I believe that we may have repositioned our relationships during our restlessness" as the others just nodded in agreement. "So, what happens next?", asked Jack.

Sanjo replied "Well, as fate would have it, I've actually given that question quite a bit of thought Jack, and have decided that it would be best for me if I were to just hop on the next flight back to Minnesota before things get too far out of hand", he said. "It really has been wonderful meeting up with all of you again, and I did very much enjoy our recent close encounters of a third kind, however, I never intended for this to be a long engagement, and Marissa is probably wondering when I'll be getting back." Sarah pouted slightly, briefly biting her lip, remembering how much fun she had with Sanjo back at the ranch in Kansas when they first met; but she also knew what was best for Sanjo, as well as her own well being when she announced, "We understand Sanjo, and we'll miss you, but I should be getting back as well; so maybe I'll just hop on that same return flight, and head back to the states with you. I should be getting back to work anyway, and try to sort things out in my own mind. I just want to add that you guys are my three most favorite 'guy' friends in the whole wide world, and I've had a great time being with all of you down here while working on my tan, but I really can't decide which one of you I'm attracted to the most, so I best be getting back to Topeka", she declared.

So that just left Jack and Joe, along with Laney and Estee, to decide how they should round things out and move forward. To which Estee then asked, "So, as Jack just said a minute ago "What happens next?" "Hahaaa, well, I believe that we've just cleared up the most confusing part", answered Jack. "My plan still holds; so I'll be setting sail for 'Bodden Town' on the southern side of Grand Cayman at the first opportunity to see what kind of trouble I can get into over there; then I'll be steaming over to Cuba to see if maybe I can gin up some new business in Havana", said Jack. "The rest of you are more than welcome to join me, or make your own plans as you see fit, but I would welcome the company if you're so inclined. There's plenty of room for everyone that wants to join me", he said. "I'm in", said Joe. "I don't have anybody waiting for me back home at the present time, so a little travel and adventure is just what the doctor ordered", he added.

"Well if you don't mind Jack, Estee and I would also like to tag along for a while too, since we're just getting to know you, and we were trying to decide where to 'head to next' anyway" said Laney. "I also have some relatives in Cuba that I haven't seen for a while, so maybe I could look them up. We're always up for a free pony ride and some pictures and videos, and I'm a lot like Joe, with no particular place to go. In any case, I too, am 'on board' for a little travel, fun, and adventure!" she exclaimed. To which Estee just added, "Well then, count me in as well! When do we leave?" she asked.

"Well, Mister, that sounds pretty cozy to me, but we may have to cut back on the alcohol a bit, otherwise we could end up in some rather challenging and titillating relationships", added Joe. They held up their hands to signal to Gino that they could use another round of drinks out on the back terrace, as the moon rose higher in the clear starlit sky over the French Harbor horizon. Laney just asked, "What's wrong with titillating relationships?"

With their monkey business out of the way, they all ordered their favorite sandwiches - or fish & chips according to their individual tastes - then lifted their glasses to toast to favorable weather, calm seas, and new adventures, while elucidating to Sanjo and Sarah that they would miss them, but would surely meet up with them again soon enough. Sarah pondered the prospect for a second, then added "Well, you won't miss me 'til I'm gone", and winked, as she playfully lifted her skirt, and the boys all lifted their glasses one more time in unanimous agreement, remembering her delectable little dance routines.

Gino brought the whole crew their sandwiches (or fish & chips) as they continued their conversations and discussed future plans. After dinner, Jack walked back to the kitchen to talk with Gino for a brief period as the others chatted, and then returned to the table with a rather hefty 'blue camo' rucksack that he placed beside his chair. They all raised their glasses one more time prior to thanking Gino and Gabriela for their splendid hospitality and engaging conversations, hugged each other warmly, told them again that they had a 'really great set up', then bid them a warm 'Arrivederci' one last time. Jack picked up the rucksack and threw it over one shoulder as they exited Gino's Lounge, then waved goodbye in the dark, and all walked back to the boat to have one more nightcap and prepare for the following days' departure. As it happened, Sarah spent her last night discussing future plans with Sanjo in his quarters, while Estee retired to the Captain's quarters again with Jack, and Laney Minetti spent the night getting to know Joe better, as they all adjusted to their new sleeping arrangements prior to turning the page once again, while looking forward to more '*buona fortuna*', and fun in the sun.

ROW, ROW, ROW YOUR BOAT

"It only seems like a risk, until you take the risk"
- Earl Woodland Horntvedt (1922 - 2005).

The following morning they all awoke to a spectacular tropical sunrise by the sea, but with grumpy stomachs, eager to get on with their next expedition. They showered and shaved, flossed between their teeth, dried between their toes, got dressed, then took the ladder up to the main deck to enjoy a quick breakfast of oatmeal, juice, English muffins, and fresh fruit on the back deck. They poured several cups of hot coffee from the pot in the pilot house, and just kicked back for a bit after another truly satisfying evening, prior to Sarah and Sanjo packing their bags for a quick boat ride over to the Roátan airport to catch flights back to the states.

Sarah and Sanjo would return to Kansas and Minnesota, then, Jack would pilot the boat from Roátan around the western horn of the island to the northwest, and take up a heading for the Cayman Islands to the northeast. Their new best friends, Laney and Estee had already retrieved their few belongings earlier that morning from a B&B hotel that they had rented in French Harbor, and had brought them aboard the yacht prior to getting underway. The water was a little choppy as they headed out into the Caribbean, but was otherwise another gorgeous day on the bay. On the way over to the airport Sanjo turned to Jack and asked "Just out of curiosity, what was in the cute little blue rucksack from Gino last night?" Jack replied that it was just a small investment from Gino for a stake in a restaurant, bar, and casino that Jack planned to establish when he landed in either the Caymans or Cuba, depending upon prospective opportunities there. Jack had stashed the bills in a safe place aboard the boat when they all returned from Gino's Lounge the night before. Now Jack had enough cash for a stake in something special for all of them to enjoy. "Well, if something looks pretty promising, I might be interested in a piece of that as well", said Sanjo. "*No hay problema*, Sanjo! I had planned to include you anyway if an opportunity comes to light. I plan to include Sarah and Carol, and Frank, and Joe as well if they're interested. It would be a sort of 'Employee owned pension plan, with health benefits to boot, tied in with the '*Jack of Clubs Charitable Trust*' that I set up", offered Jack. "I'll keep you posted if anything positive develops", he added. Sanjo felt good about that since things were sometimes a little tight up in Duluth, and a little extra financial cushion would help. He was glad that Jack would also be including Sarah, Carol, Frank, and Joe in the mix. They were all just 'one big happy family', as Jack would say.

As planned, they soon pulled into port and said goodbye to Sarah and Sanjo. They would miss each other's companionship, although they had all truly enjoyed their short reunion, plus their trip over to French Harbor from San Pedro, as well as their brief days on the beach and in the bars, as well as Sanjo's sound advice during the interim; so after a heartfelt sendoff, it was time to move forward according to Jack's aforementioned agenda. As Jack pointed the boat to the northeast, the winds picked up a bit as the yacht began to settle into its normal rocking and rolling motion. Although Laney and Estee liked the idea of free pony rides, the choppy boat ride over to the Caymans was a little unexpected for them. They soon discovered that riding in a smaller boat with a 77-foot waterline in open water was just a tad bit different than traveling on a cruise ship, or riding on a train, or in a plane. There was a lot more undulating going on than what they were used to. It was more like riding a horse than a pony; or maybe a bit like riding in a dugout canoe through white water. It took both gals a while to get their 'sea legs' working, so in the meantime there were a few unpleasant moments when they felt the need to heave their cookies over the side. Jack and Joe kept the girls busy with a few odd chores around the boat like cooking and cleaning while Jack and Joe performed routine maintenance, stood watches, and piloted the boat. That was OK with Laney and Estee because it kept their minds off the pitching and rolling, and gave them both something to think about rather than getting in the way of maneuvering and managing the boat.

With just the two ex-sailors operating the craft, Jack and Joe found themselves thinly stretched to accomplish all of the work without Sanjo, Sarah, and Frank to help with the chores. Be that as it may, when they weren't working they would go down to the galley and make some tea or coffee and chat, or play cards, or just sit around and relax, and/or read a book. The crossing didn't take very long in any case. At a steady rate of eight to twelve knots, even with the undulating motion of the waves, it wouldn't take more than a few days to a week to cruise the three to four hundred miles to the Caymans if they maintained a steady pace. At night they would drop anchor for a while with their lights on and drift to catch up on their rest, while Jack and Joe rotated shifts to keep the boat pointed in the right direction. They also instructed Laney and Estee how to track the compass and GPS to maintain their course while adjusting for currents and wind. They would stop periodically for a short swim, or slow down for some sight seeing, or picture taking, or fishing; but for the most part, they just kept a steady pace. The strong winds that were kicking up to the southeast were still pretty far out in the south Atlantic, so the effect on their position was generally limited. So the ladies bided their time and were able to still get together with Jack and Joe when they could, as they steered steadily to the northeast toward the Caymans.

After swaying back and forth for a few days, the gals were a little surprised when they finally stepped off the boat onto the pier at the Barcadere Marina near the George Town Yacht Club a few days later. They discovered that their sea legs wanted to continue to 'sway back and forth' until they walked a block or so to shake things out. Rather than walk like a drunken sailor after being on the boat for a time, Joe suggested that they all stop at the nearest watering hole to imbibe in a couple of margaritas and some beers to get straight again. As they sat consuming their drinks, Jack found the manager of the marina and paid for a week's berthing, then joined the group back at the table to order some lunch as well as another beverage. They then called a few B&B type rental places that they found on a cell phone app to reserve a nice condo on the beach near Bodden Town for a few days. They felt like they needed a little more space after being confined to a boat for the three-day trip. Jack also rented a car to get back and forth between the condo and the marina as they all enjoyed the following several days on the beach.

After a few days of exploration though, the group found that Grand Cayman was rather sterile for their individual tastes. Too many tourists, too small, and not enough character for what they were all searching for. They needed more substance, some old world ambience, some nightlife, a greater variety of stores and restaurants, more entertainment, and generally more mojo. The girls felt that the big island had little to offer other than 'blow holes', bars, beaches, and a few buxom babes in bikinis. Jack and Joe agreed with the girls and generally had the same tedious feeling about the place.

But something else was happening to Jack as well; His outlook on life was taking a turn for the better. After departing Roátan, and saying 'goodbye' to Sanjo and Sarah, he felt a lightened load as he put his past troubles behind him. Many of his worries about the ranch, the clubs, the chaos in Cancun, and other petty problems began to melt away. Sanjo was right; he should 'just let it go'. He found that he was actually beginning to enjoy life more, as well as his time at the beach condo, and their travel with their two new friends, Laney and Estee. Joe seemed generally attracted to Laney, and Jack was also fond of Estee. Perhaps some of Sanjo's 'quantum jumping' had begun to rub off on them, as Jack and Joe rotated to a new reality and felt the strong love vibrations at 528 Hertz. So, the two new couples spent quite a bit of time together getting to know one another and having fun. Perhaps it was their lady friend's broader feminine perspective on life, their college background, their inquisitive minds or contrasting concepts, or maybe it was just their willingness to learn new things, that interested Jack and Joe. In any case, Jack was happier as he learned more about the two of them, and tended to be more 'upbeat' as he and Joe spent more time learning their ways. That was all a big change for Jack, but he was enjoying the courtship more and more.

And, as he enjoyed their courtship more and more, he found that he needed less and less. More was less, and less was more. Jack was becoming a minimalist. He began to wonder whether he truly needed other things in his life like a big ranch in Kansas, an airplane, restaurants and bars, or even a big boat to live on, as well as maintain. Maybe he didn't need any of it, he thought, as he began to obviate his previous concepts. Maybe he just needed a partner to share things; as he adjusted his appreciation for life's fundamentals.

So it was that line of thinking that prompted all of them a week later to say "let's blow this pop stand called The Caymans", as they returned to the boat for the next little leg of the trip over to Cuba. Laney had mentioned several times that she was looking forward to finding her long lost Cuban cousins, and Estee too, seemed more inclined to 'get the hell out of Dodge', and get on with their adventure. During their short time in Grand Cayman, Jack had found some time to explore the island in his rental car, look into some real estate possibilities, and ponder prices for purchasing properties there. Much to his displeasure, he found that the prices were 'way over the top' for the type of place that he wanted, as well as the general construction. Nevertheless, viewing several properties did give Jack some good ideas for the future, ... so the trip wasn't a waste of time, and was actually satisfying in that regard. He decided that he might be more inclined toward investing in an older 'fixer upper' hotel or 'old stone building' with 'good bones' and some history; and possibly work with an architect to modernize a place to get exactly what he wanted. So, that became Jack's new action plan and perspective as they rotated out of the Caymans, and headed for a distant Cuban port.

So, after about a week of enjoying their beach condo on Grand Cayman, they were again back on the water, this time heading for Havana. The sky was a tad more threatening to the southeast, but they were still in safe territory relative to any major storms. Still, they needed to keep a close watch on the weather and monitor the radio regularly. The distance to Havana from Grand Cayman was a little less than 300 miles, and was located almost straight north as the crow flies, but they would need to steer a bit northwest, heading about 320° on the compass, to approach the Port of Havana from the north while circumventing the western side of the island. For their upcoming stay, they reserved a couple of rooms at the *Hotel Armadores de Santander* in 'Old Havana' for a few nights with a 4- Star rating and location close to the harbor in the main port for convenience. Once they landed, they could survey the area for additional accommodations. They had already booked the rooms three days out, so needed to adjust their travel to check-in on the appropriate day. The hotel was elegant, had a fascinating history, a great bar and restaurant, and excellent views of the harbor for their visit. It would also be a good staging point for Laney Minetti to look up her relatives. Since Laney was in fact part Cuban, and was also fluent in Spanish, she was a great person to have along for communicating with the locals. Being from Belgium, Estee Snyder also knew a little Spanish, so would be a great help to the boys as well. For all practical purposes, they were estimating about 300 miles and a couple of days for the trip. They could make it in a day if they pushed it, but instead predicted about a two-day trip in good weather if they took their time.

Meanwhile, as they merrily, merrily maneuvered gently down the stream, life began to mimic, and manifest their dream. Sarah Reid had landed safely back in Kansas City during the prior week, and was again back in Topeka with Frank and Carol at the 'Jack of Clubs' waiting on tables and dancing for drinks, while Sanjo Casagrande was back in Duluth with his wife Marissa in their cute little Dutch Dacha on Lake Superior, snuggling in for the winter. So, all was well in their quaintly compartmentalized enchanting little world as they knew it, until Jack got the call from Frank.

Frank had been over at the farm outside of Topeka doing a little bird hunting with Ray Forbes, the foreman over at Jack's ranch, just to 'get away from the office' for a few days and traipse through the corn fields hunting pheasants. Frank genuinely enjoyed bird hunting at the farm after the fall harvest was finished because it brought him closer to nature and helped relieve some of the stress he felt from his many hours working at the club. He relished his time working at the *Jack of Clubs* with Carol and Sarah, but every so often he just needed a break from the routine. On one occasion, Frank also invited a couple of their Russian friends that had been visiting the club, to do a little bird hunting with them since the Russians also liked to get out in the field, get some exercise, and shoot some guns. Jack always kept a nice selection of shotguns at the farm for just such recreation. So after beating the bush beyond the 'back forty' one day, as they were all sitting around the barn at Jack's ranch having a cold *Holy Grail Pale Ale* and talking about their various great bird shots, one of their Russian friends mentioned that they had been talking with their old buddy Garry Odonavich down in Panama, who told them that their not too friendly foes Miguel Parás and Ignacio Escondido, had been sent to Cuba for a small operation there, and were having a gay old time. Frank was surprised to hear the news since he thought the two hooligans had been ousted from the equation altogether, and were no longer a threat. Having heard the news, he called Jack to let him know what he had learned, since Frank knew that Jack and the crew were steaming toward Cuba at that very moment, and would arrive in Havana shortly. Naturally, the news came as a surprise to Jack and Joe since they would now have to keep a sharper lookout for trouble when they docked in Havana, and would need to plan accordingly.

The group pulled into the Port of Havana a couple of days later as scheduled, and after going through customs to get their visas purchased, and passports stamped, they secured their yacht and checked into the *Hotel Armadores de Santander* in 'Old Havana' for a few days and nights to relax and enjoy the congenial old city. As anticipated, Laney and Estee found their new accommodations to be 'marvelous' saying that it was 'just what the doctor ordered' after spending a few days rocking and rolling through some raucous waves in the Caribbean. The two couples settled into their two separate rooms, then met downstairs at the bar to enjoy a beverage and discuss details for the days ahead.

Jack and Joe hadn't previously mentioned anything to the girls about the trouble they had encountered earlier in Cancun. Why worry them? So as they sat there sipping their drinks in the delightfully adorned bar, Jack thought that the girls should at least be aware of the possible peril, as Jack and Joe talked around the subject a bit, revealing that the reason 'Crazy Joe' had come down to Mexico to meet with Jack initially, was because of a local 'difference of opinion' while Jack was in Cancun. They explained that Jack had been 'restrained' temporarily until Frank, Joe, and some Central American pals were able to 'negotiate a settlement' to resolve the issue; and that, as a result of those negotiations their little group decided to leave Mexico for other ports south. Sarah then flew down to Belize to meet with Jack and the others after the discrepancy was settled. The explanation puzzled the girls a bit since they didn't really know Jack and Joe's entire history 'all that well', and had only just met them, so they wisely requested a more complete explanation. "Well, It's probably nothing", said Jack as he explained that he had recently heard from Frank by phone, and that the two guys involved in the 'infraction' over in Mexico might have relocated to Cuba after the incident; so Jack and Joe might have to keep an eye out for them during their visit there. In any case, Jack and Joe explained that 'it was no big deal' and they were confident that they could 'handle the matter' if the issue became more of a concern. Their summary seemed to partially placate the girl's curiosity, however their antennae went way the hell up, as they didn't entirely believe the story, and didn't think that their explanation was very clear.

"For a couple of guys that 'seek the truth', you sure don't tell it very well", Estee added. Her candid response troubled Jack because Estee was right, and he was really beginning to admire her character and attitude, as well as her whole demeanor. Laney then asked, "Just how the hell were you able to actually come to terms with these guys? How were the negotiations eventually settled?", she prodded for a better response, offering them a chance to 'come clean'. Joe laughed at Laney's assertiveness and said, "Well, as I recall, Jack made them an offer that they couldn't refuse", as he smiled broadly, then added "But, I don't really know for sure because, as I recollect, I was napping at the time", he said, giving Jack a little 'wiggle room'. With that last comment, Jack finally relented and began to tell the whole sordid story once again (with the grisly details deleted), about how he was knocked over the head in Cancun, thrown into the back of a van and held captive for a few days until Joe and the others came down to 'bail him out' of a bad situation. Then he told them about how they had pointed the boat in the direction of Belize with the two hoodlums, Ignacio and Miguel on board, but 'gave them a chance to escape' while traveling south to San Pedro, … and how the two banditos had decided to 'jump overboard and swim to shore' near *Banco Chinchorro* to avoid further conflict. The explanation was solid enough for Laney and Estee to at least accept the story as partly true (although there were a few holes in their story), and to give Jack and Joe some credit for allowing the hombres to escape. Still, they wanted to know what kind of danger they might face since they were all now in Cuba, as well as how Jack and Joe would handle the situation if they came across these guys again. Jack said "Well, let me make some phone calls to see if I can learn more about why these clowns are over here, and see if I can straighten the whole thing out", he finished. The last statement relieved some of the girl's anxiety, since Jack indicated that he would take a proactive approach to the situation rather than just letting the whole mess unfold without doing anything about it. *'Judicemur Agendo'*, - 'let us be judged by our actions' - they all agreed, was a good motto to follow in that case. They also agreed that it was best to stay together as a group while in Cuba since there would be 'more safety in numbers'. Jack would keep them posted on any additional details he might learn after making a few phone calls.

The 'renegade' situation wasn't the only issue that required some attention. As they were sipping their drinks and having a bite to eat, the news report on the overhead TV in the bar lounge revealed that a 'tropical depression' was forming in the Atlantic off the coast of Florida, and could possibly hit Havana, depending on the storm track. The guys weren't too concerned about the weather though, since the worst storms typically hit Havana in September, and they were already into late October. As ocean waters cooled, storms tended to be less severe. Still, hurricane season for that part of the world was said to occur from late June until late November, so anything was possible. In any case, storms were typically harsher along the southern coast of Cuba due to the direction they normally tracked, so Havana's harbor on the north coast was better protected from storms than the coastline to the south. Still, it could get a little nasty for sightseeing, so they would keep an eye on the weather, and keep an umbrella handy.

With the more immediate concerns behind them, Laney tried to track down her Cuban cousins while she had the opportunity. She called some of her close aunts up in New Jersey to retrieve some lost contact information, and was able to get the names, phone numbers, and addresses of a couple of cousins that actually lived in, or near Havana, as well as their e-mail addresses, so she was excited about her success. Then, with that information in hand, she pulled up a map on her smart phone to get their current locations relative to where she was staying at the hotel in 'Old Havana' to plan their route.

Consequently, as Laney was calling her cousins, Jack stood up from the table where he had been sitting with the others and walked over to the hotel bar, positioned himself on a nice comfortable stool with armrests and a back at the counter, put his feet on the brass foot rails and ordered a local Havana *cerveza*, while he dialed up the numbers of his two old Russian pals Garry Odonavich and Zakhar Maxikov to determine 'What the hell was going on in Havana with these two derelicts that jumped him in Cancun', and 'Why the hell hadn't he been notified' by his two 'close comrades' that had apparently set the whole thing up in the first place?

Jack first connected with Garry Odonavich who answered Jack saying "I thought you knew all about it since you met with Seumas, and talked the whole thing out in San Pedro!?", he said. Jack then learned that when Garry and Zak discovered that Seumas hadn't 'taken out' the two hooligans when he had the chance in Chetumal, Garry and Zak had talked it over and decided that maybe the best thing for everyone would be to arbitrarily 'reassign' the two gangsters somewhere distant to remove them from Mexico entirely, so as not to attract more attention from the Mexican authorities. Actually, that made a lot of sense to Jack, but again, he wanted to know why he wasn't informed, since he was at that very moment back in the same country as the two thugs. Garry repeated that he thought Jack had already been made aware of the situation, since he had met with Seumas earlier and discussed it all. Seumas had apparently neglected to disclose that little bit of pertinent information to Jack about the transfer, which also puzzled Jack. Garry then suggested that perhaps Zak could 'fill him in on more of the details' since Zak was behind the plot to launch 'Operation Highjack' over in Havana shortly anyway. That new piece of the puzzle threw him for a loop, and grabbed his attention; So Jack thanked Garry for his candid response, then dialed up Zak Maxikov who was also surprised by Jack's inquiry, since Seumas had also indicated to Zak that Jack had 'already been apprised of the current status'.

Something didn't add up, but Jack was inclined to follow Sanjo's earlier advice and 'just let the whole thing go', and give the two Russians the benefit of the doubt, … but not before he heard verbal confirmation from Zak that he wouldn't be running into any more difficulty with Miguel and Ignacio while he was in Cuba. Jack told Zak that he and Joe were now in Havana with a couple of new lady friends, and didn't really want any trouble while they were all travelling together. There had been at the least, some kind of failure in communication with all parties involved. Zak reassured Jack that everything was under control, and that he would contact both of the gang members to 'make certain that they understood the situation, and didn't do anything stupid' under the threat of ending their participation in 'everything', once and for all; As in, 'gone for good'. Zak then told Jack that 'Operation Highjack' was actually a plan to recover some gold bullion that had been stolen from them by 'people involved with the Cuban government and some mob members' a long time ago; to which Jack just replied, "Hold it, right there, Zak! I really don't want to hear another word about it! I'm not currently involved in any of this, and, I don't want to go there, or get involved in another crazy scheme right now! So please, leave me out of it!" Jack chided. Zak understood Jack's concern and reassured him that 'the boys' would steer clear of them altogether, and that Jack wouldn't see, or hear, 'hide nor hair' from either one of them, in any shape or form whatsoever while they were in Cuba. Jack promptly thanked his old Baltic buddy and told him that he was also making plans to distance himself altogether from his association with a few people up in Kansas, in any case, and would contact Zak again to let him know what was happening after he had formalized a few agreements. Jack also mentioned to Zak that he was considering unloading his personal stake in the *Jack of Clubs* anyway, and perhaps even selling the ranch for the right price, and suggested that if Zak was interested, he should let him know at his earliest convenience. Zak found the revelation interesting for a variety of reasons, and likewise thanked Jack for the information; then promised to stay in regular contact with Jack with any new knowledge going forward.

After his phone calls, and while still seated at the bar in the *Hotel Armadores de Santander* in 'Old Havana', Jack ordered a double 'Scotch on the rocks' reflecting on his recent conversations, satisfied that he had sufficiently reconciled the current hassle in Havana. He could relax and ruminate prior to informing 'Crazy Joe' and the girls about the current status, and look ahead. He felt content on the comfortable bar stool, quenched in his own contemplation, remembering a quote from the famous Russian writer and historian, Aleksandr Solzhenitsyn that stated, *"A man is happy, so long as he chooses to be happy."* Jack slowly downed his dainty double scotch, and chose to be happy at that one remarkable moment in time, as he pondered his past, and contemplated a propitious future, while also recognizing that he was daydreaming about Estee more and more. Love was risky, but so too, was loneliness.

PRADO ESPLANADE

Love is a rose but you better not pick it It only grows when it's on the vine A handful of thorns and you'll know you've missed it You lose your love when you say the word "mine"
  - Neil Young, recorded 1974

When the two of them were alone together, it was like their hearts and minds were one. Jack felt that he had known Estee Snyder his entire life, or more than that, for all of time. Estee felt a similar metro-magnetic, Cuban-kinetic connection with Jack. Time didn't matter. Was it better to love, or be loved? That didn't matter either. Their auras merged; their comingled vibrations reciprocated like sine waves of an alternating current, and were instantaneous. What mattered was, they forever wanted to be together, and were not as happy when they were apart.

So as Laney Minetti began tracking down her Cuban cousins to map their respective locations on her GPS phone app, the two couples reveled in their lively new *Español* environs, enjoying the warm equatorial Cuban air as Laney searched for her long lost relatives. In every sense, the positive pulses were substantially multiplied in Havana for all that they sought, contrary to what they had found in the Caymans. Joe Melnik and Laney Minetti had tenderly connected too. Where was it all headed? They didn't care.

One of Laney's cousins, Elise Lopez (on Laney's mother's side) lived in a sleepy little coastal suburb, located about fifteen minutes west of Old Havana called Santa Fe. So following her GPS coordinates, the four friends took a cab over to the western section of Havana to locate Laney's cousin Elise. The languorous little town was not as hectic as the city, nor was it as 'well to do' as Havana, but being there felt friendlier; and the people that resided there were most gracious. They discovered that Elise Lopez was about the same age as Laney Minetti, and although they had forgotten the event, the girls had met previously when they were small children, yet neither one of them could recall that earlier encounter. Still, the cousins connected when they met, and were very glad to set eyes on each other once again. There was a familiarity and a family resemblance that they could embrace, and even their voices had a similar ring to them. So it was, that they fit in with their new Cuban family, and there was good cheer all around as they chatted and compared notes about their past relations. Laney was also able to connect with other cousins while she was in Santa Fe, since, after Laney had called Elise, many of her local relatives had joined in when they heard about their 'long lost cousin Elena', and agreed to meet at Elise's *casa* to greet 'Laney' along with her other friends.

Although Elise Lopez resided in the little town of Santa Fe, Laney learned that Elise worked near Old Havana at an architectural firm there, with a small office located near the *Paseo de Marti*, an attractive street in a most fashionable part of *Habana Vieja*. Elise had been studying to be an architect herself, and had obtained her 'decorators license' analogous to that trade. She also had a friend that had his 'masonry license' as they had both recently moved back to Cuba after several years working in London. Upon their return from England, she and her friend bought and renovated an older guesthouse overlooking the *Castillo De Los Tres Reyes Del Morro* in Havana near the older section of downtown, which they occasionally rented out for extra income.

The architects at her workplace had been involved in a few recent renovation projects involving older hotels and apartment buildings, so the potential for getting another project initiated with the same firm appeared to be good. The news was serendipitous to Jack since he had, in the back of his mind, been trying to figure out how to 'put two and two together' to gather additional information about older buildings in Havana, as well as purchase a hotel/restaurant to refurbish, and perhaps add a casino some day. He could learn a lot from Elise, but also from the people that she worked with, including the names and contacts of those associated with buying and renovating commercial real estate in Havana. The architects might also help Jack to acquire the proper real estate licenses and permits in Cuba, as well as introduce him to people that could assist in the operation of the businesses long-term. Depending on Cuban law, it might be necessary for the building 'owners' to be residents of Cuba, or at least be associated with an international organization. Jack wasn't sure. Maybe Garry and/or Zak could help him with those delicate details. Perhaps Elise and her friends might also know additional 'associates' in Miami, Montreal, Vancouver, and/or Toronto, or Detroit that could help with their endeavor. So the meeting with Elise Lopez could lead to additional knowledge along numerous lines. It would take some time, but it was a good beginning. In addition, Joe Melnik and Laney Minetti might be interested in monitoring the project, and perhaps even operating a hotel and restaurant in Havana at some future date, if they too were involved in putting the plan into motion and had a share in the business. So for Jack, quite a few pieces of his future puzzle were falling into place, … and Joe, Laney, and Estee could all be part of that big picture. So it was, that their meeting with Laney's cousins in Santa Fe, Cuba resulted in a big boost to Jack's efforts, as well as broadening their extended family in Old Havana, as they continued their tour of that old metropolis, and began to decide what they might be doing next.

They had enjoyed their first few days at the *Hotel Armadores de Santander*, in *La Habana Vieja*, however, upon familiarizing themselves with their surroundings they decided to switch to a more affordable hotel, central to the happenings within 'Old Havana' that would be closer to other attractions they all enjoyed. Although Jack's boat would be fine secured in the main harbor for the interim, Jack decided that he would later move it to another pier nearer to Santa Fe, closer to Laney's cousins. Indeed, based on his recent discoveries, Jack was developing various other 'long term' strategies since ultimately, his plan was to 'pull the plug' on his current activities and escape to other realms altogether; essentially unknown even to Jack at that point in time. Meanwhile, the group changed their accommodations to the *Estancia Bohemia* hotel for a few additional nights, and would plan to move the boat to the *Hemingway Marina* closer to Laney's relatives after they found new accommodations - possibly an apartment or a house near Santa Fe - for an extended stay. Still, if they were serious about staying a longer period of time in Cuba they decided that they would all need to apply for a Residence Permit to realize any real benefit, so that's what they did. With Laney actually having relations there, it might be easier for her to accomplish that task. However, they would all apply and hope that they could find some angle to allow them to come and go more freely, as well as enjoy their privilege while 'in country'. Perhaps Garry and Zak, being initially from Russia, could also provide some suggestions along those lines. It might be that they would also have to establish a charitable organization for 'community development' reasons that could possibly provide them with a permit under the guise of 'Humanitarian Project Work' to be seriously considered, ... but they planned to explore all options.

Meanwhile, with their reunion at Laney's relatives behind them, and their week's hotel accommodations decided, the two couples Estee and Jack, and Laney and Joe, began to explore other areas of the city to enjoy the local neighborhood and partake in the festivities there. They found a couple of great nearby bars and restaurants just a few blocks from their hotel near *Prado Esplanade*, to casually sit and chat over some cool drinks, and relax. One of the bars *El Floridita de Cuba Bar,* had a colorful history, and had been a hangout for Ernest Hemingway when he resided there. Another favorite bar with local ambience was the *Bar Monserrate* found near the same location. Nevertheless, there were bars located in every nook and cranny of Old Havana that were overflowing with character and energy. The *Prado Esplanade,* or *Paseo del Prado,* or *Paseo de Marti,* was a tree lined, ornately paved and tiled boulevard in the heart of Old Havana that led to the *Malecón* (officially *Avenida de Maceo*), another prominent *esplanade* and seawall, along the northern coast of Havana that stretched for over eight miles, ending in the *Vedado* section of the city. During their tours there, Jack kept an eye out for potential properties to investigate, as well as a sharp lookout for unsavory characters like Miguel and/or Ignacio. But if they were anywhere to be found, they were keeping a low profile just as Zak had promised, since Jack never saw 'hide nor hair' of them in the days that followed. That meant more quality time to enjoy their surroundings and continue their courtship with their two favorite and attractive young ladies who were fast becoming more fun and familiar with each passing hour, of every delightful day.

As the days and weeks progressed, November came calling and swaddled their lives in the cocoon called Cuba with all of its mystery, warmth, and energy until the area became quite familiar to Jack and his friends. The wind and rain came and went, followed by wonderful days of warmth and sunshine by the sea, as Jack eventually moved his boat to the *Hemingway Marina* closer to Santa Fe as planned. They found a delightful little 'Cuban Colonial' apartment to rent on a short-term lease close to the marina where Jack's boat was tied up, but also not too far from the city center where they could call 'home' for a while. The two ex-sailors shouldn't have even been thinking about love at their age, but were now lost in love, and loving every minute of it. Estee and Laney were just lost in life, looking for a raft, or something to latch onto at that particular portal in time, while Jack and Joe were just the two lucky lugs that landed in their laps. Since they all very much enjoyed each other's company, they were more than happy to make the most of the situation while it lasted. In the days and weeks that followed, the two couples blended right in with the *'Habana'* community and became familiar with the best bars, the Cuban people, restaurants, and nightclubs until they felt as if they had been in Havana forever. Jack even implemented some of Sanjo's sound advice, as he 'accentuated the positive; eliminated the negative, latched on to the affirmative, and kept his distance from Mister In- Between' ♪♪♪ ♪. Jack was also able to find a few potential properties to consider for purchase, as he began to work with Laney's cousin Elise and her friends in the architectural firm, to eventually renovate and upgrade a place to its fully fashionably and trendy potential. A couple of the buildings that Jack was considering for purchase had some additional room for future expansion, so that everything was moving along nicely, as Jack began to plan the next phase of his own retreat.

Consequently, in early December as Jack discussed options with Elise, Estee, and the architects, he settled on a very nice, almost ancient, 'Spanish Colonial' architecturally pleasing stone faced hotel near the *Prado Esplanade*, with high arched windows, old glass, ornamental iron, beautiful and huge old wooden doors with large iron hinges, wood beams in the grand ballroom with large ornate antique glass chandeliers, curved stairwells, and with a fabulous old restaurant on the ground floor. He also bought some adjacent properties that he would tear down and reconstruct in a more contemporary 'Revival Spanish Colonial' fashion to provide additional hotel space for guests, and probably another restaurant. Depending on the layout, Jack also wanted to include a 'brewpub' attached with the restaurant where he could offer beverages similar to the *Holy Grail Pale Ale* and *Flying Tiger Pale Ale* products that he offered at the 'Jack of Clubs' up in Kansas, as well as take advantage of the 'liquor business' in the area too. The brewing business could be expanded to the production and sale of rum as well, since that particular alcoholic beverage was also quite popular in Cuba as well as the rest of the Caribbean. Eventually he could export the products to Miami and elsewhere, he proffered. Being that Gary and Zak were also in the *Bottled Water* and *Oil refinery* businesses down in Panama, they too could benefit from Jack's interest in process equipment and the 'pumps, tanks, pipes, valves, and controls' end of the business and might participate in those lucrative promising ventures along with Jack and the others. Ultimately, he would also add a 'showroom' or theater for floorshows and entertainment to attract a variety of crowds from around the world. The buildings would need a lot of work to renovate, but the architects were more than happy to sink their teeth into the project as well as provide suggestions to Jack and his team on just how each of the spaces could complement each other to bring synergy to the whole reconstruction mission. The architects would also design a couple of very large penthouse suites on the rooftops of a couple of the buildings, incorporating the same old 'Spanish Colonial' theme throughout, to entertain VIP guests as well as provide accommodations for family and friends, or even an occasional wedding ceremony. The penthouse suites would have sweeping views of the *Prado Esplanade* as well as the sea swept *Malecón* coast in north Havana and would include a couple of private residences for longer stays for Jack and Estee when they were in Havana, as well as Joe and Laney while they resided there. Estee was thrilled with Jack's decision since it was just the kind of 'Cuban- Spanish Classic Colonial' type project that she had been trained and educated for in college, and was happy to be a part of the project team with Jack and the others. Jack worked with a prominent London based local Cuban bank, that was thrilled to finance the project, using some of the funds obtained from Seumas, Gino, Frank, and Joe, plus a couple of 'outside partners' (with first names Garry and Zak), to put the whole plan into motion. Jack's plan was to fund the renovation and reconstruction with a low interest loan to leverage the costs using some of his cash as collateral. When the reconstruction was complete he would attempt to attract Russian, Chinese, American, European, Middle Eastern, and other international 'players' and gamblers to participate at his casino, then pay back the long term loans with the winnings from the 'foreign investment' to fund the operation, along with charitable contributions to Cuban ventures and government that might also benefit the Cuban people. So in a sense, he was using other people's money to build his own productive asset portfolio. He would need government backing for the endeavor otherwise he could end up just like Lucky Luciano and Meyer Lansky when they tried to do a similar thing in the 1950's. Garry and Zak were more than pleased to work with Jack again since they believed that the project had a great chance of success with Jack at the helm. They needed to invest their capital in promising asset producing projects with great potential for their other partners, in any case, so supported the effort. Garry and Zak's 'partners' also had important contacts in high places within the Cuban government since the Russians and the Cubans had a long history of working together to make the right things happen in their economies from oil refining and sugar production to healthcare, agriculture, breweries, and tobacco production, to shipbuilding and marine engineering in areas like Santiago, Cuba, and many other cooperative enterprises; So, as Sanjo might say, 'it was all good'; Except that, where Garry and Zak were concerned, there was usually another 'catch' to any participation on their part; and so it was, in this case too.

Garry and Zak had both been intrigued by Jack's earlier proposal to sell the *'Jack of Clubs'* up in Topeka as well as the ranch and some other properties. They were quite familiar with the whole operation since they had been to the club in Kansas many times themselves, but also knew the 'Management Team' since they were good friends with Frank, Carol, Sarah, and others at the club, and also knew Ray Forbes' capabilities out at the ranch. Therefore, it was a 'move right in, and set up house' sort of investment that they felt could be easily managed with the correct people already in place. That worked in Jack's favor as well. Also, although they kept Miguel and Ignacio 'out of sight, and out of mind' throughout the whole 'Operation Highjack' scheme to retrieve the 'stolen Russian gold bullion' in Cuba, the operation had not gone off as 'slick' as they had anticipated. The operation was a success in that they had retrieved the gold as planned; however, they were never quite able to transport the bullion out of Cuba, so the Cuban authorities were hot on their trail to get the bullion back from the Russians. So, as Jack was briefed on the details of the operation and learned more about their future plans, he became genuinely curious, but also quite concerned, … but was willing to listen. "Zak, I told you and Garry to leave me out of this whole mess, and that I didn't want to hear any part of it!" Jack repeated, as he sat down to discuss the subject with the two of them. "We understand your position Jack, and we're not here to put any pressure on you going forward; however, if you are open to discussing it, we may have a 'win- win' situation for all of us that may be to your liking, and we'll handle every facet of it. You won't hear, see, or know hardly a thing. However, you stand to benefit from the operation greatly! Are you interested in learning more?" Jack certainly found their last comment to be intriguing, and knowing Garry and Zak as he did for so long, he was beginning to see where the conversation was leading, so Jack responded, "Well, sure, I've heard all this before but you know me, I'm always willing to listen to a good business proposition; So, … shoot!".

Garry and Zak knew that Jack and Joe were quite fond of Laney and Estee as they were tracking their every movement and had, with various 'boots on the ground', watched their relationships grow since they landed in Havana. Also, based on Jack's earlier comments about wanting to separate himself from the operations in Kansas, and knowing Jack as they did, and his propensity towards wanderlust, as well as his desire for a simpler life, they were prepared to make Jack 'an offer that he couldn't easily refuse' but that would also benefit 'their old friend Jack' in the long run. By now, Jack had made his final plans for the purchase and reconstruction of the buildings that he bought in Havana, put up the money, and signed the necessary contracts to get the work started. He had also paved the way with 'Crazy Joe' and Laney Minetti, suggesting to them that when the project was successfully completed, they might consider being ' part owners', as well as possibly managing and running the operation while Jack 'oversaw' the project vicariously. Since Laney hadn't gone far beyond being a cocktail waitress in Las Vegas, but had her degree in 'Communications', she jumped at the idea of having a stake in the operation as well as managing it. Joe had pretty much fallen for Laney, and didn't really have anything going back home in any case, so he too agreed to the arrangement. So, the plan was coming together, which just left Jack and Estee to decide where they wanted to be next. Jack had proposed that they 'travel to various parts of the world' seeking adventure and intrigue, as well as discovering new places, which Estee found acceptable as well. She wasn't sure about Jack's offer initially, and had actually contemplated settling down someday, but decided that the exploit might satisfy some deep-seated anxiety and fill in some gaps at that point in her life. She also very much enjoyed architecture, as well as different cultures so, "Sure!" she said, and agreed to travel with Jack with an occasional stop back in Cuba to check on the new operation in Havana from time to time, visit their friends, share a dinner, and enjoy a glass of wine while talking over old times. So with the die cast, Jack made preparations to transition to the next phase of a prolonged plan.

Knowing that, Garry and Zak made their proposal to Jack. "It's pretty simple Jack", said Garry, "We need to get our gold out of the country and back over to Russia as soon as possible, and we need a foolproof plan to make that happen. You, on the other hand, want to travel with Estee to foreign lands and explore new regions with each other. We're proposing to help you facilitate those desires, and we'll make all of the arrangements. We have friends in the shipping business that have a few tankers that travel regularly between Havana and St. Petersburg, Russia. We actually have a vessel coming into port next week, returning on the following week. You also know the area around Helsinki- Finland quite well, as well as Tallinn, Estonia, and St. Petersburg, Russia from our earlier projects together. We'll make all of the necessary arrangements to load your boat *Victory Liner 504* onto one of our oil tankers heading back to Russia, so that you won't have to worry about a thing. We've already made the necessary adjustments with the right people in port for the day that your boat is loaded on the tanker. Miguel and Ignacio will load the gold bullion onto your boat a night or two before the tanker sails, and make sure that your boat gets loaded on the tanker with the gold safely hidden onboard. We'll just need access to your yacht a couple of days prior to you moving it to the main harbor so that we have some flexibility. The guys will use a Rigid-Hulled Inflatable Boat (RHIB) with a quiet motor to transport the bullion through a rear deck hatch at night. The gold will be sealed in containers that they'll just drop into the bilge, or some other non critical area for quick recovery when the tanker docks in Russia. When the tanker sails, we'll pay you $50,000 in gold bullion deposited in a Swiss bank account under your coordinates, plus another $50K when we remove the gold in Russia; plus, we'll pay you a $25,000 bonus for your troubles, including airfare and hotel accommodations for you and Estee to fly to Helsinki, Finland where we'll make additional plans to meet up with you. You may want to take the *Tallink* ferry over to Tallinn, Estonia from Helsinki, then rent a car and drive over to Narva, Estonia on the border. From there, we'll get you over to St. Petersburg where one of us will meet you to get you to your boat. After the two of you have satisfied your sightseeing appetites, we'll make additional arrangements to have your boat brought back to Cuba on a similar tanker at a later date on our tab, if you so desire. How does that sound? You won't have to get involved in any part of the operation other than moving your boat to the port where the tanker docks after we move the gold, and then flying to Helsinki to retrieve your boat, all expenses paid by us! Agreed?"

"Well you also mentioned an interest in buying my controlling stake in the club and the ranch, if I decide to leave for a while and do a little traveling. So, what about the *'Jack of Clubs'*, and the ranch?" asked Jack. "I promised Frank, Sarah, Carol, Sanjo, Joe, and the others that I would take care of their interests, so I don't want to leave them 'hung out to dry' with any agreement I make", said Jack. "On top of that, Frank Valero and Carol Mulhaney are both part owners in the *Jack of Clubs* with a 10% minority interest each, so we'll need a nod from them before we can consummate a deal", he added. "And of course, they'll need to be compensated proportionately for their stake in the entire business", Jack continued. "No problem Jack", said Zak "We'll take good care of them all and give them each a small stake in the businesses, including Sarah. We'll also 'kick back' some of the profits to you if we're able to expand the business further. That should help your regular cash flow situation. In addition, we'll pay you ten times earnings, plus the appraised value of the buildings and land, for both the club and the ranch to take possession. In addition, we'll give your friends an increase in salary for running the place. The whole package should be worth at least $30 Million in US dollars, maybe more, for you alone, to allow you to participate in other deals", said Zak. "You can then use the money to expand your operations here in Havana, as your newly renovated Spanish Colonial revival hotel, restaurant, and casino take off over here. Of course, we'll participate in that operation as well with our external partners since we also have a vested interest in your success. Do we have a deal?" Jack pondered the proposal for a moment, ran the numbers in his head, then looked the two blue-eyed Russians straight in the eyes, and answered assuredly, "Yes, we have a deal!" "Great!" said Zak. "We'll set it all up and keep you posted. They shook hands, and all felt genuinely satisfied with their new negotiated accord. No contract, just a solid handshake with a sound understanding amongst old friends; just the way they all liked to do business.

So another week went out, and another Russian oil tanker came into the main port in Havana, Cuba as December lost more of its days, and the days lost more of its light, and the Christmas holiday season approached. Jack liked the idea that he didn't have to get involved in any part of Garry and Zak's program, other than flying to Helsinki to retrieve his boat. So Jack just bided his time and waited for a signal from Garry and Zak to make his next move according to plan. On the other hand, as he reflected on their recent conversation, he wasn't sure that he liked the idea of Miguel and Ignacio boarding his yacht some evening to stash crates of gold bullion somewhere onboard. Where would they realistically hide it, he wondered? Would they leave everything else alone? Could he really trust them, just because Garry and Zak said that 'everything would be OK'? Could they plant a bomb? Seumas had told Jack earlier that they wanted to 'burn the boat to the waterline' when he met with him in San Pedro. So, did the two banditos still have it in for Jack? Should Jack go aboard his boat to wait for them while they did their dirty work? The more he pondered the different scenarios, the more he realized that it was pointless to worry. Jack would stay out of it, just as he said he would, and just as Garry and Zak understood that he would. The next time he would see his boat after moving it to the main port would be in Helsinki, Finland or somewhere in the Baltic when he would retrieve it there with Estee, after they both flew to Finland first class. So, it was settled, and Jack wouldn't give it another thought.

As the day approached to move his boat to the main Havana port closer to where the Russian tanker came in, Jack called his Russian buddy Zak again just to 'touch base' and see that they were all on the same page regarding their schedules. "Everything is set up, and going according to plan", assured Zak. "We've sent the specs for your Patrol Craft, YP 504, to the Captain of the oil tanker. Using the dimensions, they've loaded the correct boat cradle on to the main deck to set your boat into when it's lifted aboard the tanker with a crane. They can then secure the boat with blocks and tie-down straps for the crossing over to St. Petersburg. We'll call you when we need you to move your boat to the other harbor to be lifted aboard the tanker, and give you the location where to tie it up. Bring Joe with you if you want some company. Then just walk away and enjoy the holidays in Havana with your friends. We'll do all the rest" he assured him. "Thanks, Zak! I'll wait for your call", responded Jack; and the deal was done (almost).

About a week and a half after that last phone call, as Jack, Joe, Estee, and Laney were strolling up the *Prado Esplanade* toward the sea swept

Malecón coast in north Havana looking at shops along the decorated boulevard, and approaching their Cuban Christmas holiday, Jack smiled broadly as he recalled the previous week's events in their new Havana haven. The oil tanker had departed for Russia about a week earlier and was now well on it's way across the Atlantic to a Baltic or Russian port with Jack's prized 'Yard Patrol Craft' and the Russian's precious bullion loaded securely on board. $50,000 USD worth of gold bullion had already been deposited in Jack's private Swiss account under his elected coordinates, and the caliginous 'Operation Highjack' caper was conveniently behind them. Nevertheless, as was often the case with Garry and Zak, it hadn't gone off without a hitch, since, when the time came to finally make the switch, Jack's two Russian pals had decided to make some last minute changes as they pondered over the same concerns that were bothering Jack earlier.

The more that his two eloquent Russian friends contemplated Miguel and Ignacio trying to pull off a 'night time raid' into the *Hemingway Marina* in Havana to board Jack's boat and transfer the gold bullion from a Navy Seal type RHIB boat, the more jittery they became. They wanted to keep Jack out of the loop if at all possible, so making the switch off the northern coast of Havana at night by boat may have proved problematic with several Cuban military patrol boats cruising the coast. The last thing that they wanted to see was a shootout between the Cuban military and the two out gunned ex-*Los Santos* gang members at sea with Jack and Joe piloting the yacht. They could envision a scenario where the Cuban military might sink the boat with a blast from a deck mounted cannon with the end result being all of the gold, as well as their friends descending into a watery grave at the bottom of the *Straits of Florida* with no recovery possible. So, that option wasn't even considered. No, they needed to come up with a better plan.

So, shortly before *Victory Liner 504* was scheduled to be moved from the marina to the main port where the oil tanker was berthed, Zak asked Jack to contact the marina to inform them that he would be moving the boat later that day, but first wanted to load some essential supplies for a lengthy trip. So Jack called the attendant at the Marina and told him that a shipment of food and supplies would be delivered to his boat that afternoon, and that 'two guys in a white delivery van' would be transferring the supplies later that day. The attendant assured Jack that it wouldn't be a problem. So, around 2:00 PM that same afternoon, Miguel (still walking with a slight limp from his gunshot wound), and Ignacio showed up at the marina's gate in a white delivery van with a sign that read *'Parás-Mercado'* painted on each side panel in large green letters, and drove the van to the area next to the pier where Jack's boat was tied up, transferring the gold in broad daylight. They pulled a wooden plank from the rear of the van and placed it between the pier and the yacht's main deck, forming a gangway. Then, using a couple of hand carts from the van, they wheeled about 20 crates of 'food stuffs' from the back door of the van to the boat in about 30 minutes time. Jack had previously opened the boat for access to the galley, so the two banditos merely wheeled the crates into the aft section of the boat and lowered the crates down an aft hatch and ladder, into the midsection where they loaded each box into a food storage locker and walk-in cooler next to the small freezer in the ship's galley. Each crate contained twenty, one kilo gold bullion bars so that the value of each wooden crate was worth about a million bucks, for a total value of around $20 million USD for the whole twenty-crate shipment. After the gold was securely stowed they threw a couple more loose bags of potatoes on top of the crates to make the piles appear more randomly stacked, then latched the locker tightly. The crates were artfully marked for potatoes, canned goods, and dried fruit products so that they appeared to contain just what the boxes indicated. In fact, the gold bars, stamped with distinct Russian markings, were carefully hidden in the bottom portion of each crate in cardboard boxes placed over a metal plate with actual product placed above more cardboard 'spacers' to separate the contents, cleverly concealing the actual cargo. If someone opened the crate marked 'potatoes', they would just see some potatoes on top, with a piece of cardboard separating what would appear to be more potatoes underneath them. The same was true for the canned goods, and the dried fruit; so, it was all accomplished quite cleverly. After the bullion was all moved to the boat, Miguel and Ignacio exited the Marina in their delivery van the same way that they had entered, waved to the attendant smartly, and quickly left the crime scene. Zak then immediately called Jack informing him that the transfer had been successful, followed by Jack and Joe taking a quick cab ride over to the *Hemingway Marina* to move the boat. Upon arrival, the two sailors smartly hopped aboard the yacht and slowly backed it out of it's berthing spot, getting underway over to the main harbor located about ten miles up the coast where the oil tanker was berthed. During the short trip to ferry the boat over to the other harbor, Jack retrieved his favorite Smith & Wesson .38 Special that was hidden under the mattress in his rack, since he didn't want it on the boat during the transit to the Baltic. Joe also snatched the Taurus 'Curve 180' from its hiding place along with the two Bersa Thunder .380 ACP handguns and other weapons that the Panamanians had left aboard the boat after the rescue operation in Cancun, and placed them all into a brown leather duffle bag that Jack had in his berthing compartment. Upon arrival in the main Havana port and maneuvering to the specified pier, the two sailors secured the boat with mooring lines to the pylons, placed side bumpers in position, secured the 'colors' by taking down their American flag and stowing it properly into a metal container, grabbed the brown duffle bag with their guns off the deck, then locked the boat for the last time in the spot that Zak had indicated; They then turned and walked away, casually looking back once or twice to reassure themselves that everything was sound and secure. So finally, they could 'stick a fork in it'; because, that part of the deal was done.

Following up after the transfer was made, and Jack's boat was tied up next to the tanker, Zak Maxikov made contact with Miguel and Ignacio once again and made them another offer that they couldn't refuse. He instructed the two banditos that they could choose to remain in Cuba where he would make it his personal business to make their lives very difficult going forward, or Zak would pay their way back to Cancun where they could sit out the rest of their sorry lives doing precisely what they had been doing previously; making deliveries to the bars and restaurants along the '*Zona Hotelera*' strip beside the Cancun Nichupté lagoon. Zak added that if either of them were to ever get out of line again, their deliveries would cease to be of any value to 'management', and they would find themselves again swimming off the coast of *Quintana Roo,* near *Banco Chinchorro,* but that next time there would be no research vessel in the area to pull them out of the shark and barracuda infested waters near the reef. They fully understood their options and both nodded in agreement to the dictated conditions. Although Miguel casually shot back, *"You tell Jack that he hasn't seen the last of us. We still owe him for shooting me in the leg!"* Miguel was still nursing his right leg as he and Ignacio limped lethargically aboard their pre-ticketed flight out of Havana back to Cancun to eventually come around full circle in their licentious existence. They were good soldiers, would follow orders, and not threaten anyone else any longer, or so Zak hoped.

Perhaps Zak should have thought his decision through a bit more carefully since his new plan was going to make it somewhat difficult for Seumas back at *'Guillermo's Grill'* to contend with the two banditos. The deliveries may have been a good idea for all concerned except for the fact that Seumas was the last person that Miguel and Ignacio had seen in their hotel room in Chetumal, prior to doing a faceplant on the turquoise Formica kitchen table and waking up in Panama. Now the banditos would be back in Seumas's backyard in Cancun. They also knew too much about Jack's initial abduction, the Havana project, and the 'Operation Highjack' gold bullion transfer to Jack's boat, loaded on the Russian oil tanker heading back to St. Petersburg. In addition, they would now be closer to the Mexican authorities as well. Jack handed the brown duffle bag with his S&W .38 Special revolver and other weapons over to Joe for safe keeping in their Cuban Colonial digs, as the two American hombres caught a cab outside of the Havana Harbor main gates back to their old apartment in Santa Fe, as the whole ordeal ended.

THE CITADEL

"By all means marry, if you get a good wife, you'll be happy. If you get a bad one, you'll become a philosopher"
— <u>Socrates</u>

So with a big concern out of the way, and no boat to call 'home' during their travels together any longer, the two couples, Estee and Jack, and Laney and Joe, continued to explore other areas of Havana beyond *La Explanada de Prado* and partake in the many fun festivities as the Christmas season rolled around. Havana wasn't like other cities, all decked out with flashing lights and fancy fake flora, but did have an appealing old world charm during the holiday season, even with its recent history as a communist citadel. Perhaps some of that stigma was wearing off as the world turned, along with a changing geopolitical climate and some changing weather. The four friends were able to find some unique and memorable gifts for each other to celebrate the special holiday dedicated to *Feliz Navidad para el bebé Jesús*. Jack and the others were also able to find some artful and attractive pastoral Christmas cards to send to their friends back in Minnesota, Kansas, Nevada, Louisiana, and elsewhere, as was their custom during that time of year.

Along with some selective sightseeing, and with their holiday shopping well underway, the group found more time to spend with Elise Lopez, and their 'extended family' within the Cuban community. The experience prompted Jack to ponder 'peopled communities' around the world in general. What made a community 'good', compared with one less amenable? What made this place special? If all people were connected through their subconscious by some 'universal karma', was humanity, in and of itself, one big happy connected community? If so, why didn't people take better care of each other, Jack wondered? Did density matter? If thoughts and subconscious energy were transmitted through some sort of electromagnetic pulse or arbitrary wavelength, did the proximity of one person to another effect the magnitude, amplitude, or frequency of the transmissions? Perhaps people living in places with more dense populations like Seattle, San Francisco, Dallas, or Detroit had similar mass mindsets as a result. Maybe it was the sunshine, or the changing weather that affected their tenaciousness; or, perhaps the transmissions were more ubiquitous. Who knew? That reminded Jack that he would soon need to reach out to his friends and family back in Kansas to extend some holiday cheer as well. He had already bought a few achromatic, but 'artsy' Christmas cards to send, but needed to find a little quiet time to sit and write the cards. Perhaps he would find time later, as he tended to procrastinate when it came to that sort of activity. Without a boat to allow him an occasional strategic escape, he found that time was a scarce commodity that should be rationed, as he felt more confined to quarters. It made him anxious. So, what was it about 'Community' anyway? Was diversity actually beneficial, or was it just more corporate sponsored 'political correctness' obtusely defined? Then again, what was 'diversity', really?! In Finland, for example, along with the 'Finns', a *diverse* populace might include some Russians, Swedes, 'Baltic' folks like Estonian, Lithuanian, or Latvian clan, mixed with a sprinkling of some Sami, and Roma. Did the combination of different peoples and cultures make a place diverse? Did their synapses singularly assimilate?

In contrast, countries like Canada, Russia and China might be considered abundantly more diverse with their numerous different French, English, Asian, Scotch/Irish, Algerian, Czechoslovakian, Cossack, and sundry other cultural ancestries spread out over very large swaths of real estate. By comparison, how were all of those people getting along, in a general sense? Was religion a factor? Probably. But what really held all of those people together? What was the bond; the attractive force? Perhaps it just came down to good versus garbage, and a golden rule; 'Do unto others, as you would have others do unto you'. Jack theorized that, if you just left people alone, they would all get along just fine (for the most part), and work out their differences over the long run. The larger problem seemed to be that whenever governments and religions became part of the equation, the result was more often one of 'divide and conquer', rather than 'commoners all getting along with their cousins'. Then again, perhaps it was just another ploy or 'control mechanism' by the 'religious', and/or governments, or those that perceived themselves to be in power, to try to manage the masses. Simply put, strong communities should 'reinforce family values', and that one single mantra should be the core precept of any productive society, with all smaller families working together as one big family, decided Jack. Conceivably, if that simple premise were followed, more cooperation, with less discord, would manifest in the world, enabling everyone to experience a more vibrant and festive 'Christmas Spirit', he surmised.

Frankly, it wasn't a subject that Jack liked to ponder for any significant length of time anyway, since there were just too many variables to consider. Still, in his quest for happiness, he was searching for a place where he could live in peace without interference from internal and/or external conflicts. Essentially, just live, and let live. Where could he find such a place? Cheboygan, Michigan? Or more reflexively, Reykjavik, Iceland? Svalbard? As he thought about it more, he decided that he should just find a quiet little corner to carefully compose his Christmas cards to his kin and colleagues, while thinking about home. As was customary, every year in December, the three ex-sailor friends, - Sanjo, Jack, and Frank - communicated through their annual cards to stay connected. That year once again, some of his friends were back in the states, while Jack was kicking back in the Caribbean with Joe, Laney, and Estee; ... Whilst, Frank was back up in Topeka with Carol and Sarah. Nevertheless, it was usually Frank that was more reticent and reluctant to give away any intimate details or disclose any personal or confidential information, and would often just scribble a short note at the bottom of his card. That year, it was Jack that was reluctant to disclose any intimate details, or convey any personal or confidential information. Nonetheless, Jack decided that he would include a note similar to what Frank usually wrote in his Christmas cards, plus a bit more detail, while also informing the others about his future travel plans, for what was shaping up to be an extended period of time. Although he didn't quite know where or why he was going, or with whom, ... Jack was trying to find a place for his later years where he could just 'kick back', relax, and be happy. Would that be Cuba, or a place somewhere beyond the shroud, where the truth lay hidden? He remembered that someone famous once said, 'The best revenge was just living well'. Jack eventually found a quiet little corner in their leased Cuban Colonial apartment where he could communicate to his family members and friends through cards, as he scribbled the following little note to Frank and the others;

Dear Frank, Carol, and Sarah –

I hope this card finds you all doing well up in Kansas, and basking in the spirit, peace, and joy of this very special Christmas season, while the rest of us lounge in the solar minimum of this celestial winter solstice in Cuba (lol). I wanted to send you a short greeting at this very special time of year to let you know that, due to some rather unusual events involving our Baltic friends, I was encouraged to load my boat aboard a Russian oil tanker that is presently steaming towards St. Petersburg, Russia for the holidays, with 'Victory Liner 504' secured in a cradle on its main deck.

You may be hearing from Garry and Zak shortly, as I have also decided to relinquish my share of the 'Jack of Clubs' as well as the 'Redhouse Ranch' to fund some future travel, as well as begin our next palatial project with the purchase of an old 'Spanish Colonial' hotel in Havana with help from Joe, Laney, Estee, and others. Garry and Zak have promised to take good care of you all up in Kansas while we take the next steps in the transition. As you know, I don't like to let too much grass grow beneath my feet, so feel it's time to undertake some additional travel to explore new realms and perhaps find the true meaning of Christmas. Nevertheless, you're all welcome to visit us in Cuba anytime.

Estee is planning to travel with me to Europe, as I retrieve my boat in the Baltic States and we extend our travel together. We aren't quite sure where any of this is leading, yet believe that better times are ahead, as we 'just adjust' to dynamic changes aboard this small blue planet we call earth, and sail away into a setting winter solstice sun. Again, wishing you all the best during this very special time of year knowing that there is still peace, love, and joy in the world, and that we'll continue to stay in touch. Because, if everything eventually gravitates to logic, we can still depend on the one pure premise;

"You can't make footprints in the sands of time, … while sitting on your ass!" Wishing You All a Very Merry Christmas!

With that little detail done, Jack decided to write some additional cards to Sanjo and Marissa up in Duluth, Garry and Zak in Panama, Elise and her Cuban cousins and other friends in Havana, as well as Joe, Estee, and Laney ... while still in the Christmas card calligraphy spirit. Jack would try to make them all aware of his perpetual plans to punch through the envelope, and pursue new perspectives in some pastoral space.

With Joe Melnik, Laney Minetti, and her cousin Elise Lopez taking on more of the hotel and restaurant reconstruction project, along with plenty of planning and detail coming from the architectural firm, Jack was able to spend more time with Estee Snyder planning their upcoming travel to Helsinki to pick up Jack's boat, as well as plan extended travel from Finland. Nevertheless, Estee was beginning to feel a bit homesick for her folks back in Belgium during the Christmas season, so decided that she would alter her plans to some extent to meet with her family first, then reconnect with Jack later. So, as they reworked their schedules, Estee decided to fly directly to Brussels to visit her folks for the holidays, extended into January, while Jack would fly directly to Helsinki and try to hook up with Zak depending on the Russian oil tanker's schedule. It would probably take the tanker three weeks to a month to make the Atlantic crossing from Havana to the Baltics in any case, so they cut short the rest of their stay in Cuba and instead just flew to Europe straight away, planning to work out the details later. They would communicate by phone or text going forward.

Europe had a great mass transit system, so Jack could put in at any major port with the boat, then take a train, tram, car, cab, or plane fairly efficiently to all points in between, while in Europe. Looking at logistics, Jack planned to initially head back over to Helsinki for a week or two, and then hook up with Zak when the tanker landed in St. Petersburg. Upon being reunited with his boat, he planned to spend some additional time with Zak in Russia, then, drop down to Gdansk, Poland, or Lübeck, Germany as the weather warmed. He would probably use Helsinki as a 'base camp' for a time, traveling back and forth from there as his plans changed; so a quick hop over to Brussels, or anywhere else in Europe by plane or train from there would be relatively simple. Perhaps Zak would join him in the transit south just to keep Jack entertained. From Lübeck, Jack considered heading back north to Bergen on Norway's west coast for a spell to just relax, practice some Norsk, and kick up his heels for a few weeks, before heading further north to Tromsø, on Norway's northern coast. He wasn't sure how his plans were going to play out with Estee, but would take the transition one step at a time. Nothing was cast in concrete, so he would discuss options with her later.

Be that as it may, in all honesty, as much as Jack and Estee felt a fondness for each other that they hadn't experienced earlier in their lives, and as pretty and perfect as Estee was, she was just too young for Jack. They were happy when they were together and uncomfortable when they were apart; But, were they really a match made in heaven? Perhaps it was just the allure of the Caribbean that lit their lamp at a convenient moment in time. Or, maybe it was their proximity to the Bermuda triangle, … but time was not always as static as statistics, as Estee sought to reconcile her true feelings for Jack as well as her own needs and wants. If Estee sincerely wanted to settle down some day and have a family, it wasn't going to be with Jack, so they both needed to factor the facts into the equation. Estee's biological clock was still ticking, and priorities were pointing to a different path, as they sought to recognize their differences while separating for a spell. Was theirs' a lasting love, or just two ships passing sublimely in the night? In contrast, Joe and Laney were a much better match since they pretty much enjoyed their relaxed relationship as friends and lovers, and were satisfied with just being together and having fun working on the restoration project, and generally enjoying their lives in Havana with Laney's Cuban cousins, one day at a time. Since Laney had 'Cuban' in her DNA on her mother's side, as well as close family in Havana, the authorities were more inclined to grant her special treatment related to a 'resident visa' there, to her benefit. If that were the case, Joe would just go along for the ride and firm up his partnership with Laney to make the whole package work in their favor. That was good for Joe and Laney, but didn't work as well for Estee and Jack. So, that was just one more niggling little anomaly that was gnawing at Jack as he hopped a plane to Helsinki in late December.

Helsinki was a stark contrast to Havana when Jack landed at the Helsinki- Vantaan airport a few days after bidding farewell to Joe, Laney, and their Cuban mates. He was now significantly north of Belgium at coordinates 60°10'15"N 24°56'15"E, where days were short and nights were long, around the same latitude as Bergen, Norway. Whereas, Jack had earlier enjoyed temperate tropical weather, plenty of sunshine, and more daylight in the Caribbean, ... Helsinki was cold, crisp, crunchy, and overcast by comparison. Still, the eternal light, bright character, and extracurricular energy of the Soumi people seemed to compensate for the cold, and kept Finland festive. Jack checked into a favorite hotel near the 'Bulevardi' avenue, between Lönnrotinkatu and Uudenmannkatu streets where he had easy access to the 'No. '6' and '6T' trams that allowed him quick transit to the Central Train Station and city buses, the City Center, *Stockmann's* department store, the Helsinki-Vantaan airport, as well the new *Tallink Ferry* terminal that provided transit to Tallinn, Estonia. He would later look for an apartment in that same 'Bulevardi' avenue area where he could lease a place longer term, and use it as a base while in northern Europe. If Jack were to eventually head further north to Norway, he would find a similar type of climate to Helsinki. Nevertheless, Tromsø was situated quite a bit further north of Bergen at a latitude of 69°40'58"N 18°56'34"E. But, as Sanjo would say, 'it was all good'! When Jack was back in the Baltic and Nordic countries he felt centered; which, along with the colder weather, stoic solitude, warm hearts and independent thinking of the people, and all inclusive sumptuous saunas, were some of the reasons why Jack very much enjoyed the 'Viking north' with its old world version of vintage 'Yin and yang'.

It could have been that the combination of shorter days and longer nights, combined with the colder weather, whilst all bundled up to stay warm, helped Jack to reflect inward while squarely facing the future. What did he really want? What would make him happy? What would quiet his soul, and cultivate contentment? He had done it all. What he needed was a new program; a precise paradigm; a change of venue within a watery and wild world on a small spinning blue planet. It really came down to personal choice, strident desires, and expectations. A person could *choose* what they needed and wanted. If expectations outweighed their needs and wants, the result was often dissatisfaction. If worldly desires were small, and could be more easily wrought, perhaps the result would be 'happiness'. It just came down to personal choice. Less was more, - more or less.

Nevertheless, he didn't dwell on the matter much longer, since after a couple of week's waiting in late January, Zak Maxikov called Jack and offered to meet with him in Narva, Estonia to travel together over to St. Petersburg to check on Jack's boat. The oil tanker had arrived that same week where a team of special forces Russian Spetsnaz troops met the tanker at the port of entry and removed the precious metal cargo from the walk-in cooler and food storage areas in the boat's galley and lowered the gold down into some heavily guarded high security government vehicles situated on the pier for transfer to safer storage. So Jack checked out of his hotel in Helsinki and took the number '6' tram down to the *Tallink Ferry* terminal the following day for the crossing through the Gulf of Finland over to Tallinn, Estonia to meet with Zak. He took a limo from Tallinn over to Narva, where Zak met him at a hotel that was already booked for a one- night stay. Since Zak was from St. Petersburg originally, he knew the area like the back of his hand as well as the proper authorities and paperwork required to get Jack processed into Russia for travel to Zak's home town for a short stay. Just as Zak had promised earlier, after the gold was safely transferred from Jack's boat, Zak promptly deposited another $50K in gold bullion to Jack's numbered Swiss storage account using Jack's coordinates. Jack elected to take the additional $25K bonus that the Russians had promised in various fiat currencies (Euros, Rubles, and some Norwegian Krona), for travel expenses later. So again, 'it was all good', and the two gentlemen, along with the Russian Federation, were satisfied with the successful results.

    Now, Zakhar Maxikov, who hailed from St. Petersburg, was quite a likeable person anyway, but was also a person that was well respected in his 'hometown'. He had lots of friends in high places and important positions in both the business world as well as the government. At 6 foot, 4 inches tall, and a solid 190 pounds, with some special military training earlier in his life and a strong 'Cossack' heritage, Zak was just a good guy to know as a friend and compatriot, as well as a good travelling companion. He could open a lot of doors in a number of very creative ways, and could go places where others might not easily venture. Jack and Zak had been friends for a number of years and their combined experience had been useful to both of them in their varied careers. They covered each other's back, trusted each other's instincts, and worked as a team rather well. Which was also why they liked doing deals together, and why Zak and Garry Odonavich liked being partners with Jack in businesses like the *'Jack of Clubs'*, the

'Redhouse Ranch', and Jack's newest venture with the Spanish Colonial Hotel and restaurants, and possible future casino businesses in Havana, Cuba. So, in St. Petersburg they both had a chance to talk, exchange confidential information, and breathe the fresh winter air of that exotic metropolis with its fascinating history, where Zak grew up. Moreover, they had a chance to discuss past and present life changes as Jack confided in Zak about Estee Snyder to get his valued opinion. Zak understood Jack's situation and advised him matter-of-factly that he should probably 'just let it go'. He understood Jack and Estee's relationship quite well and his instincts told him what Jack already knew; that if he really loved her, he should just release the tension and let nature take its course. Estee was just too young for Jack, especially since she wanted to have a family someday. Jack acknowledged that reality, which was the first step required to help redirect his energies. He reluctantly agreed to refocus his internal lenses to try a few new different F-stops, as the two of them hit some of Zak's favorite cabarets and watering holes in the surrounding area to ease the strain. Since it was his own 'backyard', Zak knew the best adult nightclubs and bars in St. Petersburg where the two of them could relax, have a few 'brewskys', and do their best to decompress. 'Love is a rose, but you better not pick it; it only grows when its on the vine. A hand full of thorns, and you'll know you've missed it, you lose your love, when you say the word "mine" ♪♪♪ ♪

Jack spent about a week in St. Petersburg with Zak while they talked over old times, visited Zak's old neighborhood, and met a few of his old time friends. All in all, it was time well spent, and helped Jack to get his act together. The other major issue that Jack had to face however, was that there was no way that Jack was going to be able to move his boat out of the Russian port of St. Petersburg during one of the coldest months of the year. In addition, his boat was still strapped in a saddle on the tanker's main deck, with plans to place it on the pier in the following weeks. So, the boat would sit there until the winter ice thawed at which time Jack could return to St. Petersburg in the following months to retrieve it. Uncharacteristically, he hadn't quite factored that little piece of important information into his previous plans as reality finally set in. Since the ferries were still running between Helsinki and Tallinn during that time of year, he thought maybe the channel would be open to maneuver his boat to another port, yet hadn't quite factored in the ice on the rivers. In any case, it would ultimately work to Jack's advantage since Zak agreed to travel with Jack out of the Russian port when he returned sometime around late March or early April. In the interim, Jack would return to Helsinki the way he came, settle into a cozy little apartment on the 'Bulevardi', and take in as many occasions as time would permit to enjoy the hot Finnish saunas in the winter time. He would also call Estee to have a good long talk.

Frozen River, Port of St. Petersburg, Russia

Back in Helsinki, Jack settled into a fairly modern 'Scandik' type Finnish apartment with beautiful older wood beamed ceilings, lots of colored glass with a view of the boulevard and a very 'Finnic' ambience. The place also had a couple of saunas on the lower level, which could be used by residents with similar apartments in the building. Apparently, 'sex in the sauna with rock music' was something else that the Finns enjoyed to help them stay warm and fuzzy in the winter; so there was some of that going on as well. Jack on the other hand, preferred Jazz or Classical, with a bit of Glenn Miller or Tommy Dorsey's 'Big Band sound' mixed in; but in the end, everything eventually came down to personal choice. In any case, having finally settled in, Jack soon found the occasion to call Estee as planned to discuss her holidays with her folks, and eventually get around to the subject that they were both trying desperately to avoid, but needed frankly to discuss. After they had both spent some time back in their separate worlds, and had discussed their positions with family and friends, they had collectively and correctly come to the conclusion that, although they had loved each other faithfully for a time, they now understood that the best thing for both of them was to just cherish their memories, and move on. They spoke for about an hour together passionately over their cell phones from afar, with some fairly gut-wrenching uneasiness and grief, but eventually, both relented to their fate, and let go. They would keep in touch as best they could for a while, but in the end, they would both just get on with their lives as time progressed.

Even after the call ended it took Jack a while to come to grips with the realization that Estee was gone. He would never forget her, nor would she forget Jack, but it was water over the dam. They would move on. So as Jack reflected, he decided that it was probably a good time to check back with Joe and Laney in Havana to see how the Hotel restoration project was coming along, and possibly make plans to return to Cuba for a while to cool his heels, or warm his feet, or mend his heart (whatever), and take some long strolls again along the *Prado Esplanade* in the center of Old Havana that led to the *Malecón* (officially *Avenida de Maceo*), and enjoy some better times in the bars and bistros of old Cuba like the *El Floridita de Cuba Bar*. It felt like a rather long time since he had connected with his Cuban comrades in any case, as he dialed up his old pal Joe Melnik. Indeed, Jack found that things had been proceeding at a proper pace as the Cuban work crews were nearing completion on the initial phases of some of the projects. The entire reconstruction project would probably take the better part of a year to complete, however, since the hotel had been a very nice hotel in the early part of its life, the team had planned to renovate the various buildings in stages to allow them access to a portion of the properties earlier, and begin to attract customers from around the world. In that way, they could begin to build a revenue stream for further refinements. More in, less out, to meet expenses for the reconstruction, and payroll for the working crews and newly hired staff people. Many of the hotel rooms had also been renovated on a few of the upper floors to accommodate guests. They had also established a good relationship with the bank to fund the projects under the prevailing circumstances.

In addition, Laney had been granted a 'resident visa' for a longer stay by the Cuban government, and as it happened, Joe could remain in Cuba as well, as long as the two of them got 'hitched'. So Joe, who was willing to just 'go along' with the program, had therefore proposed to Laney, who promptly accepted the offer, as they were planning a small wedding in the newly renovated Grand Ballroom of the updated Hotel. The work crews were making good progress on the new restaurant and café, so they too could be put into play during the ceremony. All in all, the wedding was a timely incentive to help all of them focus on making more progress, and to move the schedule along quickly to have the buildings in some semblance of suitability by mid-March. Since the wedding would be smaller, Joe and Laney would have comfortable rooms for their guests while they attended the service and reception. On another note, the architects were chomping at the bit to finish up their plans and wanted to know if there were a few new names for the properties that Jack might have considered? That being the case, Joe and Jack had a few discussions with Laney Minetti and Elise Lopez on a conference call, where Jack had suggested that he would like to name the new hotel *'La Citadel Grandé Hotel & Suites'*, with one of the restaurants named the *'Prado Promenade'*, and a café called *'Café de Marti'* renamed in tribute to the renowned Cuban national hero *José Marti* from Havana. In contrast, Jack decided that the ballroom should be named *'Tsar Nicholas Grand Ballroom'* after Tsar Nicholas II of Russia who was assassinated, along with his entire family by the vile, vicious, and murderous Bolsheviks during the Russian Revolution in the early 1900's. They all liked the new names, and agreed to inform the architects of their consensus, prior to planning the wedding.

Moving things right along, they selected a date to recite their wedding vows in mid-March to give them all some time, then addressed several 'Save-The-Date' cards that Laney had made up at a local card shop in Havana to send out to some close friends and family for the nuptial ceremony. So, in mid February, Laney sent invitations out to Jack's good friends, Frank Valero and Carol Mulhaney up in Topeka at the Jack of Clubs, as well as Sanjo and Marissa Casagrande up in Duluth, Minnesota, as well as Zakhar Maxikov and friend, and Garry Odonavich, and friend down in Panama, the two Panamanians Fernando and Eddie, and Sanjo's Mom Anita Kelly (and guest) out in Albuquerque, New Mexico; Gino

Giovanni and Gabriel over in French Harbor near Coxen Hole, as well as Elise Lopez's many relatives in Havana. An invitation was also sent out to Seumas Santaña, and guest in Cancun. Needless to say Miguel and Ignacio were excluded from the master list as they were to be forever in 'lock down' back on the hotel strip on the Yucatán Peninsula in Mexico. Of course, Jack would need a date too, and because he was so very fond of his little dancer friend, Sarah Reid (aka *Enchanté*), Jack asked if she would consider being his very special companion at Joe and Laney's wedding; to which she accepted his kind offer without hesitation, knowing that Frank and Sanjo, along with Joe the groom would be attending also. They also extended an invitation to Laney's good friend Estee Snyder over in Belgium, who RSVP'd back saying 'Thank You Very Much', but who decided that her attendance would be quite awkward under the circumstances, so respectfully declined the invitation; as everyone perfectly understood her sensible hesitation. Perhaps she would visit her good friend 'Laney' sometime after the wedding to revisit Havana and review some of her handy work, as she had been a very integral part of making the new hotel and restaurant renovation project a great success.

Needless to say that, when the special day finally arrived in March, after all the festive preparations were hastily assembled, the wedding was a fabulous affair. The males, all 'dressed to a T' in splendid tuxes, ties, and summer suits, and the ladies in their gorgeous gowns and flowered dresses, boogied the night away as the lively music filtered down into the warm and bustling streets below. They celebrated and partied like there was no tomorrow, as if they were in a great Viking Hall with all manner of music and dancing with a band the likes of the great Dámaso Pérez Prado, playing the timeless tunes of his magnificent 'mambo' magic ensemble, with drinking, and hugging and kissing well into the next morning, until they all eventually went to bed drunk. But, not before the professional staff from the '*Café de Marti*' brought them all fresh hot Italian late-night pizzas baked in the wood fired ovens installed under the direction of Laney Minetti from the newly renovated café and grill. While, throughout the long evening 'Joe Melnik, the groom', behaving at his boastful best, reminded all who would listen that "without alcohol added to the mix, there would be a lot fewer relationships, let alone fewer marriages". Then he would drop the subject, remembering where he was, as he took another sip of his rum while the room continued to spin well into dawn on their piece of the small blue planet, under the fabulous shimmering glass chandeliers in the new *Tsar Nicholas Grand Ballroom*. As the crowd slowly dwindled away, and guests retired to their individual suites, the ball room was left rumpled and well used, and 'broken in' sufficiently with tablecloths, coats, hats, and scarves all strewn haphazardly across tables and chairs as a morning cleaning crew arrived to put the whole place back in order before the breakfast banquet that followed. That night, Joe ended up with Elena Minetti (aka *Laney Melnik*) in the palatial bridal suite on the top floor, as Sanjo spent the night with his wife Marissa Casagrande (aka *Cassandra*) in another sumptuous suite, and Frank Valero bunked down with Carol Mulhaney (aka *Pernicious*) in a similar well appointed suite, and Jack enjoyed a special night with Sarah Reid (aka *Enchanté*) in the newly renovated penthouse on the hotel's magnificent rooftop overlooking the *Malecón* coastline to the north. And, all was well in the world.

La Citadel Grandé Hotel

From Old Town Habana
To Copacabana
Youthful time travelers tell
There's so much more fanfare
And no place quite grander
Than 'La Citadel Grandé Hotel'

La Esplanade Prado
Flows past it like moon glow
While ladies and gentlemen yell
From the beaches and bars
And from old classic cars
They come to relax for a spell.

The Malecón coast
Up the road from that post
Too sea-swept and fancy to quell
Keeps everyone gleeful
And full of good people
Where ladies and gentlemen dwell

They all come to party
At the Café de Marti'
With customers doing quite well;
Where wood fired pizza
And smart looking matrons
Offer their wares for sale

The proud Prado restaurant
With Promenade patrons
And Cuisine that rings a bell
With great menu fare
More people go there
And placate their stomachs quite well.

So, come to the party
Along with the hearty
And escort your favorite gal;
In Cuba, Habana
Along Prado de Marti'
At La Citadel Grandé Hotel

Jaak Tallinn - 2017

SMALL BLUE PLANET

"Don't waste your love on somebody who doesn't value it."
- <u>William Shakespeare</u>, <u>Romeo and Juliet</u>

  The Cuban architects were to be commended on their outstanding commitment to detail and excellent assimilation and implementation of Spanish Colonial design within the newly reconstructed hotel, as it was truly their pinnacle achievement. They were ardently transforming a turn of the century stone building into a modern masterpiece and gem at the center of the old city. All who attended the wedding were awestruck at the design group's vision, and what they had cultivated as a team and a community. The local inhabitants within the immediate vicinity of the hotel also felt a special pride in what their comrades had accomplished to date, and felt a part of it. Estee Snyder too, should have been congratulated for her prescient input into the entire 'Spanish Colonial' design concept. From Elise Lopez and her family over in Santa Fe, to the people at *El Floridita Bar*, to the young and old people strolling up and down the *Prado Esplanade* all the way up to the *Malecón* along the sea swept northern Havana coastline; they had all watched the reconstruction evolve and become a prominent part of their vibrant proud community, and a crowning crystal of contentment. Of course, it had been Jack's vision initially, but became everyone's crested creation. They were all well aware of their inclusion in the process, and felt fulfillment as integral players in its success. The new '*La Citadel Grandé Hotel & Suites*' was now a firm feature of the *Habana Vieja* landscape, as well as a distinguished travel destination to be included within every new visitor's 'bucket list'.

  Nevertheless, that was a little hard to imagine looking at the wedding guests who began to roll out of their racks for breakfast the following morning with hard hangovers and bloodshot eyes. The new bride and groom, Laney Minetti (who decided that she might just keep her maiden name) and the grizzled groom Joe Melnik, were trying to remember what had happened as the male staff members, wearing crisp white shirts and jackets with black bowties, and the waitresses with their crisp white aprons and black sashes over black cotton dresses, and wearing crisp white paper crowns in their hair, delivered food from the partially renovated *Prado Promenade* restaurant serving them all breakfast in the newly renovated *Tsar Nicholas Grand Ballroom*, with the tables all rearranged and set up on crisp white cotton tablecloths with beautiful floral centerpieces, for the 'morning after' breakfast buffet. Actually, the new bride and groom couldn't decide whether they were now Mr. and Mrs. Melnik, or Mr. and Mrs. Minetti, or maybe just still Laney Minetti and Joe Melnik, but it didn't really matter much. It was sort of like the red stoplights in Rome; they were really just a suggestion, and no one actually paid any attention to the rules anymore. Rules were made to be broken, regardless. Was their wedding even really legal in Cuba? Nobody seemed to care, as long as they could all just remain in Havana and operate the hotel. Not even the government seemed concerned anymore, as they too, were proud of the accomplishment, and just wanted to feel a part of it. So, 'It was all good', … as Sanjo liked to say.

    The wedding ceremony had been like a large family reunion since many of the guests hadn't seen the other guests for several years, if ever at all. Their new Cuban friends had a chance to meet the 'whole family' of distant friends and relatives so that they welded new communal relationships in a big family way. The event had also been a good opportunity for Jack, Zak, and Garry to discuss their plans with Frank Valero and Carol Mulhaney regarding the sale of the '*Jack of Clubs*', and '*Redhouse Ranch*' in Kansas, and discuss their participation in the transition of the properties. In any case, Jack and his pals felt as if all of Havana now knew their names and had welcomed their presence there with open arms and hearts, as if they were all natural citizens. It was a renaissance and enlightenment for 'Habana' and a great Grand Opening for the new *Citadel Grandé Hotel*. They could let the good times roll from that day forward. Be that as it may, Jack thought it would also be a great time to make a reticent exit, to 'get out of Dodge' while the getting was good; to retire at the peak of a performance, so to speak. So, that is what Jack decided to do. Bolt.

Jack found plenty of time to discuss his current situation with his good friend and casual companion Sarah Reid again (aka *Enchanté*), to explain the situation with his boat still sitting in the frozen port of St. Petersburg, as well as his split with Estee Snyder as he tried to decide his next play. Zak had already agreed to meet with Jack back up in Narva to escort him back to his boat in St. Petersburg, and make the transit over to Helsinki. So, that part was well taken care of, as Jack felt quite comfortable with the arrangement. Nevertheless, what was Jack going to do after he returned the boat to Finland? Initially, he had planned to travel down to Lübeck or Gdansk, then visit with Estee for a while and possibly take her with him as they explored the north together. However, that whole program fizzled, and had now been effectively scrapped. Therefore, after the wedding ended and Jack and Sarah retired to their penthouse suite, Jack popped the question to see whether Sarah would consider taking Estee's place and perhaps travel with him up to Bergen instead. Then perhaps they could follow the coast of Norway up to Tromsø for a time, to see the 'Northern Lights' and play 'Viking' for a while. Sarah was a little surprised by the timing of Jack's impromptu proposal, but it was also rather 'spur of the moment' for Jack as well. "Why not!", he thought; "Why not!", she thought; it's not as if either of them had any pressing engagements at that particular moment anyway, as they both agreed that it would be a great time to make a strategic escape back to Helsinki together, and perhaps try a little 'sex in the sauna to some rock music'. Following that, she could join Jack and Zak to retrieve '*Victory Liner 504*', then sail away into the sunset to go 'Viking' as a proud warrior couple. It was almost like being in a gang again, thought Sarah; they could even get matching Viking rune tattoos in Helsinki to laud their fearless raids, if desired. However, Sarah already had one tattoo on her right butt cheek that just said "*Esse non videri*", so perhaps she could put an image of '*Thor's Hammer*' or a raven on the left one.

So, as the wedding guests mulled around for a time after the festivities began to dwindle, Jack and Sarah booked a late night flight out of Havana north to Helsinki, and slipped quietly away as the other guests eventually did the same, leaving Joe and Laney, as well as Elise to get back into their regular routines as the new resident managers of the *'La Citadel Grandé Hotel & Suites'*. Nobody remembered the guests coming or going in the following frantic days, as they all got back to work completing their daily chores. Nevertheless, most of the plans had been set in motion and the activities were mostly on automatic as the work in Havana resumed. About a week later, Garry and Zak found some time to visit Frank and Carol up at the *'Jack of Clubs'* in Kansas to finalize their agreements and put that deal to bed as well; So, everything was copacetic and working according to plan. Garry and Zak took over the day-to-day management of the *'Jack of Clubs'* and the *'Redhouse Ranch'* near Topeka, and reconciled their positions with Jack's foreman Ray Forbes out at the ranch as well. With the slight increase in pay that Zak offered to feather his nest, Ray had no qualms with continuing what he had been already doing for many years; just running the ranch and 'Gettin 'er done' as he completed his daily chores 'Come Hell or High Water'.

In the end, Jack's profit from the sale of the properties actually came in well north of $50 million USD, but then again, Jack knew that it would. When Zak had offered him ten times earnings for the businesses, plus the appraised value of the buildings, Jack knew that he would make out well enough. With 200 acres of farmland and 100 acres of it planted with crops up in Kansas, plus many of his beef and veal cattle being used for organic meats, along with the microbrewery which was producing the *'Holy Grail Pale Ale'* and *'Flying Tiger'* brands, Jack knew that he was already pulling in a strong profit of over $5 million USD after taxes, depreciation, and amortization just in those assets alone; Especially, since he had recently set up national distribution for the beer products. So, once Garry and Zak actually saw his 'books' they understood that Jack was already doing quite well on his own, and it was just a matter of a little simple math to see that ten times earnings, was going to pull in a nice final figure for Jack, Carol, and Frank after the purchase was completed. After all, Sales, minus the cost of sales, equals profit. 'Earnings', equals net profit before taxes. Ten times five, equals fifty; then when Jack added the sale of the buildings, the whole package began to take shape. Jack knew his numbers, and knew what he had built. More in, less out, to cover expenses and payroll; The rest he kept, and deposited some of his share into the *'Jack of Clubs Charitable Trust'* in his offshore trust account down in Panama where he had the funds invested in properties, Treasuries, and Bonds, that were also growing at a profit; so that too, was 'all good'. Jack would also establish a *'Health Care Insurance Package'* within the trust fund for his pals to benefit from in their retirement years, so that everything was coming up roses. Since Frank and Carol also benefited sufficiently from the sale, and had elected to retain their smaller stakes in the 'Sports Bar', as well as to continue managing the club at increased salaries for their continued participation, they were sufficiently satisfied with the final arrangement. In any case, all of the businesses were still growing at a healthy 10% - 30% pace, so everybody benefited from the transaction, while it also helped their 'cash flow'. Frank and Carol also agreed to help Jack and the others in the logistics of setting up the new hotel, restaurants, and other businesses in Havana since they were both good managers, knew the pitfalls of hiring and retaining good people to facilitate a smooth operation, and could participate in the Cuban venture as well. The transition would also give Frank and Carol an opportunity to 'get out of Dodge' on occasion to enjoy some warmer weather in the Caribbean, as well as visit with their special friends down in Havana. From Gary and Zak's perspective, they planned to 'piggyback' off of Jack's success and put in another microbrewery down near the new *'Citadel Hotel'* in Havana to produce more of the *'Holy Grail Pale Ale'* and *'Flying Tiger'* brands in Cuba, with the addition of producing their own brand of rum, and use Jack's distribution channels that had already been established to increase sales further, while also dodging some of the taxes since the brewery and distillery plants would be licensed under Garry and Zak's own 'Russian' businesses, while some of the products would be distributed outside of the already established channels. So again, 'it was all good', and everything was progressing in a very favorable way to their combined satisfactions. 'Win, win, win' situations for everyone involved. One of the only loose ends was Jack's '50's era blue-and-white Cessna 170 tail dragger airplane, which was still in a hanger near the sports bar in Topeka. Maybe he would sell the plane too, he thought. That, and the future casino might have to wait a while longer until conditions were more favorable for implementation.

    Upon landing at the Helsinki-Vantaa airport about ten hours after their departure from Cuba, and taking the airport train to the *Kauppakeskus CityCenter* near the *Central Train Station* in Helsinki, Jack and Sarah hopped on the No. 6 tram up 'Bulevardi' avenue, between Lönnrotinkatu and Uudenmannkatu streets to Jack's furnished apartment to settle in for a spell and get comfortable. Sarah was impressed with Jack's temporary digs and made a special point of letting him know that she was quite happy to be there with him, and was looking forward to their upcoming travel together. She was excited to be with Jack again, and felt like she needed a change at that particular point in time anyway. The dance routine at the bar in Kansas was getting a little old, and she much preferred to just dance for Jack. So it was all looking good to both of them finally, and they were glad to have some private time together once again, as they headed down to the misty sauna to detoxify, and listen to some satisfyingly smooth and soothing jazz.

In Finland, they could feel the intoxicating vibrations of the earth, water, and air, even in the winter months, while the days were shorter and the sun was diminished. The soothing jazz helped to amplify the virtuous vibrations, stimulating the world around them in alternating frequencies and amplitudes. So, along with visiting some very fine Finnish restaurants and quaint little diners in the area, Jack showed Sarah some of the other attractions in the vicinity near Jack's apartment; like *Stockmann's Department Store* with eight floors of shopping offering everything and anything that one could imagine or want from clothes, to furniture, to appliances, to a shave and a haircut, or even a nice meal if needed. *Stockmann's* also had a Forex currency exchange office on the eighth floor, which Jack used as a lower cost alternative and convenient venue for trading different currencies; So, the location was excellent for conducting all manner of personal and business trade. Jack also took Sarah for walks down past *Stockmann's* and along the tree-lined and well groomed *Esplanadi* central park to the outdoor *Market Square* centered between the popular and attractive *Pohjoisesplanadi* and *Eteläesplanadi* avenues, with their 200 year old Russian designed architecturally attractive stone faced buildings, and fashionable stores with more great shopping. They could easily walk to the *Central Train Station* located just a few blocks from the apartment, or take the tram, which then offered access to everywhere else in Finland. So for a couple of days they took the train up to Tampere to have a look around and enjoy that very fun and fascinating little city, and enjoy the area. Next, they traveled west by train over to Turku (oldest city in Finland, settled in the 13th century) for a few days, to have another look around and enjoy some of the fine riverboat restaurants along the *River Aura*; and the following week they visited the old and peaceful seaside port of Porvoo to the east, to enjoy the many fine shops, restaurants, and local attractions there as well. So, Sarah was beginning to get more comfortable and familiar with Finland also, just as Jack had.

In early April, they caught up with Zak again as he headed back to Europe to help Jack retrieve his boat over in St. Petersburg, as earlier promised. Sarah would have to decide whether she wanted to remain in Helsinki at Jack's apartment for a while and wait for his return, or just travel with Jack to St. Petersburg, to make the transit back with Jack and Zak. She decided on the latter. Therefore, around mid-April, as the weather began to warm and the ice went out, Jack and Sarah retraced Jack's previous route back over to Narva, Estonia, taking the No. 6 tram down to the *Tallink Ferry* Terminal for the two hour crossing through the Gulf of Finland over to Tallinn, Estonia, then rented a limo for the scenic ride over to Narva to meet Zak. They stayed one night on the Estonia/Russian border in Narva at the same little inexpensive *Elektra* hotel where Jack had stayed several weeks previously. They met Zak the next morning for a hearty breakfast and a little meet-and-greet between the three friends (they hadn't seen each other since the wedding in Cuba the month before), signed some paperwork for the visas, showed their passports to the authorities, then drove with Zak in his Mercedes for about an hour and a half east over to the port of St. Petersburg to reunite with Jack's motor-yacht. Zak and his crew had removed the boat from the saddle on the oil tanker's deck several weeks earlier, tidied it up a bit, then moved the boat upstream to a small marina in the *Reka Srednyaya Nevka* River a short span away. They secured it to the pylons on the pier where it sat proud as a pearl, ready for its next mischievous mission. It was good to see the old girl again. Zak would leave his car parked in the Marina lot on the river as he rode the boat back with Jack and Sarah prior to tying up in Tallinn. Zak would then leave Jack and Sarah on their own as he returned by Limo back to Narva and St. Petersburg to recover his car before returning home. After a short 'pre-flight' inspection to make sure that everything was in proper working order on his boat, Jack raised the American flag colors, fired up the diesel engines, and backed the boat away from the pier into the middle of the river, as the three close comrades got underway heading back towards Tallinn. It felt good to be back at the con again as Jack piloted his boat under the A-118 highway bridge, adding power heading out into the Gulf of Finland for the fresh and fairly lengthy multiple hour ride back. Sarah and Jack would spend a few nights in the 'old town' section of Tallinn at a Boutique hotel that Jack had reserved, to do a little shopping and sightseeing within the old world city gates, relax in a sauna for a while, take in some good restaurants, and enjoy a little Baltic cuisine with some good red wine, before making the crossing back to Helsinki. It was all good, as Jack set off to settle into one of his favorite old world ports for a short sojourn with his favorite dancer girlfriend, and all around 'good sport', Sarah Reid.

So, *Victory Liner 504* became Jack's own floating fortress, and his new mobile 'Citadel Hotel'. After several days of exploring Tallinn, Jack and Sarah boarded the motor yacht once again for their return trip to Helsinki across the choppy Gulf of Finland. After their trek from St. Petersburg, the trip across the Gulf was a 'piece of cake' since it only took a few hours. Back in Helsinki, Jack secured the boat to a pier close to the downtown Market Square as the two adventurers returned 'home', walking past the Market Square and along the tree-lined and well groomed *Esplanadi* central park to Jack's cozy little Helsinki apartment near the 'Bulevardi', stowed their luggage and packages, and headed down to the sauna to listen to a little jazz. Indeed, they were beginning to enjoy their regular sauna episodes so much that it became a kind of addiction. They found that it was a great way to unwind from the stress of the day or troubling travel; So, as a result of that noteworthy observation, Jack decided to have a couple of local craftsman install a swank little shipboard sauna using Finnish Red Cedar, in one of the many berthing spaces aboard his boat. He also installed a quality sound system to pipe in a little jazz and classical music as they amused themselves. With just the two of them traveling together in the near future, they didn't need the extra berthing compartments for guests anyway, yet a sauna would be 'just what the doctor ordered' as they planned their expedition north, and as Jack reflected on the premise, '*if you get a good wife, you'll be happy*'.

Jack also called his old pal Joe Melnik down in Havana after he landed back in Helsinki, just to touch base and see how the reconstruction project was coming along. Joe was happy to report that the reconstruction was on track and that about half of the '*Citadel*' hotel rooms had been renovated and/or updated. The restaurant renovations were also well on their way, and close to being completed. In any case, as they remodeled more hotel rooms their revenue stream increased proportionately, with the new room rates also increasing as they approached full occupancy. So, the project was progressing according to plan with the current management in place. With Jack's blessings, Garry and Zak had also begun construction on a new brewery and distillery adjacent to the '*Citadel Hotel*', that was scheduled to be completed within about six months time. So, everyone seemed satisfied with the steady progress and new business growth.

To that end, as Jack and Sarah settled into their digs in Helsinki and began to plan their next gig through the month of May, Jack suggested that a good travel route might include a cruise across the Baltic Sea to *Stockholm* for a few days, then down to *Visby, Gotland* for a time, then over to *Malmo*, before heading north through the *Helsingør* straits north of *Copenhagen*, into the *Kattegat*, and along the southern tip of Norway through the *Skagerrak* to *Kristainsand*. While traveling, they could choose to either get a swanky hotel room in the various ports they visited, or remain on the boat if it was more convenient. So Jack's boat was a great mobile base and useful platform for everyday life while traveling. Following their stop in Kristiansand, they could track the Norwegian coast north to *Stavanger*, before moving further north to Bergen, Norway, another well known Hanseatic League port situated on Norway's temperate (but often rainy) west coast, as they visited more towns to the north.

Now, people around the world came in a variety of shapes, sizes, and colors, allegorically speaking, but their dispositions varied. Much of the population was inclined to be rather 'socially' oriented, as they enjoyed the company of others, reveled in the exchange of ideas, and liked interfacing and networking, as they generally felt delighted in close relationships. Others tended to be more introspective, and attempted to keep their distance while allowing some space between themselves and others and keeping their personal liaisons private. In that regard, they enjoyed their solitude, interacted well with others when required, but generally preferred the 'arms length' approach, as they relished their peace and quiet. People typically fell somewhere between those two types of personalities, Jack decided. So, in trying to determine what would make *him* 'happy', Jack began to appreciate that '*solitary*' trait within his own persona, as he also spent more time interacting with Sarah. In reality, Jack and Sarah were a lot more alike than they cared to acknowledge. Although Sarah enjoyed being with others on occasion, especially dancing for drinks, a dinner, or tips, she preferred her alone time, and was actually a rather private person, Jack discovered. That quieter side of Sarah intrigued Jack, as he found her to be more like him, yet evermore alluring and exotic at the same time. So, as the two began to spend more private time together, in the saunas and on the ship, they began to delve more deeply inward, as they expanded their envelopes, while their relationship and love affair blossomed.

Jack soon realized that he had finally found most of what he had been searching for in his heady new relationship with Sarah. He had his motor yacht, which provided him with shelter and mobility on a small blue planet, whose outer sphere was covered in three fourth's water (yet whose internal surface was said to be only a quarter water), ... as well as his privacy, along with a lady friend that viewed the world much the same as he did, and would behave passionately within that world to satisfy mutual objectives. Jack also discovered that Sarah had an ear for jazz and classical music and enjoyed dancing to the sound of a piano, saxophone, a little fiddle, and some snare drums, while noting that there was nothing quite as seductively libidinous and head-poppingly salacious, as watching a licentious young 'laplander' doing a titillating lap dance on the wooden deck of a graciously appointed shipboard spa.

In that way, Jack also kept his independence, since there was no rule advocating that they had to get hitched in any case. Sarah found that she too, had finally found what she wanted; a guy who would shelter, comfort, and protect her, as well as satisfy her innermost worldly desires, needs, and wants, along with someone that she very much enjoyed spending time with. So, the combination worked. Less was more, more or less. They also had a nice steady cash flow to augment those aspirations as they ventured into new realms, keeping them both stimulated and satisfied. Furthermore, Jack and Sarah had together established some semblance of anonymity, as they were slowly slip- sliding away from an austere world that they were seriously attempting to escape, as they sought more solitude, self sufficiency, and sophistication, with several degrees of separation from a dissolute civilization, situated just outside of their planet-skimming 'Citadel'.

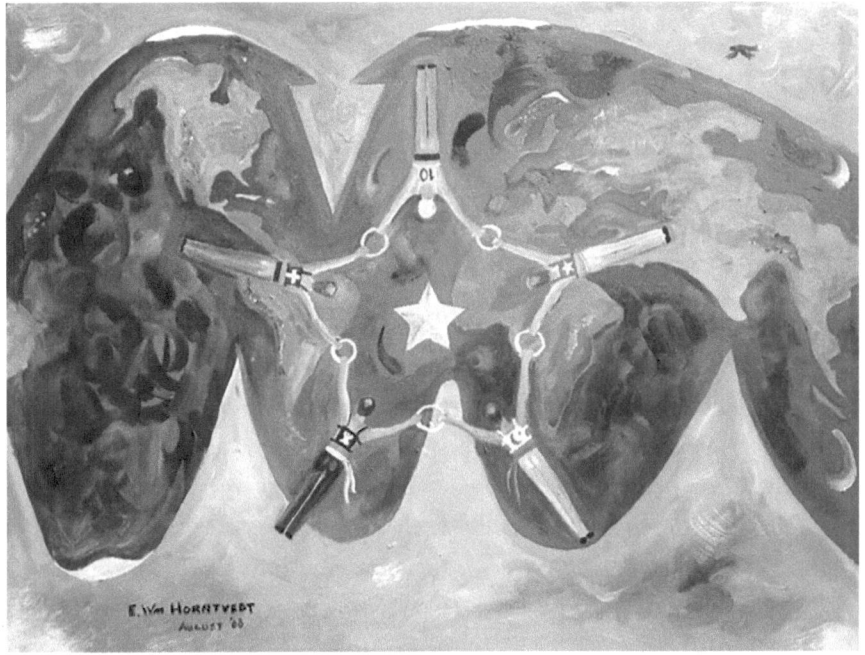

Small Blue Planet

TROMSØ TRISKELION TRYST

> "[The Triskelion] is related to Odin once more, and symbolizes the act of obtaining the mead of poetry (The skáldskaparmjöðr) a powerful source of power or the power of the words, speech and knowledge. Summarizing the tale, Odin stood with the giantess Gunnlöð in her cave for three nights and had sex with her. By doing so, he gained access to the mead of poetry, which she was guarding. Odin drank three times, three horns filled with the mead of poetry. After drinking the mead, he fled in the shape of an eagle directly to Asgard. The name of the three horns were so called, Óðrærir, Boðn and Són."
>
> - Arith Härger - http://whispersofyggdrasil.blogspot.com

The mist began to lift but was still a steamy shroud that required penetration to realize any invocation, as Jack and Sarah entered their sensuous shipboard sauna upon pulling into Stockholm. The melodious jazz music had a magical and mesmerizing effect as it engulfed their amalgamated auras and beseeched them inward toward their lascivious love grotto. Seated on the wooden bench against the cedar slat bulkhead, Jack dipped his ladle into the wooden water bucket and dropped another load of distilled water onto the hot rocks as more steam rose toward the ceiling, sending out sizzling sounds of saturated satisfaction as the searing stones released their reticent superheated vapors. The sweet smell of heated cedar ripped through the olfactory neurons in their nasal cavities as they settled back and inhaled the hot vapors, sensing the steam seeping into every open pore of their stressed and strained bodies.

Jack and Sarah felt exhilarated as they settled back into their newly installed shipboard sauna after miles of walking through the stony streets of Stockholm. Although they were in Sweden for a short stay, the particular port didn't really matter much since the different destinations all had their own unique fine qualities and attractions, and were fascinating in any light. What mattered was that the two of them could enjoy exotic new havens together, but could always return to their enchanted waterborne abode to relax after a long day to ruminate, reflect, and relax. So they began to morph a bit as they traveled, and would blend into their unique environs, as the two observed contrasting customs and cultures. Jack began to grow his hair and beard longer and don local attire, as Sarah began to wear her reddish locks in a Nordic maiden braid like a crown, and dress in a variety of leather and wool woven vests, with slim wool slacks, as the two assimilated within the Skandic settings. Sarah even braided some of Jack's longer locks to help him get into character, as they normalized to Nordic nuances.

Stockholm had a captivating history in any case, with its occult ties to Viking proclivities, as Jack and Sarah continued to play their impromptu parts in Nordic ports. Nevertheless, after steaming to a wide variety of cities and towns, to *Kristiansand* and *Stavanger* and beyond to take in the local attractions, the two tentative teammates began to feel like they had 'seen that movie before' as the attractions began to blend together and look a lot alike. As the 'sameness' began to sink in, they began to look forward to returning to their own little familiar floating hovel and private dwelling at each day's end, to take another sauna and get mellow. Many times they would also bring fresh fruit, fine fish, grains, and/or vegetables from the local markets to prepare their own dinners in the boat's well-equipped galley, if they were so inclined. They also encountered a lot of other work since the boat had become their 'home away from home' and needed to be maintained. In fact, they developed a pretty close relationship with their yacht since, like any home, if they took care of the boat, it took care of them. Therefore, they did routine maintenance on machinery together, as well as cleaning and other chores to make sure that everything was 'ship shape', equipment was secured and stowed in the proper places, and everything was in good working order; 'A place for everything, and everything in its place'. Sarah became pretty handy with working on the shipboard machinery and helping Jack with some of the duty, so they both began to feel as if they were part of the boat, and the boat was part of them. Jack would also demonstrate how to take readings on equipment, and show how various devices functioned so that Sarah understood the operation of each apparatus and how the parts worked together as a system. Jack explained sundry other components like the navigational aids, radios, engine performance, and how to control the boat in rougher water so that Sarah felt more self assured with the procedures while underway. So, the boat began to take up more of their time along with the trips to new and exotic places, as they both enjoyed being on the boat as well as getting away once in a while, to see many of the same old things.

Sure, they enjoyed some very fine restaurants and saw quite a few famous sites, some 'Saint Olav' type churches, as well as several 'Viking' and 'Whaling' museums on their walking tours, but after awhile much of it just became 'old hat'. Bergen was a little better as it seemed to them to be more like San Francisco with its seaside bistros, fun gift shops, a mountainside *'Mount Fløyen'* tram ride, and blossoming boulevards. But after that, they decided to just set a course for Tromsø, stopping to rest in a variety of ports as they made their way north, but mostly remaining aboard the yacht. They verily embraced the unscheduled routine more and more, as the days wound down and the daylight hours increased, since time began to lose its significance as the moments all began to meld together. There was no pressure to be anywhere, or do anything after a time, other than just enjoy their sauna sessions and motor north. Eventually, after spending several weeks on the churning Norwegian Sea, stopping in many charming seaside ports like Alesund, Brønnøysund, Narvik, Harstad, and Finnsnes, while occasionally venturing up some fabulous fjords, they finally reached Tromsø at the northern edge of Norway, and felt elated to ultimately reach an endpoint on their trek, for the allotted time of travel. By then, the two decided that they had 'enjoyed about as much as they could stand' of their semi-solitary existence, and agreed that the warmth of Havana and *'La Citadel Grandé Hotel & Suites'* would look pretty good to both of them for a while, as they began to plan a journey south and looked forward to seeing their fun loving fellow compatriots and time travellers again.

Be that as it may, their lengthy time at sea, as well as some mind-altering ports that they had visited, allowed Jack and Sarah to clear their heads and embrace some proxy perspectives that had previously lain dormant in Jack's metaphysical mind (and were never even considered by Sarah), for as long as Jack could remember. Jack posited that the world previously presented to him may have indeed been just a fabrication, and that it was probable that the world was actually quite different than most people were willing to acknowledge or accept relative to the small blue planet's formation and composition, as well as people's misinformed, and often times, incomplete perception of reality.

No, Jack believed that the earth was actually alive, and was a living pulsating planet with a heart and a soul, enveloped in a dynamic electromagnetic flux with a central sultry sun emitting energy, as well as being a formidable force of convulsive contention. Perhaps it was all just a test as well. So, as Jack reflected upon the writings of <u>Willis George Emerson</u> and his novel '*The Smoky God: Or The Voyage To The Inner World*', and other 'conspiracy theories', where the author compared the construction of the earth to that of a 'Geode', a hard rock and spherical boulder on the outside, yet hollow, with a thin crust and crystalline composition on the inside, it naturally gave Jack more food for thought. In the story, the author presupposes that the earth's crust is on average about 300 miles thick, and that the center of gravity is 'centered within that 300 mile circumference' at a depth of about 150 miles, and that the force of gravity can be felt on either side of the 300 mile thick crust, externally as well as internally. An interesting premise in any case! So, combined with his own travel experiences, and as he and his sensuous shipmate and sauna partner Sarah Reid traversed the raw wide surface of the watery planet to the north, Jack began to rationalize that the 'real world' might not actually be as 'straight forward' as what he had previously understood; and that the current citizens of planet earth may just actually be visitors in a place where they certainly participate, but whose origins may have been concealed from them by nefarious and obscure forces, yet hidden in plain sight. Though, perhaps his eyes were just playing tricks on him as he fancied fierce trolls and fairies flitting amid the jagged rocks while the two travelers twisted through the fabulous fjords, - or maybe they were elves - or perchance it was just the mysterious miscibility of the misty vapors mixing musically amongst the many waterfalls and cliffs as their motor yacht wound merrily, merrily through the quilted waters near the *Lofoten* Islands, and spun in and around the many rocky archipelagos within the *Vestfjorden*.

Be that as it may, Jack and Sarah began to pontificate those particular postulates more pensively, as Jack made preparations to put his boat into storage in Tromsø while he and Sarah also made additional plans to fly down to Havana for an extended period of time. The two of them spent about a week just getting to know the area in and around Tromsø with its Arctic University, famous Space and Physics Departments and universal good cheer as Jack contracted with a local marina to make some modifications to his boat to add an auxiliary fuel tank in the engine room, to extend the range for future travel. He paid a little extra to have some maintenance done on the diesel engines and auxiliary machinery, along with some general 'tender loving care' to get the boat in shape for the next cruise. He also contracted with the Marina to have a high-speed shipboard WiFi system installed with a dome for receiving satellite signals installed above the superstructure to allow him to get better service when venturing further out to sea. The fuel tank conversion would give him added assurance whilst he strayed further away from the coasts, while also improving efficiency underway. He had already installed a Reverse osmosis desalination system aboard the boat with a sizeable potable water tank for fresh water storage, so felt pretty good about his long term sustainability, reliability, and seaworthiness under adverse conditions, but wanted that extra edge.

So with that project in play, and with the boat being well cared for, Jack and Sarah hopped on a *Scandinavian* airline flight with Business Class tickets bound for Havana about a week after arriving in Tromsø. The two shipmates (and sauna mates) were thrilled about boarding an international airline flight south, as well as having someone else do the piloting after spending so many weeks on the water dodging whatever calamity came along. So as they settled into their comfortable leather sofa-bed seats to watch movies, sleep, and casually chat, they looked forward to the seventeen-hour flight to Havana via Oslo, without any outside cares in the world as they fantasized about the future. As they waved farewell to Odin, Freyja, Thor, Gunnlöð, and the other Norse spirits, they fancied that it would be fun to feel the warm ocean breezes off the northern coast of Old Havana along the *Malecón*, as well as visiting their old pals at '*La Citadel Grande Hotel & Suites*' once again, while strolling near the *Prado Esplanade*, and just casually sitting and chatting over some cool drinks or fine red wine at *El Floridita de Cuba Bar* once more, and relax, while talking about their travels.

The newlyweds down in Cuba, Joe and Laney Melnik, met Jack Redhouse and Sarah Reid at the Havana airport when they landed, and hailed a classic '54 Cadillac convertible cab outside of baggage claim for their return trip to '*La Citadel Grandé Hotel & Suites*' located in the older section of the city. The four embraced each other as they met, while Joe couldn't get over how much the two appeared to have just stepped off a Viking longship prior to landing in the island country. Back at the hotel they also met up with Elise Lopez and some friends as they all gave Jack and Sarah big hugs and began to fill them in on the wonderful progress they had been making with the property developments. They also discovered that Frank and Carol were planning to fly down from Kansas a few days later, after they heard that Jack and Sarah were flying in from Norway. Within a couple hours of their arrival though, Jack and Sarah confessed that they were just too exhausted from the long flight from Tromsø to keep their heads off the table, and needed to get some rest. So Joe handed Jack the keycards to the penthouse suite on the rooftop of the '*Citadel Grandé Hotel*' for the couple to crash for a day or so, and catch up on their sleep. They would all get together again later to talk and party, after Jack and Sarah partially recovered from their jet lag.

So, to put things into perspective, it was sometime in early June when Jack and Sarah emerged from the penthouse suite on the rooftop of the *Citadel Grandé Hotel* and rejoined their friends to celebrate, and tour the grounds around the hotel. Frank Valero and Carol Mulhaney were expected to arrive from Kansas that same afternoon so they could all get together to compare notes while in Cuba. Garry and Zak had also heard the news about Jack and Sarah, and were expecting to meet up with everyone the following week as well. Meanwhile, Joe Melnik and Laney began to take the two new arrivals through the various renovated buildings to show them the upgrades in the individual hotel rooms as well as the new

'*Prado Promenade*' restaurant, the '*Café de Marti*' café and improvements to the outside façade, while Jack and Sarah began to acclimate to the new time zone. Work crews had either replaced or sand blasted the outside stones of the hotel so that it looked like a brand new building with a new *façade*, and was spectacular compared with some of the adjacent buildings. They had also replaced whole window sections throughout the hotel, as well as some of the doors and carpeting. They kept some of the older huge wooden doors but refinished them as appropriate, to keep their 'old world charm', while making them appear more elegant. The architects managing the project were doing a wonderful job keeping everything on track with a Gantt chart detailing which task needed to be tackled next. Although Joe and Laney were busy 24/7 with work, they enjoyed their new roles as 'Hotel Directors' as the renovation project advanced. Every day, several new issues arose that they needed to confront and/or resolve but they were handling problems and customer concerns quite well. If things became too chaotic, they could hand the responsibilities over to Laney's cousin Elise Lopez for a few days while they skipped across the water to Key West, Florida, or Miami, or over to Cancun for a few days for a short break, so the two newlyweds had found their 'sweet spot' as far as work was concerned, and the positions paid pretty well to boot.

As Jack and Sarah began to loosen up a bit, and acclimate to the time change and the temperate climate, they began to talk more about their recent travel experiences as well as their iconoclastic personal perspectives. Laney was the first to recognize a subtle change in Sarah's views with her deeper appreciation for the world around her, and a more grounded 'sophistication' compared with her earlier sophomoric slant on reality. She also noticed her closeness with Jack, as well as Jack's more caring character towards Sarah. So it seemed that their travel together had benefited them both. Laney recognized that Jack's earlier courtship and subsequent split with her good friend Estee had also happened for all of the right reasons, so was quite comfortable with the couple that was standing before her that had ascended above that fray, and was impressed by their resultant metamorphosis. As Laney began to question Sarah more about their recent travels, she became even more intrigued as Sarah began to explain their many sensuous sauna sessions as well as their discoveries around the Norse countries, their cultures, customs, and behaviors. Laney wanted to learn more, so Sarah mentioned that many people in the northern realms still adhere to assorted pagan beliefs and rituals, as well as summer and winter solstice celebrations like 'Midsummer' (summer solstice), and 'Mayday' (traditionally the 1st day of summer), which Sarah also found intriguing. "Thor, Odin, Freyja, and other Gods are still very much alive and well, and a significant influence in their cultures", explained Sarah.

"Although many people converted to Christianity several hundred years ago, the Scandinavian people truly venerate their Viking past, and still associate with sundry rituals and social behaviors that reflect those religious rites, while finding pleasure in less conventional pastimes, which we found to be quite intriguing relative to our own needs, wants and desires, and the enjoyment I personally draw from dancing and music", revealed Sarah. "Tell me more", said Laney. "Were your sauna sessions really that stimulating?', she asked. "Well actually, it goes beyond that" said Sarah. "In fact, Jack and I have had many intimate conversations over the past month or so about truth, morality, and alternative lifestyles", she continued. "Why is it that we behave the way we do; where did we learn our social behavior? A lot was passed on from parents, friends, or siblings, while other aspects were learned from watching the behavior of others in large and small groups. But what if another world exists, from which many of these behaviors and beliefs may have originated earlier? Jack and I have discussed the possibility of additional journeys to forgotten lands further north, beyond the known realms we currently understand or acknowledge, through a silent misty shroud that may lead to another world within the earth's interior, that may be much more elegant than the world we've known, yet with limitless and perpetual possibilities", added Sarah, passionately.

"Perhaps you two need another nap", said Laney with a laugh. Nevertheless, Laney began to think about what Sarah had said, and still wanted to know more about their recent trip, as well as where they might be heading next. But first she wanted to head over to the Havana airport with Joe Melnik to greet Frank Valero and Carol Mulhaney who were arriving that afternoon. In a similar manner to Jack and Sarah's arrival, when the two Kansas passengers landed at the airport, Joe hailed a classic '56 Chevy convertible cab as Frank and Carol emerged from outside of baggage claim and they all made their way back to the *Citadel Hotel*. The time zone was not all that different between Cuba and Kansas, so the two new arrivals didn't suffer the same jet lag that Jack and Sarah had. Therefore, they were in their prime party personalities as they pulled up to the parking area in front of the hotel, grabbed their bags from the trunk, and as Joe handed their room keycards to them both, they headed up to one of their favorite suites at the *Citadel Hotel*.

Frank and Carol had a few days to acclimate and see the progress on all of the renovated portions of the hotel, restaurant, and café just as Jack and Sarah had previewed the project previously. It would be a few more days until Garry and Zak would arrive to go through a similar routine, since none of the other partners had seen the progress since a few months earlier when they had attended Joe and Laney's Havana wedding in mid-March. That being said, they were all impressed with the updated décor and were genuinely pleased with the way the whole restoration project was progressing. So, with that part of their reunion accomplished, they all decided to celebrate at a few of their favorite hotel and 'stand alone' bars in the area, and just enjoy the warmer weather over some delicious Cuban drinks in delightful 'Old Havana', near the *Citadel Hotel*. It was almost the weekend anyway, and Garry and Zak weren't scheduled to arrive until the following Monday. That gave them all a few days to get reacquainted before they would need to put their thinking caps back on and talk a little business. So they used their special time to just relax and enjoy the whole Cuban Colonial ambience of the Old Havana area along the *Prada Esplanade* to the group's total, complete, and utter satisfaction.

When Gary and Zak finally arrived in Havana from Panama the following Monday, their gracious hosts Joe and Laney Melnik went through the same 'classic convertible' routine once again, only the next time, the cab outside of baggage claim was a 1955 maroon and white 'Buick Special' ragtop for the return trip to the hotel. Garry and Zak were quite pleased with the reception and fan club at the airport, but were not quite as cheerful as they had intended to be due to some recent news that they would need to impart to all of their good friends and partners in Havana. Joe and Laney could see the sadness in their Russian friend's faces as they waited to hear the dire news. Upon checking into the *Citadel Hotel* along with the others, the whole group quickly got together down at the newly remodeled *'Prado Promenade'* restaurant and bar for an impromptu pow wow, prior to their planned tour. They all ordered a few of their favorite drinks from the new bartender while Zakhar Maxikov presented the group with the unfortunate news they had only just learned themselves that same morning. As it happened, while Miguel and Ignacio had been making regular scheduled deliveries along the Hotel Strip in Cancun, Mexico for the past couple of months as instructed, it turned out that they were not the 'good soldiers' that Zak had assumed, as the recent bad news had obviously proven otherwise. Zak had a rough time getting the story out initially, but after a couple of quick sips of the Bloody Mary he was nursing, he just sort of blurted out the announcement that "Seumas Santaña is dead". Then, with the hard part out of the way, he was able to reveal a bit more about the regrettable event, along with the current status. Evidently, while making their delivery to *Guillermo's Grill* the day before, where Seumas had just started his afternoon bartending shift, Miguel and Ignacio delivered a couple of boxes of liquor as usual, but then Miguel turned quickly and shot Seumas twice in the chest and once in the head before the two casually walked out of the grill back to their delivery van, and sped away.

Seumas had been fearful of the two unruly characters since their arrival about a month earlier, since Seumas clearly understood that he was probably the last person the two bandits had seen, prior to their waking up in Panama after Seumas had spiked their bottle of rum down in Chetumal a couple of months earlier. As a result, Seumas kept a pistol handy beneath the bar counter in case the two hombres ever became reckless, but unfortunately for Seumas, he was about 10 feet away from his revolver when Miguel got the drop on him. In retrospect, he should have taken the two punks out as soon as they landed in Cancun, since he figured that they would eventually put two and two together and the needle would then point directly at Seumas as the guy that betrayed them. Seumas was reluctant to act for fear of reprisals from the local police if he took them out as intended. In any case, most everyone in the *Grill* having lunch at the time of the shooting had witnessed the incident, and had given multiple descriptions of the assailants to the local police, who quickly identified Miguel Parás as the shooter, and Ignacio Escondido as his accomplice. Following the shooting, they immediately issued a public statement saying that it appeared to be a 'gangland slaying' as both the assailants and the victim had once been members of the same notorious *'Los Santos'* gang that had recently been behind many other grizzly acts in the Yucatan peninsula. The police also announced that the 'assailants were still at large, and their whereabouts were unknown' at that time. The police and Mexican military had cordoned off the area and conducted a thorough search of businesses, warehouses, and dwellings immediately after the shooting, but it appeared that the perpetrators might have escaped the immediate area. Other departments in adjacent cities had been notified, as well as a bulletin issued to apprehend the suspects as soon as possible for further questioning. As a consequence, the group then sitting at the table all faced a much larger problem.

If the two suspects were immediately apprehended, they might sing like canaries about a whole slew of info known prior to the event, including confessing their earlier kidnapping of Jack Redhouse in Cancun, the subsequent armed rescue by his pals, Frank, Joe, Garry and Zak, and their Panamanian pals, the eventual unscheduled swim along the Mexican coast of *Quintana Roo* when Jack made them an offer that they couldn't refuse, their subsequent meeting with Seumas Santaña in Chetumal after the two assailants were rescued by a research vessel that just happened to be cruising off the coast as the two thugs swam for their freedom, their unconscious trip down to Panama after being drugged by Seumas, as well as the pièce de résistance, 'Operation Highjack', and the transfer of the stolen Russian gold to *'Victory Liner 504'* and its successive crossing on a Russian oil tanker to St. Petersburg, Russia. Surely, the Cuban authorities would be most interested in that little bit of information, which could implicate many of the members seated around the table at the time, who were then surreptitiously sipping their drinks at the moment of revelation, and contemplating their next moves. Sadly, what Garry and Zak had just revealed was probably just a small portion of what the two banditos knew, and could therefore reveal, so all of a sudden, their whereabouts became a major concern to both Garry and Zak, as well as the others.

As Jack began to read the tealeaves in his smooth double-trouble on-the-rocks scotch in front of him, he thought, 'How perfect!' It was almost as if Garry and Zak had planned it all along!' he thought, as he knew how their minds worked, and began to see the writing on the wall. If the two Russians played their chess pieces correctly they could control every aspect of the game. You could almost see the smoke coming out of Jack's ears as the wheels began to rotate at about 18,000 RPM, while he quickly began to formulate a 'Plan B', and maybe 'C, D, E, and F', as his metaphysical mind rapidly morphed ahead at warp speed to find a solution to the complex equation that had been thrust upon him.

"So, what's your next move Zak?", asked Jack. "If you've known about this for the past several hours as you flew up from Panama to Havana, surely you've considered what is at stake here, as well as the possible consequences if something isn't done quickly, and have considered what needs to be done next!" Jack asserted. "As you well know, Joe and I didn't want any part of the fun and games with your Cuban gold heist and the oil tanker plan, but went along with the program to try to make it a little easier for you. Now we seem to be neck deep in Kansas cow dung waiting for the 'Gendarmes' to come over and kick the door down. That doesn't give us a warm fuzzy feeling, as I'm sure you're well aware", continued Jack, a bit peeved. Zak was quite remorseful with his response knowing that, had he taken care of the two gangsters while they were still in Cuba, he wouldn't be telling his sad story at that time. Zak could have just as easily flown the two thugs to Panama or anywhere else for that matter, but after they had been so helpful with the transfer of gold a couple of months earlier, he thought that they might straighten out and fly right. Also, since the two goons had previously made liquor deliveries along the hotel strip in Cancun for a good duration, Zak figured that they could be trusted to behave going forward. In retrospect, that was a mistake. So, Zak wasn't vying for more action, he just wanted the situation to stabilize. "Well, yes, of course we've thought about it quite a bit Jack, and as you well know, time is of the essence here. We have our antennae out as well as people on the ground out looking for the two of them now, and will take care of the situation quickly in any case. This is no longer your concern as the scope of the problem is now much larger than even I can convey to you in confidence at this time. I can say that we have our own intelligence, and that as a result, we believe that we have the situation under control for the time being. Nevertheless, due to our close proximity to Cancun, here in Havana, it's possible that changes can come quickly, so we need to take some precautions. We also believe that Miguel and Ignacio are headed to Havana next, since Miguel's last threat to me was, and I quote, *"You tell*

Jack that he hasn't seen the last of us. We still owe him for shooting me in the leg". Of course, we know that it wasn't you that popped a cap in his leg since you were the one being rescued. Nevertheless, he blames you for the incident, even though *they* were the ones that committed the crime of kidnapping. But that's how their minds work. Nevertheless, it is our recommendation based on our current intelligence, that we immediately make plans to return Frank and Carol to Kansas, and that you and Sarah, as well as Joe and Laney take a short vacation somewhere out of the country until this whole mess blows over. If it's any consolation, we know where these guys are presently, and we've taken precautions to contain the situation, and will shortly take them out of the picture permanently. We also feel confident that they won't be arriving in Havana within the next 12 hours due to their current mode of transportation, but that's all that I can reveal to you at this time. In any case, our team needs to make certain that they'll never disclose additional information from this moment forward. So, that's where we stand. Also, we don't recommend that you tell us, or anyone else where you are headed next, although we can guess, and you should make plans to get there quickly!" Zak concluded.

"OK, Zak. I get it. So, I guess we pack our bags right now and catch the first flight out. Sarah, Joe, Laney, please pack your bags in the next 20 minutes and meet me in the lobby in thirty. Frank and Carol, I suggest that you follow suit as well. We can all go to the airport together and decide on our destinations later. We're out of here beginning now!", said Jack, as they all stood up and stepped away from the table, waved a single salute to Garry and Zak, and headed up to their rooms to pack. As they were walking away Jack turned back to the table and said, "Zak, could you please call us a couple of cabs? We'll be back down in about 30 minutes. Thanks", then turned again and walked away.

BEYOND THE SHROUD

> *"He is the God who sits in the center, on the navel of the earth, and is the interpreter of religion to all mankind"* – Plato *(From 'The Smoky God' by Willis George Emerson)*

Down in the hotel lobby, Jack, Sarah, Joe, and Laney met up with Carol and Frank, as they all hopped into one of the two cabs waiting with their engines running at the front entrance of the hotel. Garry and Zak waved goodbye as the six of them sped away toward the Havana airport in hardtop classic cars for their departure flights. Elise Lopez and her relatives were not at risk in any case, since they were never included in the previous conversations about Jack's operations with Garry and Zak, so the main concern was for the six people that had just left the hotel.

Upon arrival at *José Martí International Airport* (HAV) in Havana, Jack and the others gathered their roller bags and walked directly over to the ticket counter area where Jack paid the difference for Frank and Carol to make their return flight back to Kansas City with their round-trip tickets, then purchased four more one-way Business Class tickets to Helsinki, Finland International airport (HEL) for himself and his three other close friends. He would fill them in on the details after they checked their bags through airport security and were settled in the Business Class lounge waiting to board their flight. Once there, they could relax, enjoy some stiff drinks, discuss their options, and grab a sandwich prior to boarding the ten-hour flight across the Atlantic to Jack's favorite port of all ports, Helsinki, Finland. Frank and Carol said 'farewell' to the others as they passed through security and headed to their respective gates, and all agreed to stay in touch as they learned more. Since neither Joe Melnik, nor his new wife Laney had been to Helsinki previously, they were actually quite thrilled about the quick switch in plans, and were looking forward to a change in summer scenery away from the hotel (although they would miss Elise Lopez and the others, but hoped to be away for only a couple of weeks at most). In fact, in many ways it would be like a honeymoon for the newly wedded couple, since they hadn't really had one yet with all of the work they were doing at the hotel. Garry and Zak would take over the daily operation of the hotel and renovation projects in the interim while the dust settled, and as the situation in Havana stabilized. The Russians had plenty of work to do as well in any case, since they were right in the middle of their new microbrewery and distillery construction project adjacent to the hotel, and needed to oversee that operation anyway while in Havana. The little group at the airport all had questions, but few had answers except for Jack, since he knew exactly what he was doing. So the rest of the group just followed Jack's lead.

Within a couple of hours from their arrival at the airport the four travellers settled into their business class seats aboard their *Finnish* airline flight as they rotated out of Havana and headed across the North Atlantic to Helsinki. The flight was actually quite enjoyable for all four passengers as they soon landed at (HEL), took the train to the Central Train Station in Helsinki, hopped on the number '6' tram on the south end of the station exit heading northwest, and rode back to Jack's apartment on the Boulevard. Although the overseas flight had been comfortable enough, the four of them felt a bit exhausted after the past traumatic 24 hours, so after Jack put away his roller bag in his apartment, he asked Sarah to get some rest as he walked Joe and Laney over to a very nice hotel just up the street from the apartment. He booked a room for the two of them at the hotel, revealing that he would check in on them later the next day after they had all gotten a good nights rest, and would get together with them for dinner the following evening. They then bid each other farewell as Jack walked down the boulevard about two blocks away, back to his apartment.

The following day, after about ten hours of sleep and a solid breakfast, Jack and Sarah headed downstairs to the sauna for a little relaxation and entertainment to dial down the stress from the previous couple of days, and relax. Afterwards, they went for a walk down to *Stockmann's* near the City Center to do a little shopping and just have a general walk around town to loosen up a bit. The two of them knew that Joe and Laney would still be adjusting to the time difference and may not even be out of bed yet, so they took their sweet time looking around, and picked up a few needed items for the apartment before walking back up the boulevard to their place. Later that same afternoon around 5:00 PM Jack received a call from Zak with some relevant news. The time difference between Helsinki and Havana was seven hours, so that 5:00 PM in the late afternoon in Helsinki equated to 10:00 AM the same morning in Havana. Zak filled Jack in on some of the intelligence that Zak had known about earlier, but couldn't convey to Jack due to the seriousness of the situation at the time. Nevertheless, after Jack heard the information he better understood what had happened. Zak gave Jack some peripheral details over the phone, but since it was an open line, he held some of the information back. Eventually, after a couple of weeks had passed, Zak flew to Helsinki on business, and met with Jack and Sarah for dinner and drinks to explain the whole episodic chronology of events in more detail.

So, as they later learned, after Miguel Parás shot Seumas Santaña at the grill and the two thugs, Miguel and Ignacio sped away together in their delivery van, they immediately boarded a cruise ship bound for Miami with some simple disguises, with the intention of catching a flight back to Havana after they reached their destination port in Florida. That mistake bought Zak and his comrades a little time since they had some of their people on the same cruise liner bound for Miami as a precaution. Zak withheld that information from Jack Redhouse for everyone's safety when they had all met in Havana, since he couldn't reveal the source of the intelligence at the time. In any case, while still aboard the cruise ship, a couple of Zak's people located Miguel and Ignacio down at one of the shipboard bars brooding and boozing on some cheap rum and kept a close eye on their actions. As they left the bar area later that evening and were returning to their cabin, the two of them met up with a couple of very large Russians who persuaded them to take another swim in the Gulf of Mexico; but this time they were too far out at sea to be rescued by any passing ships. Indeed, the two banditos didn't even struggle much as they knew they were guilty and were already dead. As they were physically lifted off the main deck, they watched the ship's waterline race toward them at 32 feet per second squared while being tossed overboard like two crumpled up paper cups, falling into the ship's wake as they were both washed out to sea like yesterday's garbage. As it happened, Zak had a back up plan if the situation had gone south, since they also had people positioned in the local police departments, the jails, and in the Mexican military who might have been called upon to serve their country if necessary. Zak had withheld that knowledge from Jack when they all met at the hotel bar in Havana, but he couldn't take any chances or leave any loose ends during the crisis, so had to let the whole thing play out. So in the end, that was the sad seditious story of Seumas, Ignacio, and Miguel that was afterwards just a page out of history, as Jack and his friends eventually returned to their normal work routines following the tragic incident.

Joe and Laney Melnik eventually flew back to Havana from Helsinki after the problem had been buried at sea, while Frank and Carol were never in any real danger from the start, since the whole situation had been sufficiently contained within about 48 hours after the crisis had originated. As icing on the cake, Joe and Laney were able to experience a little slice of northern Europe while they were sufficiently entertained by Jack and Sarah for a couple of weeks in Helsinki, Finland. They also learned to enjoy the fine hotel sauna facilities during their short sojourn in Helsinki while visiting all of the usual attractions in Finland with their gracious hosts. Nevertheless, after a couple of weeks of lounging around and getting a bit restless, Joe and Laney decided that it was time to return to Havana to check the progress with the reconstruction project, and to just generally get back to work with their busy lives. So upon thanking Jack and Sarah for their hospitality, they all took the train back to the Helsinki- Vantaa airport together where Laney and Joe caught another business class flight back to Cuba after the situation in Havana returned to normal. That being the case, it was now time for Jack and Sarah to continue their journey north, revisit their boat in Tromsø, and decide where they would be heading to next.

By then, mid-June was behind them as the weather turned fabulous in Finland at that time of year. They spent another week just milling around the area, taking trains to and fro, while planning their next journey. They also had quite a few discussions about what would make them both happy relative to their combined futures now that they had gotten to know each other a little bit better. To be honest, they were both beginning to feel quite content with their present situation as it was structured, but were trying to look ahead a bit toward the future. Nonetheless, it was also a perfect time of year to head back up to Tromsø to inspect the modifications to Jack's boat, as well as conduct some sea trials if the boat conversions had been completed. If the modifications had been completed they might take the boat out for a short cruise north of Tromsø up to Svalbard, to check the yacht's performance. It would also be good to visit the local areas around Tromsø again, especially during the warmer summer months, they concluded.

Now, as unfortunate and tragic as the deaths of Seumas, Miguel, and Ignacio had been, their auspicious timing may have been judicious, since they probably left the small blue planet during prime time. And, although they paid the ultimate price for their pain and suffering, and sins, if and when the world economic bubble finally broke, the anguish that the rest of humankind might face would make their plight pale by comparison. Remember, there was no 'real' money in the Western world, only digits in cyberspace filling the void of confidence, backed by nothing but debt (notes) and credit (more debt), so that if and when the holding bar eventually snapped shut, and the hammer struck the plate, overdue chaos would follow. So, the system was broken. The puzzling thing to Jack was why people still believed that money was real, though as long as people accepted what the government told them, the scam stayed afloat. It was global musical chairs; and the music was still playing, but if the music stopped, there weren't nearly enough chairs to go around.

As a backstory, some of Jack's earlier ancestors had emigrated from Norway to North America in the late 1800's during a previous mass migration when things were similarly a little hectic in the world. Some of Jack's early relatives had hailed from around Bardu, Norway, up around Trondheim, but later settled around Tynset, Norway prior to eventually turning up in Minnesota. Jack's Great Grandfather had been a 'Master Builder' in Norway, and the third son in a rather large family, so knowing that he wouldn't be getting the family farm, he left Norway to find more fertile ground in the young developing country across the big pond. So some of Jack's DNA had originated near a place where he was now having some work done on his boat. As a result, Jack felt a kinship to the area around Tromsø, and thought that perhaps it might even be time to return the favor, and just emigrate back. Consequently, in late June, Sarah and

Jack took the four-hour flight from Helsinki to Tromsø to get back into the swing of things, and booked a few nights at a nice hotel near the water in downtown Tromsø before checking in with the marina regarding the boat. The additional time would allow them to decompress and enjoy the area prior to getting on with their future travel plans.

After a couple of days in Tromsø, Jack and Sarah took a cab over to the marina where Jack's motor yacht was secured next to the dock ready for Jack's personal inspection. The craftsman at the marina had gotten a little creative and had installed two new ample sized doubled walled fuel tanks made of type 316 stainless steel on both the port and starboard sides to provide more capacity as well as to balance the load within the hull. They had also curved the tanks to fit within the frames of the hull, and painted them to match the bulkhead, so that if a person didn't know they were there, they would think that the tanks were just part of the ship's hull. They also installed some SST ball valves in the fuel line for fuel shut-off, along with a bypass line to allow for maintenance if necessary, and connected the new lines to the main fuel lines, so Jack was more than pleased with the results. He could isolate the tanks for normal operation while underway and just use the tanks when required for extra capacity. In addition, the work crew had serviced the Detroit diesel engines, performed some general maintenance on the auxiliary equipment, and scrubbed the boat down from fore to aft, and port to starboard, so that it sat there shining like a brand new boat. The new satellite dome for the WiFi internet system also gave the boat a 'High Tech' look that made it appear important. Again, Jack was more than impressed with their work. It was as if the work team enjoyed the boat more than Jack. One could almost see a broad smile painted across the bow as it sat there proud as a penguin. So, with the boat overhauled and ready to go, Jack settled up with the marina and decided that he would take the boat out for a check ride the following day. The two shipmates also stocked the walk-in cooler and freezer with an added supply of groceries like fish, meats, bread, grains and fruits and some good red and white wines for a long trip. He then asked the work crew at the marina to go over the boat one more time to double-check their work as well as top off the tanks for an extended cruise. He also informed them that he would probably be heading up to Svalbard to check out that area for a short spell, but would most likely be returning within a couple of weeks. The crew at the marina understood Jack's instructions and made the necessary preparations for Jack and Sarah's next excursion, as Jack and Sarah returned to the hotel to pack.

So it was sometime on a crisp blue morning shortly after the summer solstice, heading into the warmest time of the year, that Jack and Sarah loaded their gear on Jack's refurbished patrol boat and 'set sail' for Svalbard. Sarah was dressed in a fitted pair of blue denim jeans and low cut boots, wearing a denim jacket over a light green knitted sweater top with her reddish hair pulled back in a braided bun, while Jack was wearing what he always wore, a cotton shirt with blue jeans and a ball cap. It was a beautiful day on the water with brilliant sunshine as Jack did a quick check of the shipboard equipment and lit off the diesel engines, pulling away from the dock and out of the Tromsø harbor toward the port of Longyearbyen, Svalbard, Norway. With nearly 24 hours of daylight during that time of year in Nordic northern Europe, it all seemed like one long day anyway, but it was a delightful morning nonetheless. The trip up to Svalbard would take them several days to a week regardless, since the distance from Tromsø to Longyearbyen was roughly 1,000 miles. Jack and Sarah could always head down to their shipboard sauna for some additional fun and relaxation in any case, if they wanted to take a break from the daylight or the cooler summer weather on the water. Of course, in that case Sarah would need to shed her denim jacket, but she could keep her boots on. Jack would need to lose the ballcap. Jack had booked a few nights at an attractive *Radisson Blu* hotel in Longyearbyen for their short stay to give them both a little break away from the boat when they arrived, while allowing for some comfortable accommodations, and a bit more elbow room. Since neither of them had ever been to Svalbard previously, they were both looking forward to seeing the well kempt little Arctic Circle town and doing some sightseeing during their layover.

Now, as many people in the modern world know (and according to the text on page 39 of Willis George Emerson's novel entitled '*The Smoky God*', where he writes "Olaf Jansen claims that the northern aperture, intake or hole, so to speak, is about fourteen hundred miles across", we are often kept in the dark regarding what is real, and what is not. So, one of the things that had been gnawing at Jack's sense of reality for quite some time, and might subsequently lead to some satisfaction on his part, was to know for certain whether a large opening at the top of the world did indeed exist, that might lead to an inner world with its own radiant sun and green pastures, populated by benevolent and amiable giant humans, with 'three hundred foot tall' trees and woolly mammoths, along with many lost species of birds inside the inner earth? And, if so, why weren't other people curious about that possibility? Especially since most people in the northern hemisphere had seen the northern lights at one time or another radiating spectacularly from that very same magnificent hole for multiple millennia! And of course, Santa Claus had to have his workshop somewhere; so who's to say that he and Mrs. Claus, along with Santa's elves didn't actually reside in the inner earth, with an opening up near the North Pole where they could come and go as they pleased without outside detection and/or interference? Indeed, 'Rudolph the Red Nosed', along with Dasher, and Dancer, and Prancer, and Vixen, Comet, and Cupid, and Donder and Blitzen, were probably all reindeer that hailed from the Svalbard area where most all of the hardiest reindeer were harbored. It was all beginning to make some sense to Jack. For that matter, since Jack was originally from Minnesota, perhaps even Paul Bunyan, along with Babe his blue ox also came from that same region. There was so much that Jack didn't fully understand, while the answers may have all been sitting directly ahead of him for some time. The other myth that needed clarification was 'why did icebergs consist of frozen fresh water that contained no salt', if they were sitting right in the middle of a salty sea? There were multiple explanations as to why that was the case (ice from snow, glaciers, icecaps, etc.), but the explanations were not necessarily correct. Where did the fresh water originate? Furthermore, since Tromsø was actually one of the northernmost cities in the world (even north of Duluth, Minnesota where Sanjo lived with his wife Marissa), situated within the Arctic Circle, and Svalbard was 1,000 miles north of Tromsø (so, even closer to the Arctic Circle), how difficult would it be for Jack and Sarah to just casually motor up that way during the warmest time of the year to see for themselves whether an opening existed at the top of the world, Jack wondered? Why the hell not? They were up that way anyway, and their boat had been fitted with extra fuel tanks, thought Jack. Furthermore, for good measure, Jack could strap on a few barrels of diesel fuel to the aft deck for safe measure while in Svalbard, and easily investigate the big gaping hole at the top of the small blue planet personally. Meanwhile, Jack and Sarah could continue to enjoy their sensuous little sauna sessions all the way up to the Arctic Circle and back, whiling the time away.

After breaking out of the fjords into the Norwegian Sea leaving Tromsø, the two shipmates spent a couple of days with the boat's compass pointed pretty much straight north until they finally arrived in Longyearbyen, and tied the boat up in the harbor alongside quite a few other boats and ships, some of which were much larger than Jack's little 81 foot long patrol craft. Upon securing the boat they checked into the *Radisson Blu* hotel, and stowed their gear. The accommodations were quite comfortable with a nice little 'in house restaurant' and a separate bar, as well as all of the amenities of a fine hotel, so Jack and Sarah were impressed. They decided to go down to the hotel restaurant to celebrate their little trek north with a romantic candlelight dinner and some delicious red wine, and text their friends back in Kansas, Minnesota, Havana, and Panama to say 'Hello'. They were seated at a very cozy little table by an outside window overlooking the glacier hills of Svalbard while they ordered a main course of delicious fish, potatoes and cabbage, with some white wine from the menu, as they texted with their friends on the other side of the small blue planet.

Jack had six friends listed on the same combined text message link; Frank, Joe, Sanjo, Carol, Sarah, and Zak, as he wrote a short message, and casually hit 'send';

Jack cell;

Now sitting at the Radisson Blu restaurant in Svalbard, Norway with Sarah Reid contemplating our next move. Wish you were here. :-)

Frank cell;

Glad we're not! Sounds like a cold place to eat.

Joe cell;

What are you doing way the hell up there? Thought you were in Helsinki!

Jack cell;

Just up here for a short spell, and maybe a Viking visit to see Odin and Thor in Asgard. Thinking about checking out the entrance to the inner earth up at the Arctic Circle! What do you think? Should Sarah and I go for it?

Zak cell;

Hahaa. Hello Jack, everything is going well down here. We're now back down in Panama after spending some time in Havana. Do you really think the entrance exists?

Jack cell;

Not that far away from it now. Less ice in the summertime with 24 hours of daylight. Sarah and I may cruise up that way just to see what we can find. Sound reasonable?

Sanjo cell;

I thought you were still in Havana! You're almost as far north as Duluth! Let me know when you're in the neighborhood, and I'll meet you for a cold pale ale.

Joe cell;

Go for it, Jack! You probably won't get another chance!

Frank cell;

Why not? What could go wrong, … go wrong, … go wrong …?

Carol cell;

Be careful Sarah and Jack. We miss you!

Sarah cell;

You won't miss me 'til I'm gone (lol).

Jack cell;

Ditto for me.

Jack cell;

We'll keep you posted. If you don't hear from us soon, we're probably sleeping with the giants. We'll let you know if we find some music in 'them thar hills'.

Jack cell;

PS; If you lose our signal, we're probably already inside (lol).

Carol cell;

That's not funny, Jack.

With the texting out of the way, Jack and Sarah talked it over and decided together that a little trip north wouldn't hurt in any case. If they ran into some resistance, like lots of ice, or rough weather, they could just turn around and head back to Longyearbyen and/or Tromsø. They had come a long way already, so why not give it a shot?

So the next day they just walked around Longyearbyen touring the local museum and checking out the local attractions. Jack also went down to the harbor and spoke with a work crew near the docks about getting a couple barrels of diesel fuel strapped to the aft deck of his boat with some cargo straps if the diesel fuel was available. He asked the men to just go ahead and do it if they could find the fuel, and he would pay them cash for their troubles, so they said they would see what they could find. All Jack wanted was a little extra insurance since he had plenty of extra rubber hose and a hand pump on board to transfer the fuel later if necessary. He gave them five hundred Norwegian Krona cash for their troubles and told them to keep it in any case. Then Jack and Sarah continued their walking tour. Later that evening they had another delightful dinner at the hotel restaurant and talked a bit more about a possible trip north. They were both feeling quite satisfied at that point in their lives, and enjoyed being in the Arctic Circle where there seemed to be less focus on world troubles, less personal angst between members of the immediate population, and less chaos; where people seemed to pay more attention to where their next meal was coming from and how to stay warm rather than a crashing economy. Perhaps it was just a case of a lower density population. Less people meant less trouble. Again, less was more, more or less. In any case, they were both content while enjoying each other's company and their time away. After another good night's rest, Jack walked down to the harbor the following morning to see whether the guys he spoke with earlier were able to get hold of a couple of extra barrels of diesel fuel. To Jack's surprise, they had already secured the full barrels with cargo straps to the aft deck as requested. They had apparently found the fuel on another one of the vessels in port, and had requisitioned them. Jack thanked the gentlemen and paid them for their trouble, giving them some additional cash for their efforts. He and Sarah would head north the following morning just to have a look around. Jack was excited about the prospect of actually exploring the ocean extremities north of Longyearbyen, but really had no idea of what to expect. Other ships, like Russian research vessels, were traveling up that way also, so it seemed like a harmless enough adventure. Jack had also heard rumors from people living in the area that there was less ice up in the Arctic Circle than years past, as the earth was changing and more of the ice cap was melting. Perhaps it was freezing again elsewhere, but nobody seemed to know. In any case, the people that lived that far north were mainly concerned about the conditions in their own community, and not so concerned with conditions in other areas of the small blue planet.

The following morning they checked out of their comfortable Longyearbyen hotel and made their way down to the docks again with their gear. Upon getting settled aboard the boat and conducting the normal checks, Jack fired up the diesel engines and gently eased the boat away from the docks out into the open harbor of the *Isfjorden*, then out into the open waters of the *Greenland Sea*, before pointing the yacht north again. From there, Jack headed to where the northern lights normally appeared ahead of their location and set the controls on automatic pilot to maintain his course. The water was a little rougher as they made their way north with a few higher wavelets with longer wavelengths for several hours into the second day, but there wasn't a lot of ice, and after a short time the sea calmed down as the air became warmer, almost balmy, as they continued to motor further north. Jack had no idea where he was headed, but had plenty of diesel fuel in his main tanks, plus the auxiliary tanks that he had installed in Tromsø, plus the extra barrels of diesel fuel strapped to the back deck, so wasn't too overly concerned. A slight evanescing mist began to rise gently from the calm warmer waters ahead with the misty air on the horizon gradually changing in appearance, turning a variety of polychromatic colors through a light watery haze. Indeed, it was some of the calmest ocean water and most beautiful environments that Jack had ever encountered, as he set his tracking equipment on a straight course to venture a bit further beyond the misty shroud that nevertheless grew warmer and more opaque as the two of them motored north. Perhaps there was something to the Norse mythology after all, he thought.

After a couple of more days on the water, as they both began to lose track of time again while the evening darkness never came, the mist began to lift. Sometime after that, without really knowing how long, or why, or where, or when, they broke out into a boundless ocean once again with nothing else in sight but their boat, a purplish hazy sky, a strong northbound current, and a warm southern breeze that seemed to pull them like a tractor beam into a vast expansive watery unknown. The magnetic compass needle began to act more erratic as well, and didn't seem to know which way was up, but for some reason the GPS seemed to be working fine as Jack kept a steady course. With nothing ahead of them, there wasn't much else to consider, as they decided to just cut the engines for a while, let the anchor hang in the watery depths, and drift for a spell to enjoy some soothing music below decks, while laying their heads back and getting some rest. Every once in awhile as their stomachs began to get grumpy, they would whip up a quick meal from the food stored in the galley, like bacon and eggs, pancakes, or a fresh piece of seared Atlantic cod with a green salad and oil/vinegar dressing, plus a little wine, to satisfy their hunger; followed by their regular routine of minding the boat, watching the water, searching for wildlife, and enjoying the stark and stoic arctic scenery. They also played a few card games like spades, hearts, or gin rummy to while away the hours if things became a bit mundane. Either that, or they would head down to the shipboard sauna for a spell to just relax and revitalize. They bided their time in that extemporaneous manner for several days and nights until sometime later, during one of their glittering sunlit/moonlit evenings, they both just fell into a deep sleep while lounging on the back deck for an unknown period of time. When they awoke, their watery world appeared a bit foreign to them, while Jack and Sarah both experienced an overwhelming ethereal happiness that they had very rarely felt before, almost like they were stoned, as their awareness amplified.

As they gazed lazily across their seascape to the North, a slender silhouette of land manifested like a mirage on the developing horizon with a purplish haze painted like a palette above the lifting mist, but was still a steamy shroud that required penetration to realize any invocation. Sprinkled amidst the velvety veil they could make out a small fleet of dancing orbs in the distant empyrean sky as bright blue light reflected at adjacent angles off the flickering spheres. Questioning their sagacity, while slightly sleepy eyed, Sarah and Jack went below again for another sauna session to relax and resuscitate, as the boat drifted along its delicate tractor beam path. The melodious jazz wafted through the warm cedar walls of their sumptuous shipboard sauna and had a magical mesmerizing effect as it engulfed their amalgamated auras and beseeched them inward toward their lascivious love chamber. Firmly seated on the wooden bench against the cedar slat bulkhead, Jack dipped his ladle into the wooden bucket and dropped another load of distilled water onto the hot rocks as more steam circled toward the ceiling, sending sizzling sounds of saturated satisfaction as the searing stones released their reticent superheated vapors, and the two shipmates wandered lazily into a world yet unknown. The hot sweet smell of raw wet cedar knifed past their nasal neurons as they settled back to inhale the heat, and sterile steam satiated each unsuspecting pore of their sweltering obsequious bodies.

Leonard Cohen sang 'Dance Me to the End of Love' over the sound system as Jack sent another message to his friends on the other side of the small blue planet. He wasn't sure whether the new WiFi system would penetrate through the silent shroud, yet sent the message anyway. He would check back later for a response, as the two sauna mates continued to meander leisurely north, and as Sarah did a little dance routine on Jack's lingering lap in their libidinous little grotto within the delightful decks below. They had discovered a happiness that they both so deftly and desperately desired, as Jack delivered one last text;

Jack cell;

Living the life above Lapland, land of the Northern Lights, and one exotic Arctic Circle.

Fearing nothing, going forward. No giants yet, but listening for melodic Nordic music as we follow the bouncing orbs. Catch you on the other side, … just sayin', since you likely won't miss us 'til we're gone.

Love, and healing @ 432 Hertz
Sarah & Jack
Esse non videri

Feign to Flight

A wakened water on a moonlit night,
watching breaking wavelets in a mystic light

Shifting somewhat leftwards, then abruptly right,
watching droplets dance to harmonic height

Quantum schism skimming, pulsed frenetic fright
with flickering frequency of bright blue delight

Dodging dim despair That's held dead to rights when the fake fear fades through a silent night

Facing air that's quiet In a shallow bight, Toward a final feign in a vanquished light.

As waffling winds bending sound and sight, form geometric patterns in a final fight

In a vanishing act to a fated plight,
when the made to measure checks the right to might

Then, scissors beats paper and water shines bright, when rock beats scissors in a feign to flight.

Jaak Tallinn - June, 2017

ABOUT THE AUTHOR

Picture taken in Larvik, Norway, 2003

The author was a sailor that spent two years aboard a 'Kilauea Class' Ammunition ship (USS Flint), as a Machinist Mate Petty Officer assigned to 'A' Gang (Auxiliaries), and 'R' Division during three separate 'WESPAC' cruises in the Pacific, South China Seas, Indian Ocean, and other ports west, between March 1973 and March 1975.

His earlier novel, '**Victory Liner 504**', was written around poems that he wrote while in the Navy, and sets the stage for the current sequel.

Following active duty, the author returned to college on the GI Bill, earning a Mechanical Engineering degree (BSE) from Western Michigan University in 1978, and 'Master of Business' MBA degree in 1988, then worked in a variety of Engineering, Marketing, and Management positions prior to starting his own business. As a 'Project Engineer' working for a large manufacturing company in Milwaukee, he spent six years in design, manufacturing, testing, and 'start up' of desalination plants, ASME code pressure vessels, and process equipment for US Navy, marine, and commercial ship applications. Working with the company under a NAVSEA contract, he developed the first Reverse Osmosis Desalination plant for US Navy Combatant ships during the mid 1980's, installed the unit aboard a US Navy Destroyer in Norfolk, Virginia, and rode the ship to Puerto Rico with the crew in 1987 to prove the concept. Jaak Tallinn lives in Wisconsin, and has been self-employed in his own 'Business Development Consulting' company since 1991.

www.ingramcontent.com/pod-product-compliance
Lightning Source LLC
LaVergne TN
LVHW041704060526
838201LV00043B/561